"*This Side of Brightness* is one of the few novels in recent memory that I mourned ending even as I read." —*The Boston Globe*

"Absorbing...McCann's prose shines. Nothing escapes his eye." —*The Philadelphia Inquirer*

"McCann achieves a taut balance between high-minded literary effort and soap-opera-like page turner....Skillful and subtle." —*Chicago Tribune*

"A rarity in this preciously cool era—the urban saga with a social conscience, spanning multiple generations, employing the large canvas once used by Steinbeck and Algren." —*The Washington Post*

"A breathtakingly mature novel, a feat of daring...Profoundly spiritual." —*The Baltimore Sun*

"McCann's haunting, lyrical novel resonates with stark contradictions characteristic of the city in which it takes place. It unsparingly depicts violence and drug use but also captures the unearthly beauty of the world beneath the city streets." —*Newsday*

"A beautiful, lyrical novel." —*Esquire*

"Vivid, lucid, informing and poetic." —*The Village Voice*

"Bold and mesmerizing...McCann has created a rich tapestry of interwoven humanity in all its glory and horror....A fiercely original work filled with complex characters drawn with much knowing detail." —*The Portland Oregonian*

"A triumph...McCann has undertaken an endeavor of brave scope, crammed with evocative detail and memorable characters....Impressive." —*Publishers Weekly* (starred)

THIS SIDE
of
BRIGHTNESS

A NOVEL

COLUM MCCANN

AN OWL BOOK

HENRY HOLT AND COMPANY · NEW YORK

Henry Holt and Company, Inc.
Publishers since 1866
115 West 18th Street
New York, New York 10011

Henry Holt® is a registered trademark
of Henry Holt and Company, Inc.

Library of Congress Cataloging-in-Publication Data
McCann, Colum.
This side of brightness: a novel / Colum McCann.
p.   cm.
ISBN 0-8050-5453-7
I. Title.
PR6063.C335T48   1998   97-29721
823'.914—dc21   CIP

Henry Holt books are available for special promotions and
premiums. For details contact: Director, Special Markets.

First published in hardcover in 1998 by Metropolitan Books

First Owl Books Edition 1999

Designed by Iris Weinstein
The map on pp. ii–iii appears courtesy of Richard Ondrovic.

Printed in the United States of America
All first editions are printed on acid-free paper.∞

1   3   5   7   9   10   8   6   4   2

For Siobhan, Sean, Oonagh, and Ronan.
And, of course, for Allison.

We started dying before the snow and, like the snow, we continued to fall. It was surprising there were so many of us left to die.

LOUISE ERDRICH, *Tracks*

THIS SIDE of BRIGHTNESS

chapter 1

1991

*O*n the evening before the first snow fell, he saw a large bird frozen in the waters of the Hudson River. He knew it must have been a goose or a heron, but he decided that it was a crane. Its neck was tucked under its wingpit and the head was submerged in the river. He peered down at the water's surface and imagined the ancient ornamental beak. The bird's legs were spread out and one wing was uncurled as if it had been attempting to fly through ice.

Treefrog found some bricks at the edge of the path that ran along the waterfront, lifted them high, and flung them down around the bird. The first brick bounced and skidded on the ice, but the second broke the surface and animated the crane for just a moment. The wings skipped minutely. The neck moved in a stiff, majestic arc and the head emerged from under the water, gray and bloated. He rained the bricks down with ferocious intent until the bird was free to move beyond the ice to where the river flowed.

Tipping his sunglasses up on his forehead, Treefrog watched the bird float away. He knew it would sink to the sands of the Hudson or get frozen in the ice once more, but he turned his back and walked away through the empty park. He kicked at some litter, touched the icy bark of a crab-apple tree, reached the tunnel entrance, and removed both his overcoats. He squeezed his way into a gap in the iron gate and crawled through.

The tunnel was wide and dark and familiar. There was no sound. Treefrog walked along the railway tracks until he came to a large concrete column. He touched the column with both hands and waited a moment for his eyes to adjust; then he grabbed onto a handhold and, with spectacular strength, hauled himself up. He walked along the beam with perfect balance, reached another catwalk, and shunted himself upward once more.

In his dark nest, high in the tunnel, Treefrog lit a small fire of twigs and newspaper. It was late evening. A train rumbled in the distance.

A few pellets of ratshit had collected on the bedside table, and he swept them off before opening the table drawer. From the depths of the drawer Treefrog took out a small purple jewelry bag, undid the yellow string. For a moment he warmed the harmonica in his gloved fist above the fire. He put it to his mouth, tested its warmth, and pulled in a net of tunnel air. The Hohner slipped along his lips. His tongue flickered in against the reeds, and the tendons in his neck shone. He felt the music was breathing him, asserting itself through him. A vision of his daughter whipped up—she was there, she was listening, she was part of his music, she sat with her knees tucked up to her chest and rocked back and forth in childish ecstasy—and he thought once again of the frozen crane in the river.

Sitting there, in his nest, in the miasmic dark, Treefrog played, transforming the air, giving back to the tunnels their original music.

chapter 2

1916

They arrive at dawn in their geography of hats. A dark field of figures, stalks in motion, bending toward the docklands. Scattered at first in the streets of Brooklyn—they have come by trolley and ferry and elevated train—they begin to gather together in a wave. Hard men, diligent in the smoking of cigarettes, they stamp yesterday's mud from their boots as they walk. A trail of muck is left in the snow. Ice puddles are cracked by the weight of their feet. The cold inveigles itself into their bodies. Some of the men have big mustaches that move like prairie grasses above their lips. Others are young and raw from razors. All of them have faces hollowed by the gravity of their work; they smoke furiously, with the knowledge of those who might be dead in just a few hours. Hunching down into their overcoats, they can perhaps still smell last night on their bodies—

they might have been drunk or they might have been making love or they might have been both at once. Later they will laugh at these stories of drink and love, but for now they are silent. It is far too cold to do anything but walk and smoke. They move toward the East River and cluster near the tunnel entrance, stamping their boots on the cobblestones for warmth.

The snow turns to slush at their feet.

When the whistle calls the sandhogs to work, they take a last pull on their cigarettes. The red tops of the butts flare and are dropped to the ground, one by one, as if swarms of fireflies are laying themselves down to rest.

In the middle of the line, Nathan Walker watches as men from the nighttime shift emerge from the tunnel, mucked head to toe, exhausted. Walker realizes that he is looking at his future, so he doesn't stare too closely, but every now and then his hand stretches out and slaps a finished man's shoulder. The weary man raises his head, nods, lurches on.

Walker resists the urge to sneeze. He knows that to have a cold means losing a day's pay—his nose or his ears might leak blood in the compressed air beneath the river. If a cold is telegraphed, the foreman will pull him out from the crowd. So Walker sucks his coughing and his sneezing down into his stomach. He takes an amulet from his pocket, a piece of stone, and rolls it around in his fingers. The good-luck charm is icy to the touch.

Walker whispers to his partner, Con O'Leary. "What say, bud?"

"Sick as a small hospital. A hangover to beat the band."

"Me too."

"Sweet Jaysus, it's cold though," says O'Leary.

"Ain't it just?"

"Heads up, son, here we go."

The foreman nods at the two sandhogs, and they join the group at the mouth of the shaft. They stand close together and inch forward. Walker hears the whine of the compression machine from underground. It's a long hard high sound that will soon become nothing in his ears; the river is a grabber of sound, taking it, swallowing it. Walker adjusts his hat and gives a last look out over the distance. Across the river the three-arch customs house is gray in the morning; longshoremen are busy at the docks; a couple of cargo ships are negotiating floes of ice; out on the water, a young woman in a bright red coat stands on the deck of a ferryboat, waving her arms back and forth. Walker recognizes her as Maura O'Leary; just before he disappears from view her husband, Con, touches his hat in a gesture that could be dismissal or boredom but is in fact love.

Walker grins at the sight, lowers his head, and begins his descent beneath the river toward another day's digging on this, a morning so cold that even his heart feels frozen to the wall of his chest.

In the manlock, the door is closed tight and air hisses in around the sandhogs.

Walker opens the top button of his overcoat. He can feel his toes loosening now in the hot pressurized air. A bead of sweat forms on his brow, and he flicks it away with his thumb. Beside him, O'Leary stands slumped against the wall, breathing deeply. The two are soon joined by Sean Power and Rhubarb Vannucci. The air grows torrid as the pressure rises. It is as if a heat wave has decided to accompany them underground dur-

ing winter. The four men hold their noses until their ears begin
to pop.

After a few minutes, Power crouches down and takes a deck
of cards from his dungarees. The men search in their pockets
for coins and play hog poker while the air compresses their
bodies to thirty-two pounds per square inch. Walker wins the
first round, and Power slaps the young black man on the
shoulder.

"Look at you, hey, the king of spades!"

But Walker takes no offense. He knows there is a democracy
beneath the river. In the darkness every man's blood runs the
same color—a dago the same as a nigger the same as a Polack
the same as a mick—so Walker just laughs, puts the winnings in
his pocket, and deals the second hand.

Out of the manlock, still in their hats, the sandhogs enter the
compressed air of the tunnel. More than one hundred of them,
they slosh through the mud. Waterboys and welders, carpenters
and grouters, hoist runners and electricians, they remove their
caps and overcoats in the heat. Some have tattoos, others have
potbellies, a few are emaciated, most are sinewy. Nearly all of
them have worked as miners before—in Colorado, Pennsyl-
vania, New Jersey, Poland, Germany, England—with legacies
of blackening lungs to prove it. If they could reach down into
their throats they could chisel out diseases from their lungs.
The tar and the filth would come away in their fingertips. They
could hold a piece of flue-colored tissue and say, This is what
the tunnels have done to me.

There have been many deaths in the tunnel, but there's a law
the sandhogs accept: you live as long as you do until you don't.

Bare electric bulbs flicker, and the men move through a liquidy light, casting fiddleback shadows on the walls. The shadows melt and skirt and coalesce, growing longer and then shorter. In the middle of the tunnel runs a thin rail line, which will later be used for transporting equipment and mud. The men step along the tracks, and at various points they leave the convoy. Metal lunch boxes are thrown to the ground. Rosary beads are produced from pockets. The men remove their shirts in the temporary exuberance of beginning work. Here, the closure of a fist to show up an arm muscle. There, the pullback of shoulders to reveal a massive chest. Behind, the thumping sound of a fist into a palm.

But the four muckers—Walker, O'Leary, Vannucci, and Power—don't stop to talk. They have to walk the full length of the tunnel, under the cast-iron rings, past machinery and vises and bolts and giant wrenches and stacked bags of Portland cement. Walker goes out in front, balancing on one of the metal rails, while the three others place their feet carefully on the wooden ties. Their shovels swing down by their legs. Walker's has his name carved into the shaft, O'Leary's has a bent metal lip, Power's has toweling wrapped around the handle, and Vannucci's, once minutely cracked, is held together with a metal sleeve. They continue along, right into the belly of blackness.

"Hotter than a whore's kitchen today," says Power.

"Ain't that the truth?"

"Ever been in a whore's kitchen?"

"Only for breakfast," says Walker. "Grits and eggs over easy."

"I swear! Listen to the youngster!"

"And a little sizzling bacon."

"Whooeee, I like that."

"Backside bacon. With a little on the rind."

"Now we're talking!"

At the head of the tunnel they reach the Greathead Shield, the last safety precaution, a giant piece of metal that is pushed through the river by hydraulic jacks. If there is an accident, the shield will hold the mud back like a lid on a cylinder. But the four men must go even further. They each take a deep breath and then stoop to enter the door in the shield. It is like entering a tiny room at the end of the world: seventy-five square feet, all darkness and damp and danger. Here, the riverbed is propped up with long breast boards and huge metal jacks. Above the men's heads a steel ceiling juts out to protect them from falling rock and sliding mud. Right in front of their eyes hangs a wire-caged bulb, revealing mounds of dirt and puddles of filthy water. The bulb has a pulse to it, the electricity not constant. Sloshing through the water on the floor of the room, Nathan Walker and Con O'Leary reach out and touch the planks for good luck.

"Touch wood, buddyblue."

"I'm touching," says O'Leary.

"Goddamn, even the planks done got warm."

By the end of the day the muck behind the planks will be gone, carted out on the narrow railway track, loaded on carriages, and pulled by wheezing draft horses to a dump site in Brooklyn. Then the Greathead Shield will be pushed forward once more. Silently, the men challenge themselves to penetrate the riverbed further than ever before, maybe even twelve feet if they're lucky. They set up a platform to stand on. Walker unwinds a jack and Vannucci takes down two breast boards to create a window for their shoveling. Power and O'Leary step back and get ready to load the mud. The four will swap places throughout the day, shoveling and loading, loading and shoveling, slashing their shovels into the soil, burying the metal edges deep.

. . .

Nathan Walker will later sit shivering in the hospital lock and say to his friends, "If only them other guys knew how to talk American, nothing bad woulda happened, nothing at all, not a damn thing."

He is the best of them, even though he's only nineteen years old. The work is brutal, but Walker is always the first to begin digging and the last to finish.

Tall and muscular, he sends ripples along his arm with just one movement of the shovel. He drenches his skin in sweat. The other riverdiggers envy his fluidity, the way the shovel seems to meld with his whole torso, the quiet mastery of his burrowing, the blade making repeated ellipses in the air: one, two, three, strike, return. He stands wide-footed on the platform, wearing blue overalls ripped at the knees, his red hat sideways on his head, a string sewn into the brim so he can tie it under his chin. Every ten seconds the oozy muck comes out from between the breast boards at hip level. Walker turns up shells as he digs, and he rubs them clean with his fingers. He would like to find a slice of bone, an arrowhead, or a piece of petrified wood, but he never does. Sometimes he imagines plants growing down there, yellow jasmine and magnolias and huckleberry bushes. The edges of the Okefenokee swamp come back to him in waves, murky brown waters that pile into the Suwanee of his home.

Walker has been digging for two years. He arrived on a train from Georgia, the steam whistle ringing high and shrill in his ears.

The steel shield extends above his head, but much of the

time he has to go beyond the shield where there's no protection. None of the men wear helmets, and all that's left is just them and river soil.

Walker takes off his shirt and digs bare-chested.

Only the river's muck is cool against his skin, and at times he smears it on his body, over his dark chest and ribs. It feels good to the touch, and soon he is filthy from head to toe.

He knows that at any moment an avalanche of muck and water could sweep the men backward. They could drown with the East River going down their throats, strange fish and odd rocks in their bellies. The water could pin them against the Greathead Shield while the alarm sounds—a frantic *rat tat tat tat* of tools on steel—while the men further back in the tunnel scramble toward safety. Or escaping air could suck them against the wall, hurl them through space, shatter their spines against a breast board. Or a shovel might slip and slice a man's forehead clean open. Or fire could lick through the tunnel. Or the bends—the dreaded bends—could send nitrogen bubbles racing to their knees or shoulders or brains. Walker has seen men collapse in the tunnel, grasping at their joints, their bodies ribboned in sudden agony; it's a sandhog's disease, there is nothing anyone can do about it, and the afflicted are taken back to the manlock, where their bodies are decompressed as slowly as possible.

But these things don't scare Walker—he is alive, and in yellowy darkness he uses every ounce of his body to shove the river tunnel along.

The muckers have a special language—hydraulic jack, trench jack, excelsior, shimmy, taper rings, erector shield—but after a while their language is mostly silence. Words are precious in the compressed air. "Goddammit!" brings a bead of sweat to the men's brows. An economy of hush and striking shovels, Walker breaking it very occasionally with his own gospel song.

"Lord, I ain't seen a sunset
Since I come on down.
No, I ain't seen nothing like a sunset
since I come on down."

As he sings, Power and Vannucci time their digging to the rhythm.

A tube sucks out the water from around their feet. The men call it the toilet, and sometimes they piss right into it so the smell doesn't hang around. Nothing worse than stale piss in the heat. They hold back their bowels so they don't have to shit, and, besides, it's difficult to shit in air that's twice its normal pressure; it all stays in the gut until later, when they hit the water of the hog-house showers. Sometimes it comes out without warning, and they yell through the mist of hot air, "Who spiked them barbecue beans?"

Two hours of work and the tunnel is three feet deeper in length than before. The excavated muck has filled many small carriages, the containers shunted back and forth on the railway track with great regularity.

Vannucci watches Walker and learns from him. The Italian has a long stringy body, with blue veins striated on his arms. For this, the men call him Rhubarb. He first came down as a dynamiter, lighting and blasting and uncoiling his way through the tunnel's opening, but the blasting was finished early and there was just pure muck left. A man can't blast muck, much as he might want to, but Rhubarb still keeps a wrapped fuse in his pocket as a talisman. He has few English words with which to talk to the other men, so he speaks in his work and they respect him for it. Rhubarb hefts another shovelful of muck, while beside him Walker grunts.

One, two, three, strike, return.

Con O'Leary pants as he leans into the work. To his left, Sean Power sucks blood from his palm, having cut his hand on a sharp edge of the shield.

The men are beating the river and they are happy.

Soon the assembly gang will come along and put in a ring of steel—the pieces jammed into place by a small derrick, rotated by a powerful erector arm, then bolted on—and the tunnel will snake further toward Manhattan. The foremen will be delighted; they will rub their hands together and think of the day when trains run under the East River.

And then, at 8:17 A.M., when Nathan Walker has his back turned to the wall of mud, Rhubarb Vannucci lets out his very first attempt at a full English sentence. His shovel is in mid-swing, one shoulder high, the other low. Unseen by Walker, a tiny hole has appeared in the tunnel wall, a weak spot in the riverbed. The pressurized air hisses out. Vannucci grabs at a bag of hay to stuff the hole, but the dirt whirls from around it and the air escapes and the hole grows wider. At first the weak spot is the size of a fist, then a heart, then a head. The Italian can only watch as the young black man is whipped backward. Walker's feet can't grip the soil. He slides toward the widening hole and is sucked into it, shovel first, then his outstretched arms, followed by his head, right down to his shoulders, where his body stops, a cork in the tunnel. His upper torso belongs to the soil, his legs to the tunnel. Pebbles and river dirt greet him. The escaping air pushes at his feet. The soil sucks around his legs. Vannucci steps to the blowout and grabs Walker's ankles to try and drag the riverdigger down. As he pulls, the other two muckers come forward, and both of them hear the echo of the Italian's sentence around them.

"Shit! Air go out! Shit!"

On most afternoons before the blowout, the four men emerge from the hog-house showers, where the water jets out in irregular spurts from black hoses above their heads and the dirt makes puddles at their feet. Steam rises from beneath their overcoats when they hit the cold air outside. In the saloon off Montague Street they laugh at the sight of one another's clean faces. For the first time all day they can see the cleft in Con O'Leary's chin, the scars around Nathan Walker's eyes, the rude bumps in Sean Power's nose, and Rhubarb Vannucci's sleek brown skin.

It is a dark bar, all wood, no mirrors.

The men pick sawdust from the floor and roll a few tiny pieces into their cigarettes. They sit in a corner snug, pass around a single match. Blue clouds of smoke rise above their heads. The barman, Brickbat Jones, carries a tray of eight beers toward them, his hands trembling with the weight. A garter swallows his tiny forearm.

"What's up, boys?"

"Nothing much. You?"

"Same ol' same ol'. You boys look thirsty."

"I've a mouth as dry as a farmer's sock!" shouts Power.

Brickbat is the only barman around who lets black men drink in his pub. Walker once saved a hammer from splitting open Brickbat's head. He caught the weapon mid-swing and afterward never said a word about it, simply tossing the hammer in a garbage can on the way home. From then on, Walker's beer cost a penny less for the week and free tobacco was dropped in his overcoat pocket.

"How's the tunnel, boys?"

"Halfway along."

"Takes a brave man," says Brickbat.

"Takes a stupid man," says O'Leary.

"Or a thirsty man!" roars Power, raising his glass.

The men drink in big noisy gulps, no method to it, as if they were a million miles from the rhythm of the tunnel. Their words come hard and gruff at first: a dime less in last week's pay, the grouter in the manlock cheating at cards, the shredded remains of British soldiers that they hear about at home on their wirelesses, the possibility of American troops joining the fight in Europe. But their words and their throats are soon softened by drink. They relax and laugh. Stories are summoned up and melodeons are taken from pockets. Music coughs around the bar. Different languages blend. The men arm-wrestle. Sometimes a fight erupts. Or a man pisses at the bar counter and gets thrown out. Or a whore walks by the window, all red lips and drama, decoratively lifting the hem of her dress. Wolf whistles sound out and the men stare at the passing woman, their hearts growing huge and quiescent with lust. A clock lets out a gong on the quarter hour.

Rhubarb Vannucci is the first to leave, after two beers and four gongs, turning his overcoat collar up around his neck even before the last swallow.

"*Ciao, amici.*"

"See ya later, Ruby."

"Hey, Rhubarb!"

"*Sì?*"

"A word of advice."

"No understand."

"Don't forget the custard."

It is Power's joke—rhubarb with custard—but he has never explained it to the Sicilian.

The men chuckle and order another round. Empty glasses pile up around them. Smoke swivels in the air, and the seashell ashtrays become full.

Con O'Leary is next to leave, walking the cobbled streets toward the docks. He takes a ferry to Manhattan, stands in the cabin with the ferryman, then descends the gangplank and meanders through the darkening streets. His body is a father to his real age, rheumatism in it, feeling seventy although he's only thirty-four. His belly jiggles as he walks. The studded heels of his boots raise sparks. Soon the tenement houses of the Lower East Side greet him. When he turns a corner he sees his wife, Maura, leaning out of a window, waving from under her umbrella of electric red hair. He waves back and she hurries to the kitchen, where she pours two mugs of tea.

Third to leave the bar is Walker, nodding to Brickbat Jones as he goes. He shoves some chewing tobacco in his mouth at the front door and spits as he strolls the streets. Back at the Colored hotel where he lives, he hangs his boots on the doorknob so they don't stain the carpet. The room is tiny. It smells of old shirts and socks and sadness. Walker lies down on his orange bedspread with his arms folded behind his head and drifts off to sleep, dreaming of Georgia and days when he took a boat through the swamps.

Power is always last to go, reeling out to the wet streets at final call, lifting his cap to the moon. There are sunrises on Power's fingers, big oval nicotine stains, and sometimes he staggers around in such a drunken stupor that there are the beginnings of sunrises in the sky too.

· · ·

The shout rips along the tunnel, from mucker to assembly man to grouter to waterboy all the way back to the man who controls the compression machine: Blowout! Lower the pressure! Take it down! *Abbassa la pressione! Obnizyč cišnienie!* The pressure! Hey! *La pressione!* Lower it!

But the shouts get twisted and distorted in the languages they pass through, and, instead of being lowered, the dial on the compression machine rises.

With a million years of riverbed in his mouth and his shovel above his head in an attitude of ascension, Nathan Walker is trapped in blackness, his legs held down by Rhubarb Vannucci. Sand and muck and pebbles in Walker's eyes ears mouth. Watery ooze fills up his throat. His face is ripped from thrashing around. A pebble has lacerated the base of his throat. Blood soaks into the mud. He is a stopper in the ceiling of the tunnel. The escaping air leaks in around him for an eternity of seconds until, with a slow, wormlike wiggle, Walker twists the shovel above his head to create an air pocket and the soil gives minutely.

Vannucci attempts to pull him down again.

Let go of my legs! thinks Walker, as he thrashes in the muck. Let go of my goddamn legs!

He wiggles the shovel some more, and air fills up around him. He inches his head sideways in the muck, and for a second there is the ghost of his dead mother at the train station in Waycross with a blue dress on and a yellow sunflower at her breast, waving goodbye as a steam whistle blows.

He twists the shovel more, and suddenly the air rushes and Walker is released like a spat cherry stone. Still conscious, he rises through the riverbed. Past what? Dutch ships sunken centuries before? Animal carcasses? Arrowheads? Scalps with hair still growing? Men with concrete blocks attached to their feet? The dead from slave ships, bleached down to bone? All the time the air cushions Walker against the tremendous weight of soil and sand and silt. He is an embryo in a sac, sheltered as he is slammed upward, five feet, ten feet, through the riverbed, the air pocket cutting a path through the dirt, keeping him safe.

The shovel is gone from his hands but it follows him like an acolyte, as does Vannucci, as does Power, with a bag of hay clutched to his chest as if in love, a roar coming from Vannucci, and all of them feeling as if their lungs are about to explode.

And then there is water—they are rising through the river—and perhaps astonished fish, staring. Walker will remember it only as pure blackness, water blackness, not even cold at first, then a ferocious *whoosh* in his ears, a pounding at his skull, his eyeballs bulging behind his lids, a sudden soaking, the shock of water, struggling for breath, chest heaving, the panic of being surrounded by dark river, convinced that they will drown, they will all drown, pike and trout and dirt and pebbles will make a home in their bloated bellies, barges will scour the water for their bodies, seashells will nestle in their eyeballs.

And then all three men erupt through the surface of the East River, their heads just missing the floes of ice, shooting out into the air with only their overalls and boots on, their chests contracting and expanding madly now; they are spewing water and muck from their mouths, gulping down oxygen, feeling their brains thump; some tools from the tunnel accompanying them, planks spinning, a hydraulic jack cartwheeling, a bag of hay, an overcoat, a hat, a shirt, the most unlikely of flying things: it is morning, it is light, and they are up on a huge brown geyser, themselves and their dirt and their tunnel equipment. There

are ferryboats on the water. Curious seagulls in the air. Dockside workers pointing in amazement. The three sandhogs somersault in the air above the river. The water suspends them for a
moment between Brooklyn and Manhattan, a moment that the
men will never lose in their memories—they have been blown
upward like gods.

Walker's first thought when he is rescued and dragged onto a
boat, half naked, blood streaming down his face: I'm so goddamn cold y'all could skate me.

Maura O'Leary combs a single strand of hair from her cheek.
Her face is lean and spare.

Down its length the East River is quiet. She notices a few
scows and barges and some bits of rafted rubbish on the water,
the morning sun shining wheels of light in the flow. Some
movement of workers on the piers. Mules and carts beyond
the edges of the banks. And, in the river, nothing but a small
gurgle, a few bubbles on the surface from the tiny, regular
seepage of air from the tunnel below. Maura watches from the
deck of the ferry in the freezing cold, a wool scarf around her
head. Since dawn she has taken the ferry back and forth, back
and forth, back and forth—it is her daily ritual. She has done it
each morning since she found out she was pregnant. Her husband has allowed her the eccentricity. And, besides, the ferryman is Irish; he lets her ride for free. She is thinking of going
ashore and taking a trolley home. Get the crib ready for the
child, due in a month. Maybe make some potato soup for Con.
Rest a little. Chat with the other women on the upstairs floor.

She moves to go belowdeck as the river howls and erupts. A

massive funnel of water greets the city on one bank and Brooklyn on the other.

At first Maura sees only sandbags and planks of wood aloft on the geyser. She reels back, clutching at her stomach. Her feet slip on the wet deck, and she catches the railing and screams. The water keeps spurting, blowing the detritus of the tunnel twenty-five feet above the East River. Longshoremen look up from the piers, the ferryboat captain lets go of his wheel, workers on the docksides stand frozen to the vision. The sandbags crest the top of the geyser and hop around. A plank spins out from the brownburst and cartwheels down to the river. Maura watches as a bag seems to contort itself within the torrent and a curious, floppy limb emerges. She realizes that it is an arm and that a shovel is spinning away from it. A man has been blown from the tunnel! One, two, three of them! Raised from forty feet below! She sees Nathan Walker, his powerful body and the red hat that has stayed on his head like an autograph, tied under his chin with a string. But the other two bodies are hard to make out as they crest the water in their strange ascension.

Her husband's name—"Con!"—stretches out from her mouth, as if on elastic.

The three men still bob on the upshoot, although the pressure begins to equalize and—almost gently—the geyser lowers them down to the river. As Walker crashes into the water, his head narrowly misses a chunk of ice. He submerges and then comes up and after a moment he begins swimming toward safety, his arms making great windmills in the river, churning a line of white.

Vannucci and Power hold on to floating breast planks. Blood spurts from one man's head. The other lolls as if his neck is broken.

A scow is already heading toward them from the Brooklyn side. The ferryboat lets out short sharp emergency hornblasts. At the head of the tunnel shrill whistles are blowing, and a long rope of men uncoils to the light. The geyser dies down and becomes just a murmur.

"Con!" she screams. "Con!"

The next morning the newspapers report that Nathan Walker swam to the scow and was dragged aboard, blood all over his face. Vannucci and Power held on to the floating planks until rescued. The three men were brought to the manlock so their bodies could decompress. Walker sat silently. Rhubarb Vannucci tried to return straight to work, but he was bleeding and was sent home after an hour. Sean Power was brought to the lock with two broken arms, a mangled leg, and a deep gash in his forehead. Tubes were put in his ears to suck out the mud. The foreman gave him whiskey, and he vomited up what looked like a beach of sand and pebbles.

In the middle of the solid column of type—alongside an artist's interpretation of the burst—it says that Con O'Leary, 34, from Roscommon, Ireland, is still missing, presumed dead.

Neighbors arrive at Maura's fourth-floor tenement flat. They spread themselves out in a nimbus in her living room, silent in black dresses. Flowers sent by Walker, Vannucci, and Power stand on a small table.

A daguerreotype of O'Leary is being prepared for a mass card. Maura uses a kitchen knife to cut herself out of the old wedding photograph. When O'Leary is left alone, he stares up at her from the palm of her hand. She raises the image and touches it with her lips. In the photo her husband has a hard, taciturn face. The digger lived much of his life in a taciturn way, coming home, scraping mud from his boots with a knife, the slow silences at dinnertime when she would ask him to do a chore, the shrug of his shoulders, the lovely way he'd raise his chubby palms in the air and ask her, "But why?" An old white shirt of his is still hanging out the window to dry. Maura had been scrubbing the ring of dirt from around the collar. A catechism is open on the table, and Con's baseball cards are scattered beside the book: to become an American, O'Leary had decided to fall in love with the game, following it meticulously. He knew every score, each stadium, all the managers, hitters, pitchers, catchers, and basemen.

The gutted piano he was fixing stands in front of the fireplace, the black and white keys spread out on the floor. He had rescued it from a rubbish dump and dragged it through Manhattan with a rope, destroying the carved legs as he pulled it over cobblestones. Four men were employed to help carry it up the stairs, only for O'Leary to discover it was an imitation Steinway, worth little more than the wood it was made with. He had been filing the keys down; they'd been sticking against each other, causing notes to distort. At night they would summon up songs that she could play.

Maura places the daguerreotype on top of the piano and turns her head as someone knocks on the door.

A heavy man, in a suit and tie and derby hat, brushes snow off his shoulders as he enters. He asks the neighbors if they will leave.

The women wait for Maura to nod and then file out, casting suspicious backward glances. They remain on the stairs, straining to hear. Wide-bottomed, the man sits in the only chair. He hitches up his trousers and Maura can see—as a puddle forms around his feet—his polished shoes.

"William Randall," he says.

"I know who you are."

"I'm deeply sorry."

"Would you like a cup of tea?" She speaks as if there were marbles in her throat.

"No, ma'am."

"The kettle's on."

"No, ma'am, thank you."

And then a long silence as he remembers to take off his hat.

"After the blowout," Randall says, "the tunnel was flooded. The other men were lucky to survive. We had to lay a canvas sheet on the river bottom. We dropped clay on top of it. From a barge. To seal the tunnel up again. We had to do it. We will, of course, give you compensation. Ma'am? Enough for you and the child."

He points toward the bulge, and Maura folds her hands across it.

"There was no time to look for Con's body," he says. "We believe he got stuck in a second blowout. That's all we can say. Will a hundred dollars suffice?"

Randall coughs and makes curlicues at the ends of his tawny mustache.

"The body might emerge; then we can pay for the funeral too. We'll pay for the funeral anyway. Are you going to have a funeral? Ma'am? Mrs. O'Leary? I believe in looking after my workers."

"You do?"

"Always looked after my workers."

"You can leave now, please."

"There's always hope."

"I appreciate your faith, but you can leave."

His Adam's apple bobs up and down. Randall mops his brow with a handkerchief. Beads of sweat reappear immediately.

"I said you can leave."

"Ma'am?"

"Leave."

"If that's how you want it, ma'am."

Maura O'Leary watches Con's shirtsleeves flapping in the window, greeting the snow. She runs her finger around the rim of an empty teacup, curses herself for offering Randall some tea. She says nothing more, just goes to the front door and gently pulls it open for him. She stands behind the frame. The neighbors step back and let the man pass, watching him as he lumbers down the stairs, a roll of fat wobbling at the back of his neck. The women file back into Maura's room, half a dozen accents merging into one. The sound of a car outside drowns out the muffled *clip-clop* of a horse's hooves. Children are playing baseball with hurley sticks. At the window, Maura watches the children step out of the path of Randall's motorcar, some of the boys reaching out to touch its waxed body. Maura pulls across the lace curtain and turns away.

The neighbors clasp their hands and hang their heads, too polite to ask what happened. Maura stands with them—nobody wants the chair—and combs a long strand of hair away from her eye. She tells her neighbors that her husband has already become a fossil and some of them wonder what the word means, but they nod their heads anyway and let it hang on the edge of their lips: fossil.

Nathan Walker repeats the word after making a brief visit to Maura's apartment, having left an envelope full of money on the kitchen table after passing the hat among the sandhogs.

He walks the bright winter streets toward the ferry and wipes

at his eyes with an overcoat sleeve, recalling one evening last
winter after work. He was coming out early from the hog-house
showers and was set upon by four drunken welders. They used
the handles of pickaxes as weapons. The blows rained down on
the top of his skull, and he fell. One of the welders leaned over
and whispered the word "nigger" in his ear, as if he had just
invented it. "Hey, nigger." Walker looked up and smashed the
man's teeth with the heel of an open palm. The pickax handles
hit him again, the wood slipping on his bloody face. And then
came a shout—"Jaysus Christ!"—and he recognized the voice.
Con O'Leary, out from the shower, stood only in his boots and
trousers. The Irishman looked flabby and gigantic in the sunlight. He began swinging with his fists. Two of the welders fell,
and then police whistles were heard in the distance. The welders stumbled off, scattering in the dark streets. O'Leary knelt
down on the ground and held Walker's head against his white
chest. "You'll be all right, son," he said.

A patch of blood spread beneath the Irishman's nipple. He
picked up Walker's hat from the ground. It was full of blood.

"Looks to me like a bowl of tomato soup," said O'Leary.

The two men tried to laugh. O'Leary had said the word
"tomato" as if there were a sigh in the middle of it. For weeks
afterward Walker would see his friend and remember every syl-
lable: to-mah-to.

Now, moving down the streets of the Lower East Side,
Walker wipes the tears from his eyes and hefts the weight of
another word upon his tongue: fossil.

chapter 3

the first snow

*T*here is a moment upon waking when he thinks he might not wake forever. Treefrog touches his liver to make sure he is still alive and remembers the crane found frozen yesterday in the Hudson.

A jab of pain rocks his stomach. He turns in his sleeping bag, pulls the zipper down, opens his shirt, and rubs his fingers over the dent the metal has made in his chest. He pinches the dent on either side and watches a red welt rise on his skin. Cold, so goddamn cold, colder than topside even. Reaching across his bedside table, he lights a Sabbath candle and holds both hands over the flame, letting the heat slip through him. His palms hover close to the flame and for a moment his hands seem disembodied in the candlelight, the rest of him left in darkness. The closer his palms get to the candle, the higher the flame licks. Treefrog allows his hands to hover until the heat is so intense he pulls away, enjoying the pain, his two hands held high in the frigid air.

He hears a couple of rodents scuttle in the rear cave. "Fuck," he says, "fuck." He throws an empty can over his shoulder. It rattles against the wall of the cave and the rats are quiet for a moment; then they begin scrabbling once more. Time to set some traps.

Sitting up in his sleeping bag, Treefrog puts his hands down by his crotch for warmth, leans forward, and looks across the low wall of his elevated home.

The first snow falls through the ceiling of the tunnel, filtering down through the metal grill. Forty feet in the air, the grill holds the snow for a moment and then releases it. The flakes spin in shafts of light, blue winter light. They gyrate and land by the railway tracks, forming patches of snow that reach out into the tunnel, and are then swallowed by darkness. Treefrog has seen this happen often enough that he has learned not to be surprised, but still he watches for a long while and then he says aloud to nobody, "Underground snow."

Each day begins like any other. His morning ritual. He rises and dresses in the abysmal cold, lights a candle, closes his eyes. He moves, blind, to the rear of his nest. The nest is two rooms in all: an old elevated storage room and a cave.

Treefrog feels the darkness, smells it, belongs to it.

In the cave he crouches and moves around with his eyes shut. Candle wax drips onto his hand. The cave is black and damp. Nooks and crannies in the rumples of gray rock. A ledge on the wall. Hidden cubbyholes big enough to stuff his fist into. He places the candle on top of the ledge and reaches for a piece of graph paper and a sharpened pencil. Circling the small cave, he trails his hand against the wall as he goes, feeling the crevices and coldness. With each change in the landscape he opens his eyes and marks an increment on the graph paper. He returns and feels the same place with his other hand, caresses the rock, and lets the cold seep through his leather gloves. He breathes heavily and imagines the clouds his breath makes before his eyes—strange shapes and odd motions. Running his hands along the wall, he instinctively bends and twists and turns and comes to his library, tucked at the very back of the cave. Both his palms rest on a rickety wooden shelf, and he stays there as if in prayer.

Treefrog switches the pencil from hand to hand.

On the shelf he keeps his engineering journals, encased in special plastic bags, labeled with stickers. He runs his fingers along them, stopping at his favorite—tunnel building—and then moves on past his collection of maps, down the length of the world and beyond.

Ducking out from the cave, he goes back to the large front chamber; even with his eyes closed, he knows the shadows that appear in the flickering candlelight. His boots slide from carpet to dirt floor back to carpet again. He never places a foot wrong and always takes an even number of paces. Every hollow and crinkle of mud is recognized from the way it touches his feet. Most of his junk is kept here, old crates, newspapers, a sofa found bloated in the rain, cans, pots, knives, needles, three dozen hubcaps, and books stuffed into Ziploc bags to protect them from the damp. Kindling is piled around the fire pit. Treefrog stops at the Gulag, a foot-deep hole in the wall. Beneath the Gulag is a box for his cat, Castor, to sleep in. Nudging along the wall, under a clothesline strung together from ties, past his bed, Treefrog is careful not to let his feet touch the giant piss bottles lined up at the end of the mattress.

He will empty the bottles later, taking them topside to carve his name yellow in the snow where it will be illegible except to the crows.

At the edge of his nest he reaches up and touches a steel girder, spins his body, and reaches out his other hand. He marks the high edge of the graph paper with his pencil. Treefrog feels for a broken speedometer hung from the steel girder of his nest—the needle stuck at thirty-six, his age—and he says to himself, Take it easy, don't crash.

He opens his eyes, looks at the graph paper, the rows of dots and the squiggled lines. He draws a quick ordnance survey profile of where he has walked. This is his most important ritual; he cannot start his day without it. He exaggerates the features to ten times their map size, so that, on the paper, the nest looks like a rumple of huge valleys and mountains and plains. Even the tiniest nicks in the wall become craters. Later he will transfer them to a larger map he has been working on for the past four years, a map of where he lives, hand-drawn, intricate, secretive, with hills, rivers, ox-bow lakes, curved creeks, shadows: the cartography of darkness.

Fingers trembling in the cold, Treefrog stuffs the morning's map into his bedside table drawer and walks onto the catwalk with his eyelids shut. The narrow beam requires supreme balance—below him is a twenty-foot drop to the tunnel. He swings his way down to the second beam ten feet below, crouches, then leaps and drops soundlessly to the gravel, knees bent, heart thumping. He opens his eyes to the darkness.

. . .

He lives three blocks from anybody else in the tunnel. Sometimes, gazing along its length, he sees a watery movement in the
distance, and it looks to Treefrog like a canoe being paddled with
intent; or his daughter swimming toward him, arms stretched
wide; or his wife moving through the blackness, slender, night-
eyed, forgiving. But then the dark clarifies itself, and the visions
are gone.

Sitting in the stream of blue light from topside—beside the
mural of Salvador Dalí's Melting Clock—Treefrog lets the
flakes fall down around him. From his overcoat pocket he takes
a hypodermic needle, holding it to his eyes to see the marked
calibrations. He fills the syringe quarter full with air, then wets
the size sixteen needle with his tongue. Almost icy enough for
his tongue to freeze against the metal. He leaves a bubble of
spittle on the point and rummages in his other pocket for a pink
handball. He shoves the needle into the ball and pushes the end
of the plastic casing. It feels like entering skin. The ball bloats
with air and Treefrog rubs the new roundness of it. Perfect. He
takes a black pen and marks the point where the needle entered
the ball, searches in the depths of his overcoat for a second
syringe, already filled with glue. The syringe is wrapped in a
sock to keep it warm. He strokes the casing with both hands.
    Treefrog plunges the second needle into the mark on the
pink ball and lets out a slow whistle as the glue pumps into the
rubber. It will take half an hour to harden, but the air and glue
will give the ball a greater bounce. Further down the tunnel
he hears a grunt, and he turns but sees nobody.

"Heyyo," he says to the darkness. "Heyyo."

Taking a second handball from his pocket, he steps back toward the tracks and faces the Melting Clock. The mural was drawn years ago by Papa Love, long before Treefrog came to the tunnel. The clock—gray and black, eight feet high, drawn under the grill to catch the light—is curved like a woman's waist. Beside it, the wall has been slashed with a drunken line of red graffiti. Gangs of kids came down in the summer with spray cans. Treefrog watched them from his nest. Their baseball hats were turned backward. They stuck close together and were scared. After spraying the walls they left empty cans along the edge of the tunnel. But they never touched Papa Love's murals. They even knocked on the door of the old man's shack, but Papa Love never answered his door: never has, never will.

In the cyclorama of snow, Treefrog throws the ball against the wall, his black hair and long beard swinging around him. He slaps the ball first with his right hand, then with his left, there are laws to this game: he must maintain the balance of his body, keep the equilibrium, never hit out of sequence. If he hits twice with the left hand he must hit twice with the right. When he slams with the center of the right palm he must slam with the center of the left. He concentrates on the pink ball bouncing back from the mural. Most of all he likes it when he hits the heart of the Melting Clock, where the mural wiggles near clockhand four.

The ball zooms in and out from the wall.

Treefrog warms up, and there is nothing else on his mind except keeping the ball in the air, hitting underhand, overhand, from his chest, at his thigh, above his head, all simplicity, all precision, all control, in the tunnel, in the shaft of light, in the snow.

He maintains the rhythm perfectly, feeling the warmth slide through his body, its looseness, its generosity. A bead of sweat negotiates his underarm. He hits the ball too hard against a crack in the wall and it spins out of control, flies behind him, and lands on the second set of tracks. In the distance he hears a train, the 69 to Montreal, a rush of lights and metal. It comes loud loud louder and it is good night to the ball because the train is upon it and he doesn't even turn around to watch; the ball will probably be carried way up the tunnel in the underdraft of a carriage or get squashed to nothing. The sound of the train fades away as it moves toward Harlem and beyond to Canada. He slaps his fist into the palm of his hand and hears a shout from behind him.

"Yo."

Peering into the shafts of light that spill through the grates, he sees Elijah stepping out of the shadows at the far side of the tracks, a blanket pulled up over his hooded sweatshirt.

"Gimme a lighter."

"Kiss my ass," says Treefrog.

"Come on, man, gimme a lighter."

"What for?"

"I'm freezing, gimme a lighter."

"Your heater not working again?"

"Of course my heater's working. I want to smoke a goddamn cigarette."

Elijah pulls the hood away from his face, revealing a long red cut on his jawbone.

"What happened you?" asks Treefrog.

"Nothing."

"Someone slice you?"

"What's it to you, motherfucker?"

Treefrog shrugs. "Only asking."

"Don't ask. Nothing happened. Okay? Nothing. Gimme a lighter."

Treefrog reaches for the second ball in his pocket and slices it sideways, making it spin off the wall at an angle. As he stretches out his arm to hit it, he chuckles. "What you gonna give me?"

"I'll give you a smoke."

"Three," says Treefrog, and the ball is guided gently against the wall with the other hand.

"Two."

"Four."

"Okay, three, goddammit!"

"Show tell the barter man," says Treefrog.

Elijah drops the blanket to the ground, delves down into his sweatshirt pocket, and takes out a softpack of menthols. He taps the pack and three cigarettes emerge.

Treefrog lets the ball go jittering through the gravel at strange angles, way down toward the six-foot-high mural of Martin Luther King. He takes out six plastic lighters from his coat pocket, arranges them on both his palms, and says, "Choose your poison, man."

It's all one swift motion and the orange neon lighter is grabbed from Treefrog and three cigarettes are gone from the pack and already Elijah is on his way back down toward his cubicle in the southern part of the tunnel.

Treefrog puts the cigarette in his mouth, flicks his lighter. He feels a clump of snow land on his cheek, and he says aloud for a second time, for symmetry, for equilibrium, "Underground snow."

The first winter he came down it was so cold that his harmonica froze to his lips. He was sitting on the catwalk and hadn't warmed the Hohner. It stuck to his mouth, and skin peeled away when he yanked the harmonica off.

Later, topside, he was caught stealing Chapstick from the pharmacy on Broadway. He tucked the small thin tube under his tongue to hide it, but a clerk saw and stood in front of him, pushed him backward. Treefrog tried to step around the man, but the clerk grabbed him by his long hair and yanked him into a display of cold medicine, the bottles of pills clattering to the ground. Treefrog stood up and broke the clerk's nose with a single blow of his fist, but an off-duty officer came up behind him and put a gun to his temple and said, "Sonofabitch, don't move."

The gun felt cold against Treefrog's head. He thought of how a bullet might sound to a dying man as it ricocheted through his skull, and he asked the cop to put the gun on the other side of his temple. But the cop just told him to kneel on the ground and put his hands in the air.

As he knelt, Treefrog spat the tube of Chapstick out on the floor. A small crowd had gathered to watch. The clerk picked up the tube with a piece of tissue paper. All the time Treefrog had the harmonica warming in his armpit.

When the uniformed cops came he couldn't remember his real name and they shoved their nightsticks into his ribs, jabbed hard, searched him for weapons, and handcuffed him. The harmonica fell down his sleeve to the floor. They stamped down, and their black shoes crushed the Hohner. It was almost ruined; the metal was bowed down into the row of reeds, it made a sad silver lip. They asked him his name over and over again, and, with his arms stretched above his head, he kept shouting, "Treefrog, Treefrog, Treefrog, Treefrog!" Later, when he got the harmonica back—after two nights in the holding cell—it still smelled of his armpit. Not wanting to lick at his own body, he didn't play the Hohner for a week.

Warm from playing handball, he takes off his coat and drops it on the gravel, then stretches out his arms like a man crucified. He looks up to the grate and lets the flakes fall into the cups of his filthy hands, where they melt. He rubs his fingers, freeing them of tunnel dust, brings his hands together, and washes his face with the snow water, letting some of it drip to his tongue. Then he scrubs the back of his neck and feels a cool droplet meander down the collars of his shirts and soak into the back of his thermal undershirt. It has been weeks since he had a wash. He rubs the cold water on his Adam's apple and opens each of the shirts in succession. In one move he pulls the tight gray thermal over his head, throws it onto the heap of clothes near the tracks. His chest is scrimshawed with stab wounds and burns and scars.

So many mutilations of his body.

Hot paper clips, blunt scissors, pliers, cigarettes, matches, blades—they have all left their marks, the most prominent one on the right side of his belly. Treefrog once stuffed a man with a knife and it slid through the gap in his ribs; it was like puncturing a balloon, it slid in and slid out, the man let out a sad slow sigh, but it didn't kill him—the man had stolen one of Treefrog's cigarettes. That was way back in the bad days, the worst days, when Treefrog felt that he had to stab himself on the opposite side of the rib cage. On a New York City bus he punctured himself half an inch with his knife just to get the balance. He had to knock the end of the knife in with both fists. A peculiar warmth spilled over his belly, and blood ran all down the back of the bus. The driver called for assistance over the radio but Treefrog stumbled out the door, walked along Broadway, and lost himself in the neon of Times Square. Later, back in the tunnel, there was the terror of wondering whether he should balance the wound—should he stab himself on the left-hand side?—but he didn't; he just pressed his thumb into his side and dreamed of the metal shaft entering his flesh.

He rubs the water over his upper torso, though it's cold cold cold cold. His skin tingles and tightens and his nipples stand hard. He brings the snow to his veined forearms and underarms, thinks for a moment about venturing down to his crotch, decides against it.

Grabbing his clothes, he crosses the tracks. The tunnel, in width and height, is the size of an airplane hangar.

Treefrog jumps up a pillar and grabs a handhold that he has fashioned with a chisel, puts his foot between the pillar and the wall, heaves himself up with both hands, and he is on the first catwalk. With a lithe movement he is on the second, placing one foot carefully in front of the other, flicking one of his lighters as he goes, first with the right hand and then with the left, a huge cheap flame around him. His hair falls across his eyes so he can hardly see.

He reaches the edge of his nest—twelve steps and always twelve—and swings himself in.

At the entrance there is the carcass of a smashed traffic light, rescued once by Faraday. Treefrog has secured the light to a hook in the wall with barbed wire, but there's no red yellow green since he doesn't want electricity, no way; it's better to keep the nest dark; he likes it that way.

He nods to the light and moves toward his bed.

The mattress dips in the middle from the imprint of his body and he sits, listening to the sounds of the world above him: the traffic on the West Side Highway, the high-pitched yelps of the kids tobogganing in the park, the low growls of Manhattan. Treefrog pulls some extra clothes from the sleeping bag where he has kept them warm during the night—three pairs of socks, a second coat, another pair of gloves, and an extra T-shirt, which he puts in his pocket to use as a scarf. He climbs down once more from his damp nest to the frozen mud of the tunnel floor. He likes to balance on the metal rails as he walks. Five minutes along, he passes the concrete cubicles of Dean, Elijah, Papa Love, and Faraday, but all is quiet. He moves through the shafts of light, comes to the stairwell, climbs, and then squeezes himself through the hole in the ironwork gate.

Outside, in the world, the snow is so white that it hurts his eyes. Treefrog searches through his pockets for his sunglasses.

The crane is not around when he gets to the river. The ice has insinuated itself further into the Hudson, and the place where he threw the bricks has resealed itself like a wound, just a few pieces of timber and a plastic oil container frozen at the edge now. Barges are out in the channel, where the water still flows amid occasional chunks of ice. Further south, houseboats are tethered to the docks, icicles hanging in shards off the ropes.

The snow blows along the waterfront in vicious snarls.

Treefrog wraps the extra T-shirt around his face to protect himself from the blizzard. He moves through the park, along the bend of the highway where the cars are few and slow, and up the tunnel embankment. He dodges a few snowballs from teenagers, counting his steps as he trudges through the six-inch snow. In the playground near 97th Street he spreads a blue plastic bag over a picnic table that is chained to the chicken-wire fence and sits down, far away from the swings.

A few children move delightedly through the snow. He doesn't go nearer for fear of frightening them. Or their mothers. If they looked at him closely they might recognize him, although his hair used to be short, cropped tight to his head, and he didn't have the beard.

From the table he can look down onto the playground: two fiberglass dinosaurs for the children to sit on, a curved silver slide, two smaller slides, some monkey bars, a swinging bridge, a suspended tire, and six swings in a perfect row, three for small kids, three for older ones.

The bitter cold chews at his body, and the wind freezes mucus to his beard.

But when he takes off his sunglasses and puts them on his head, he sees his daughter. It is summer, years ago, and she is eleven years old, wearing an orange dress, beads in her hair, and the trees are green, the light is yellow, the playground is humming, and the earth is alive—those were the good times—and she is swinging her way merrily through the air, arms out-stretched, feet tucked under the swing, white sneakers, blue socks, her hem to her knees. He stands behind her and catches the swing, pushes her higher, and then his hands move slightly and he feels the familiar huge hollowness in his body and he pulls away, wincing at the vision.

A pang of hunger whistles through his stomach and rests in his liver. He needs to find some cans or bottles to redeem. Treefrog stands and billows air into the empty blue plastic bag; the cans will be heavy today with all the melted snow inside them. He should eat a sandwich, maybe. Or buy some chicken in the Chinese restaurant on Broadway. Perhaps another bottle of gin if he can afford it. He has heard that up north, in Maine, the places where you cash cans are called Redemption Centers.

At the edge of the playground, Treefrog waves through the sheets of snow to his daughter, puts his glasses back down to his nose, wipes a frosting of ice from his beard, and moves on, shivering, up 97th Street toward Broadway, where he becomes a solitary man dipping into the garbage cans of Manhattan.

chapter 4

1916–32

*E*ach weekday morning, when Nathan Walker descends the tunnel under the East River to continue the job of digging, he spends a moment alone and says a few words to the man coffined in the soil above him. The other sandhogs leave him be. Walker slaps his shovel against the steel ceiling, and it rings out loud and metallic.

"Hey, Con," he says. "Hey, bud."

He moves on to the end of the tunnel, mud splashing up to the back of his torn overalls. At the Greathead Shield the digging has just begun. Vannucci is already hard at work with two new sandhogs. Sean Power can no longer dig, his body mangled by the accident. Walker steps through the door in the shield and tips his hat to the new men. They nod back. In just two weeks they have already formed the necessary bonds of muckers. Silently, Walker begins his day's digging, but after a while he begins to feel the rhythm seep into him and he lets his tunnel song escape his lips: *Lord, I ain't seen a sunset since I come on down; no, I ain't seen nothing like a sunset since I come on down.*

Eleanor O'Leary is born at home nineteen days after the blowout, on Maura's thirty-fourth birthday. Carmela Vannucci is the midwife. She brings the baby out with gentle ease and whispers prayers in Italian. There is an uproar of red hair on the baby's head.

Maura lies back in her bed—the sheets, rough to the touch, are made from bleached flour bags, still faintly fragrant of something like wheat—and she thinks of her husband and his pocket watch, wonders if it is still running in the river soil. At night Maura remembers herself to sleep and wakes to find the smell of wheat even stronger. Sometimes, in her drowsiness, she thinks she has returned to the ocher fields of Roscommon with a confetti of swans beating across the sky, but when she rises to look out the window it is the gas lamplights of Manhattan that stare back at her.

When she's well enough to take visitors, she puts a dark dress over her nightgown, props herself up in bed, and says nothing about the dreams that she has of her husband's watch—it is there, ticking away in his ribs, his bones are knotted together with suspenders, and the second hand is counting the drip-away of his flesh.

After a month Maura finds work in a paintbrush factory not too far from the East River. The foreman allows her to take the baby with her. She wipes a clean circle in the dusty factory window so she can look outside and imagine Con resurrecting himself upward through the water. He will fly out with his shovel in his hands and roar at the sun. The light will glint off the studs on the heels of his shoes. He will somersault through the air and then descend with the geyser, into the river, hanging on for a moment to a floating plank. He will swim to shore with a grin on his face, and she will meet him on the dockside and hug him and kiss him. He will stroke the cheek of his unseen child and say, "Jaysus, Maura, what a beauty."

All day long Maura imagines this as she stuffs bristles into paintbrushes. Her fingers develop calluses from the work. At the end of her shift she takes the baby carriage and lifts it down the stairs, developing muscles in her arms from the weight. The mass card sits in her pocket, Con's face permanently at her hip. When she arrives home she props the card up on the piano and strikes a few notes. She looks around the room and waits for his hands to touch her shoulders.

Nathan Walker visits on Sunday afternoons, aware that his skin color would provoke too many whispers if he came late at night. He takes off his shoes at the bottom steps so his feet don't sound out on the wooden stairs, climbs the four flights noiselessly, leaves his chewing tobacco in a flowerpot, and knocks on the door.

Maura looks along the length of the corridor to make sure nobody has seen him. She guides him inside by the elbow. He keeps his eyes to the floor.

"You eating all right, Nathan?"

"Yes, yes."

"You sure now? I've seen more fat on a butcher's knife."

"I'm eating just fine, ma'am."

"Well, you look a mite skinny to me."

"Believe me, I ain't lacking."

"I have some potatoes."

"No thank you, ma'am, I just ate."

"Really, I insist."

"Well," he says, "if they're gonna go to waste, ma'am."

Embarrassed at the feast she has prepared, Maura too lowers her eyes. After potatoes and meat and tea and biscuits, she lets Walker take Eleanor into his huge arms. It is strange for Maura to watch the young man with her child, his bigness making the baby seem minuscule. Such a clash of skin. It worries her, and she keeps an eye on Walker. She has heard stories of his kind, yet she sees the gentleness in him. Sometimes Walker rocks Eleanor back and forth to sleep on his knees and when he feeds her he pretends the metal spoon is a zeppelin negotiating the sky between them. Walker always places a one-dollar coin on the mantelpiece when he leaves, and Maura O'Leary puts the money away in a biscuit tin marked ELEANOR.

Walker leaves the tenement house quickly, furtively.

Later, he must sit at the back of a movie house, and during *Tillie's Punctured Romance* the heads of men obscure the swing of Charlie Chaplin's cane. It strikes Walker that it's only in the tunnels that he feels an equality of darkness. The sandhogs were the first integrated union in the country; he knows it is only underground that color is negated, that men become men.

Not even in the gloom of the cinema can he slip like a snake through his own skin.

When he was a ten-year-old boy in the swamps of Georgia, Walker forced a water snake to stay on a rickety wooden pier for five hours. He had heard it would dehydrate in the sun. The snake fought ferociously at first, wiggling from the pier toward the water, but he kept pulling it back by its head and tail.

Remembering an old saying, he knew the snake wasn't poisonous: Red and yellow kill a fellow, red and black be nice to Jack. He didn't want to kill it himself, he just wanted the snake to die in the heat, but it kept on thrashing. The sun began to sink low in the Okefenokee sky. In frustration, the young boy put his foot on the snake's neck and slipped his knife in. Its innards were warm and he knocked them into the water. He brought the skin home to hang on his wall. Most of the house was made with logs, but his own room was composed of cinder block. He made a lot of noise hammering the nails. When the snake was stretched above his bed, his mother came in and asked him where he had gotten it. He told her the story, and she whipped him for his lack of respect.

She told him that all creatures deserved the very same treatment, that none were mightier than others, that all were made the same. They all came into the world with nothing and left the world with even less. Only belief in God and the goodness of man would bring them any happiness.

"Do it again," she said, "and I'll whip the fire out of you."

After church that Sunday the preacher told him to make amends. He kept a different snake in a box after that, treated it carefully, fed it with mice, and was amazed to watch it molt out of itself during summers, leaving sheets of clear skin in the box—much like the men he sees nowadays, a decade later, in the streets of New York, molted out of their civilian clothes into military uniforms, on their way to Europe to fight in the Great War, some of them even colleagues from the tunnels, uniforms crisp and ironed, military hats uncomfortably tilted on their heads. He has heard that, at the front, under bloody French sunsets, the sandhogs do well in their foxholes; they can dig quicker and faster and harder and deeper and further than anyone else.

. . .

One Sunday afternoon, at the end of his visit, Walker says to Maura, "There was a trick y'alls husband used to do, times, ma'am. He'd be there digging away in the tunnel with the rest of us. And see, he had this bullet that he found somewhere, on the street or something, I don't know. Anyways, we were at the front of the tunnel, and Con wasn't wearing no shirt or nothing. Most of the time we don't wear no shirts, see. And he'd up and shout, 'Look at this, lads!' He had that funny way of talking, just like y'all. Tomahto. Potayto. That sort of thing. Anyways, he bent on over, ol' Con, and put the bullet into his stomach. Right on in. It went disappeared in there! He held that bullet in his belly all day long without dropping it, not a once! Working and digging away! And the rest of us were just laughing like there was no tomorrow.

"So I know what y'all're saying, ma'am, 'cause we miss him too, he broke the darkness for us too; that's what he did, ol' Con, he broke the darkness real good."

On the morning of the inaugural run in 1917, Walker, in his red hat, makes his way along the cobblestones of Montague Street in Brooklyn. He smiles when he sees that most of the other sandhogs have come back in their working clothes too: tattered shirts, dungarees, and their favorite caps.

Many of the men have never met before, having worked different shifts. Their wives and children are with them, carrying unlit candles. The families descend the steps of the subway station and move quietly toward the platform. They walk to the front of a train where the boss, William Randall, is standing. Randall is waiting for the photographers' flashbulbs to catch him smiling. It is his first time below, and he is telling the reporters and dignitaries how proud he is of his underwater tunnel. More than anything he cannot wait to chop the red ribbon and send the first train through. As he talks, Randall preens himself for the cameras. He smells of shaving soap and hair oil, an arrogance to the smell, something the tunnel has never known before.

But instead of ducking under the black hoods of their cameras to catch Randall's smile, the photographers turn to watch the men, women, and children filtering down the platform.

As the families move alongside the train, the tunnel is plunged into darkness, the power sabotaged by the sandhogs for an hour. Matches flare and candlelight illuminates the faces of the workers as they file past. Randall lets out an indignant yell and shouts at a group of men in suits. They hold their hands up in supplication, saying, "Nothing we can do, Mr. Randall, sir."

At the rear of the group of workers, Walker grins.

One by one, the sandhogs and their families duck under the red tape at the front of the train. The men don't even look at their boss as they file past. Randall tries to stop them, but they move like water around him.

The workers tug at the brims of their hats, telling the photographers not to accompany them, just to let them be for a while; this is their moment, and they would rather be left alone.

Someone lets out a low whistle, and the sandhogs enter the tunnel carrying the candles.

"You built all this, Pa?"

"Well, bits of it."

"Wow. How long is it?"

"Couple thousand feet or so."

"Exactly, Pa?"

"Give or take an inch or two."

"It's dark."

"Of course it's dark, it's a goddamned tunnel."

Walker watches as two boys throw a baseball back and forth. The ball thumps in their catching mitts. Walker smiles to himself, thinking this is probably the first sub-aqua pitch in the history of the world. He steps between the boys and ducks the flying ball. The boys cheer.

"Spitball!" says Walker, and he goes further into the tunnel.

A few of the women, including Carmela Vannucci—heavily built with a pile-up of hair at her neck—carry rosary beads that leak through their fingers. They whisper to Saint Barbara, the patron of miners. There is melancholy in the movement of the women—they are praying for the tunnel dead—and yet a relief that it wasn't their own men who were spirited away. Long dresses swishing, hair in bonnets, the wives slip their arms through their husbands' elbows as they walk down the side of the track.

In the candlelight, Walker finds Sean Power limping along, holding his nephew's hand. Power turns and puts his hand on the boy's head.

"Meet Mister Walker."

The boy stretches out a grimy hand. "Hello."

"Mister Walker was around that day God farted," says Power.

"Huh?" says the boy.

"The day we got blown from the tunnel."

The boy chuckles but still holds tight to his uncle's hand. Walker follows behind them. He listens as his fellow mucker points out parts of the tunnel to the boy.

"That's where the foreman with the glass eye sat," says Power. "His hair went on fire one day."

"Did his eye melt?"

" 'Course not," says Power. "And the welder went on fire here. Tomocweski. Up in a ball of flames. Smelt like roast beef."

"Really?"

"The doctors saved his ass, though."

"Did he have a glass eye too?"

"No."

"Pity."

They stop and look up at the sheet of gray concrete that coats the ceiling. Power leans on his cane and takes a flask of bourbon from his pocket. He sips at it, passes it back to Walker.

"Unc, is the river up there?"

"Yeah. Right above us."

"Wow! Can I go fishing?"

"None of your wisecracks," says Power. "See here? A guy called Sarantino broke his finger in the bolt fastener right there. Popped it in, almost lost the damn thing. After wiping sweat off his forehead. His finger slipped. You can't imagine how hot it was every day."

"It's cold now, Unc."

"I know it's cold now, but it was hotter than hell."

"Can I put a penny on the tracks?"

"Why?"

"To make it flat when the train comes."

"No."

"Why not?"

"When the train comes we'll be gone."

"Awww."

"We'll have some silence now."

"Why's that?"

"Someone's going to say a prayer."

"A prayer, Uncle Sean?"

Power points at Walker. "Yeah, a prayer."

"The nigger?"

"He ain't a nigger, son, he's a sandhog." Power coughs. "Hush up now, son, and listen."

A few of the men and their families drift off and form their own prayer groups.

"Go ahead, Nathan," says Power. "Hit us with some holy stuff."

Walker clasps his hands together, asks the people to bow their heads and, instead of saying a prayer, to silently remember all the dead.

Walker unclasps his hands and puts his fist over his heart. Vannucci stands stockstill. Power closes his eyes. A two-minute silence is interrupted only by Power's nephew scuffing his shoes on the track until he is smacked on the head by his uncle. The boy lowers his head sheepishly.

The remainder is like the silence of having forgotten something very important, then remembering it and reliving it all at once.

Once the prayer is finished with a loud "Amen," Power moves down the tunnel, sipping from the silver flask as he goes. His limp is more pronounced now as he moves, and he is happy to have the other men's wives look at him with sympathy.

The baseball pitching resumes. A bottle of sarsaparilla is shared among the children: a great treat, they swish it around in their mouths before swallowing. Some women place flowers at the edge of the tracks, and more candles are lit beside the bouquets. Midway in the tunnel the men shake hands, welders searching out other welders, waterboys chatting with other waterboys. The muckers know each other from the day the two halves of the tunnel met. Bottles of champagne were smashed against the Greathead Shield that day. The men share cigarettes—no compressed air now, so the smokes last a long time.

Power's nephew goes running up the tunnel to throw the baseball with the other boys.

After a while the three muckers are left standing alone. At eye level in front of Walker is the spot that was once riverbed, where he was stuck before he was blown free. He reaches his hand out and tries to catch air in his palm, as if he could hold it, taste it, stop it, re-create the moment. Vannucci stands beside him. Above them somewhere, they are not sure where, is the body of Con O'Leary.

"Wish Con could see that baseball flying," says Power. "He sure's hell would like that. He'd get one helluva kick from that."

"He sure would."

Another silence and they stare up at the ceiling, each of them with their hands in their pockets.

"Y'all know why pirates used to wear gold earrings?" says Walker.

"Why's that?"

"So's they could buy a plot of land from God."

"That's about the dumbest thing I ever heard," says Power.

"Well, be that as it is, but it's true."

"I hope I don't go to no watery grave," says Power. "Or if I do, at least let it be bourbon."

Walker steps away toward the side of the tunnel, then says, "Hey, you two! Come over here."

As the muckers come forward, they watch Walker dig down deep in his pocket and take out a ring of hammered gold. Walker rolls the ring between his thumb and forefinger for a moment, holds it to his eye, spies the tunnel through it, and then tosses it to the side of the tracks. The three muckers watch it roll and settle in the pebbles.

"Maura O'Leary gave me that to leave here," says Walker.

"She what?"

"She wanted it left here."

"Well, I'll be," says Power. "She just gave it to you to throw away?"

"Uh-huh."

"It's hers, ain't it?"

"It is the ring of Maura?" asks Rhubarb, the Italian having learned some rudiments of the language since the accident.

"Sure is. Her wedding band. She took it off her finger this morning and gave it to me. Said she didn't have the strength to come down here herself. Asked me to do it for her. Leave it here for Con. So's he can buy his land from God."

"Well, knock me over," says Power. "That's a fine woman."

"Sure as hell is."

"How's what's-her-name? The youngster?"

"Eleanor," says Walker. "The child's growing like a weed."

"No kidding?"

"She'll be up and walking soon."

They stand complicitous in the silence and nod awkwardly, then glance away.

"My God, look at that," mumbles Walker.

"What?"

"Look at them candles," he whispers.

"Which candles?"

"Look at them candles moving."

At the end of the tunnel, the boys have tucked away the baseball and are tossing lighted candles. One by one the lights go out and then flare again with struck matches, all throwing deep-walled shadows in the distance. Power's nephew stretches out his arm to catch one of the candles. Walker watches as the lights dance back and forth in the distant darkness. The workers and their families are lit by the shimmers. Slowly the lights fade. Randall stands stockstill at the head of the tunnel, fuming. One of the sandhogs snips the red ribbon as he walks past. Randall reties it himself with shaking hands. The last few yellow lights wink. The final candle gets thrown and is gone. Walker grips his thighs through his threadbare pockets, coughs, and whispers to his two friends.

"Them candles," he says, "is about the prettiest goddamn thing I seen in my entire life."

"They was just like fireflies."

"What's a firefly?"

"Y'all never seen a firefly?"

"No."

"Well, I'll be."

"What do they look like?"

"They flick like this. *Ging ging.*"

Eleanor repeats the sound. *"Ging ging?"*

"Well, kinda. Excepting they don't make any noise. They just flick with light. Mostly when they's rising up from the grass. Ya don't much see 'em flicking when they go down. That's just the way it is. And sometimes ya can take one and pin it on a thornbush, and it'll glow there for hours."

"Ging ging."

"Ging gingaroo."

"You're strange, Mister Walker."

"Why, thank you."

"*Ging ging.*"
"*Ging gingaroo.*"

He works the various tunnels of Manhattan, sometimes digging, sometimes blasting, sometimes toiling again with underwater jobs, sometimes carting blocks or bags or cement or rubble—always the most dangerous work, at the head of a tunnel, the front hog. He works week in and week out, year after year, with a tolerable paycheck and a few dollars of danger money. No more spectacular resurrections and no more need of them—one life renewed, he knows, is enough. Walker's body remains constant, the big arms, the tough rib cage, the ripple of muscle. After work, he likes to ride the subways on the way home. As always, he hangs his boots on the doorknob. He washes his clothes in whatever sink is around. Walker seldom even buys new shirts. Working boots are his only extravagance; he gets a new pair each year. Lying down on his bed, he listens to any music that comes over his wireless, rarely bothering to flip the dial unless there is the sure promise of jazz. In a decade of flappers, he doesn't flap nor does he want to. He doesn't search out drink when it is outlawed, but he accepts one gladly when it comes his way, mostly when he meets up with Sean Power: whiskey, grappa, apple cider, bootleg beer, tunnel gut rot.

Happy enough, unhappy enough, lonely enough, alone enough, Walker is apt—like a man who spends a lot of time with himself—to laugh out loud for no apparent reason.

Occasionally he ends up in a tunnel fight that is not of his making, and he only fights if he absolutely has to. Still, he flings a powerful punch, puts muscle into it. On the street, cops sometimes shake him down and he just lets it happen, knowing better than to say anything; they will beat him to a pulp if he opens his mouth. He puts money away in a Negro bank—it gains less interest, but at least it is with his own and he feels it is safe. On his twenty-fifth birthday he splurges on a Victrola in a Harlem store owned by a famous trumpet player, pays two dollars more than he would elsewhere, but no matter. Let it roll. Let it sound on out. Two years later, he buys an even finer model with a special stylus. He carts it home and winds the handle carefully. Jazz music erupts around him, and he does wild solitary dances around his room.

Women come and go, but mostly they go—they cannot live with the idea of Walker dying in the tunnels, and besides he is shy and quiet and, although handsome, insists on wearing his ridiculous red hat and the overalls.

Only his rooms change through the years: the hotel in Brooklyn; an attic in southern Manhattan at the edge of the old Five Points tenements, bird shit obscuring a skylight; an apartment near a slaughterhouse in Hell's Kitchen, with taunts ringing out in brogues around him; a clapboard house off Henderson Street in Jersey City, with the smell of bootleg liquor seeping out from a shack next door; back to Manhattan, to a Colored rooming house around the corner from the Theresa Hotel bar; then further north to a cold-water room on 131st Street. The one and only constant in his life is his Sunday visits downtown to Maura and Eleanor O'Leary. Walker notes the passing of years by the way the tunnel dust settles down in his lungs; by the wrinkles that appear at Maura O'Leary's eyes; by the deepening curiosity of Eleanor as she leans forward and touches his elbow lightly while he tells his stories.

. . .

"See," he says to them. "See. They was building the very first tunnel in the city way back in the 1860s. A man by the name of Mister Alfred Ely Beach was in charge. Businessman. What's that they calls it? Entrepreneur. Bow tie up around his neck. Fatter than Randall, even. And Mister Beach got to thinking that maybe the thing to do was to put trains underground instead of upground. No more trains in the air, only in the earth. And nobody in the city had ever thought of that before excepting this here Mister Beach. He was pretty goddamn smart—'scuse me, ma'am, but he was."

Walker tips at a hat that isn't there, and the two women smile.

"So he tried to get a permit for digging a tunnel under Broadway, down there by City Hall. Right under their noses. But he can't get a permit no matter which way he tries, no way in hell they gonna give it to him. They're making money from the El. They don't wanna lose that. This is the 1860s, like I said. They say ol' man Beach is crazy. And maybe he is. But he goes ahead anyways. He's the sort of man who knows the only things worth doing are the things might break your heart. So he got himself some workers and they dug in secret right underneath Devlin's clothing store down there on Murray Street. At night-time they'd go smuggling the dirt back through the rows of clothes. Wheeled the dirt down the street while everyone else was sleeping. Nobody except the crew knew what was going on. Story is, the foreman was called the Tapeworm. They called him that 'cause he once cut out a digger's stomach with a knife after the digger told the secret that they was building the tunnel."

Teacups let out steam on the kitchen table while Walker talks.

"Anyways, they put in frescoes and tiles and all sorts of beautiful paintings and made that into the loveliest tunnel you ever did see. Just about the most gorgeous thing. That's no lie. And right at the front they put in a fountain in the waiting room, a great big fountain with water piped up. They'd never seen nothing like it before. And ol' Alfred Ely Beach he decided they needed a grand piano so they could welcome the customers. Just like this one here, I s'pose."

He nods across the room at Con O'Leary's piano.

"And then ol' Alfred Ely Beach sent his first train through. It must have been a day! Story is, he hired a lady, all in fancy clothes, to come down and play the piano, and all the customers arrived and saw the fountain and heard the music and must have thought they about died and went to heaven. Anyways, they ran that train through the tunnel with pneumatic pressure, two big fans at each end pushing the train along. I don't rightly know, but I reckon it might have been up to quarter of a mile or so. They ran it for a few years but they didn't make no money, and ol' Beach he was losing his shirt so he decided to close the damn thing down. So he bricked it off. Eighteen seventy-something. After a few years everyone forgot there was ever a tunnel down there in the first place. Even the men who made the maps, they forgot to put it on."

Walker looks in his teacup as if he's weighing his words there.

"Go on," says Eleanor.

"And this is where the strangest thing happens. It about jiggers my mind to think on it, but it's true."

"Go on, go on."

He pauses to take a mouthful of tea and drops an extra lump of sugar in the cup.

"True as I'm sitting here and strange as that is. Only last week I heard it. A man crossed his heart on it and ol' Rhubarb he swears it's true too. They were digging again under Broadway, see. Mind, now, it's sixty years later. And everyone done forgot about that old tunnel. They're blasting away with dynamite. Doing cut-and-cover, where they put steel sheet over the street so as none of the rock flies up in the air. So they put in the dynamite and they clear the tunnel and then one of them lights the fuse. Out they go, up on the street, and wait for the blast. Not hardly talking to each other. Tired, I s'pose. Then it goes ahead, the dynamite, and does its job. *Boom!*"

Eleanor jumps back in her seat.

Walker laughs. "And the crew they all just go back down the ladders and into the tunnel. They're walking with their scarves over their mouths to stop the dust. And one of them engineers goes first to make sure it's safe, make sure there'd be no rocks falling on them. Sure enough, the tunnel's looking good, and they all start getting that rubble out of there. Five of them. Shifting the big rocks backwards. Getting ready to put in roof supports. And all of a sudden one of them ups and screams, 'Looky here!' And he's standing with a piece of tile in his hands. And they're all thinking, Goddamn. 'Scuse me. But that's what they're thinking. Goddamn it all to hell, where did this tile come from? And then another one of them boys picks up another tile and then a piece of a face like from a building, what you call it?"

"Gargoyle," says Maura.

"Gargoyle, yeah, he picks up a piece of gargoyle, and now all of them are saying that word as loud as can be too. Goddamn. 'Scuse me, ma'am. But that's how they musta been talking."

Eleanor, fourteen years old, leans forward with her elbows on the table and her face propped up in her hands.

"Then that crew reaches in to pick off more rocks, and suddenly they hit air. Nothing there! Not a thing! So they crawl their way through that gap in the tunnel until they can stand and stretch! Now, these men, they're used to bending all day long and back again, and here they is, standing up! Tiles and paintings all around them and a train track at their feet! So they go, all five of them, walking along and not a one of them believing their eyes. Deeper and deeper and then they see that ol' fountain—'course there's not any water coming from it, but it's there, that ol' fountain and way behind it, still, that grand piano! No kidding. The piano! Covered in dust. Must about have given them heart attacks. And one of them workers, he lifts the lid of the piano and commences himself to playing, and all the men they gather around, holding their lanterns up above the keys. Ain't none of them got a note in their heads, and I don't know what song they was singing, but I s'pose it don't matter. They stood around in that ol' tunnel until the inspector came down and saw them shouting and laughing and singing over that piano."

The women sit speechless over cold cups of tea, a smile breaking at the edges of Eleanor's mouth.

"A piano underground?" she says. "My God."

"Eleanor!" says Maura. "You know I told you not to say things like that."

"Like what?"

"Like my God."

"Sorry, Mom."

They sit quietly until Walker says, "But that's something else now, ain't it?"

Maura nods. "It sure is."

"Could fool with a man's mind if he like to let it."

"Sure could."

"An underground piano."

"My God Almighty," says the girl again.

And all three of them start laughing.

Eleanor writes him a note: *Meet me under the billboard for Wills cigarettes at six.*

She arrives early, in a yellow muslin dress once worn by her mother. Passing men eye her long red hair. She avoids their stares and looks along the street. When Walker shows up she takes his hand, but he quickly lets it go and steps behind her at two paces, tentative and nervous, saying nothing. He walks in her shadow. The streets are grayed by fog. Motorcars throw fumes into the grayness. At the head of the tunnel the foreman—his face fretted with acne—says she shouldn't be accompanied by a Negro into the darkness.

"Ain't no saying what those kind'll do, ma'am."

Walker steps aside, his hands in his pockets.

The foreman takes her down the shaft and along the tunnel to show her the piano covered in dust. She lifts the lid to play a few notes, and he leans over her, holding the lantern near her head. Slyly, he puts his hand on her lower back and spreads his fingers across her hips and squeezes.

"Don't do that!" she says, pushing his hand away.

"Aw, come on. Just a little kiss."

"Leave me alone!"

She steps away and runs from the tunnel, but Walker is gone, and she searches frantically, running back and forth through

Battery Park until she finds him, shy and head-hung, standing
behind the billboard.

"It's true," she says.

"Of course it's true."

"I knew it was."

"Then why y'all so surprised?" he asks.

She shuffles her feet. "That man, he tried to touch me."

"Did he hurt ya?"

"No, but you should say something to him."

"Huh?"

"He shouldn't be allowed to do that. That's not right. You
should say something to him."

"Y'all serious?"

" 'Course I'm serious."

"I'm stupid, girl, but I ain't that stupid."

"Why not?"

"Girl."

"What?"

"Take one good look at my face."

"Oh," she says. "Oh."

Walker turns away when she leans up to try and kiss him on
the cheek, and he mumbles, embarrassed, "Y'all shouldn't do
that. It ain't right."

Although once he saw a famous middleweight boxer emerging from the Theresa Hotel with a French actress. She wore
a short skirt, high heels, and perfume and held a long thin
cigarette elegantly at the tips of her fingers. At the door of the
hotel, she brushed her lips against the black boxer's cheek.
They moved to a waiting car. When the couple was gone, young
girls on the street held popsicle sticks in the exact same manner
as the Frenchwoman's cigarette, and her perfume hung on the
air like stigmata.

"It just ain't right," says Walker.

But for years he takes her down to the bank of the East River anyway. The eyes of strangers cause him to hang his chin on his chest. He knows what they think. Sometimes he even gets violent glares from his own people. He walks way behind Eleanor to make it seem like they aren't together, and he even ignores her if people stare for too long.

At the water's edge, Eleanor says, "Tell me that story about my father again."

"Well," he says, "it was early morning. We all came down and we was just working, normal like. Digging away like we always done."

"Uh-huh."

"We was sweating and loading and loading and sweating."

"And then it happened?"

"Yeah. I had my shovel in the air just like this. And Con, he was behind me somewheres. And Rhubarb too. He was the one let the shout. First time he said something full in English. It like to broke my ears. 'Shit! Air go out. Shit!' "

Walker points toward the middle of the river.

"We rose up right out over there."

chapter 5

so slowly time passes

*A*cross from his nest an icicle hangs near the metal grate, held in static, a shaft of ice one foot long exploring its way down toward the tunnel floor. It looks like a stalactite, although he knows stalactites aren't made of ice, but of mineral deposits. No matter, he will call it that anyway: a stalactite. He wonders how long it might grow. Maybe ten, maybe fifteen feet, maybe all the way down to the ground. He nods to the piece of jagged ice. "Good morning," he says. "Good morning." The world, he knows, can still spring its small and wondrous surprises.

She arrives on the morning of the third snowfall.

A black handbag is all she carries. He is amazed to watch her from the safety of his nest. She moves under his catwalk, a huge fur coat wrapped around herself, open at the buttons, so she looks like an animal that has been sliced longways, from neck to belly button. The coat is old and tattered and yet vaguely beautiful. Underneath, she wears a red miniskirt and high heels. Her hair is threaded with multicolored beads. Some of it stands out in obscene shafts as if it hasn't been washed in years. She walks in the center of the tracks and, when she gets to the grill facing his nest, she stands in the shaft of cold blue light beaming through from topside. He can see, even from his height, that there are streaks of dried mascara on her face. She shivers in the freezing cold and pulls the fur coat tight.

She looks so much like Dancesca.

Moving toward the tunnel wall, near the mural of the Melting Clock, she looks around furtively, then squats and lifts the flap of her fur coat, careful not to soil it.

Treefrog doesn't want to watch as she pisses, so he quietly pulls down the zip of his sleeping bag and swings his feet onto the floor, careful not to step on any pellets of ratshit. He tugs on his boots, ties the laces with numb fingers. At the end of his bed, Castor stirs, and he reaches out to stroke her with both hands. Castor arches her back and nestles up close to him.

He moves quickly through the darkness of his nest toward the catwalk, and before he swings himself down he touches the carcass of the traffic light: Take it easy, don't crash.

The beams are cold; he can even feel the chill through his gloves as he swings down, twenty feet in all, toward the ground. He hits the tunnel gravel with hardly a sound and looks to see the woman stand up and adjust her skirt, a puddle of steaming piss at her feet. She glances toward him and sniffs at the air, but Treefrog pulls back into the shadows.

"Who's that?" she says.

He pulls himself deeper into the darkness.

"Who the fuck is that? Elijah? That you?"

Treefrog breathes down into his overcoat so she won't see his breath making clouds.

"Don't play no games," she says.

He can almost hear his heart thump.

"Who's that?" she says again. "Elijah?"

She rummages in her handbag, and he thinks for a moment that she might have a gun, that she may spray bullets around the tunnel, that he might end up with a hole in his head or his heart, or both, that she may even put the gun to her own head. But instead she takes out a pack of cigarettes and cocks her face sideways, lights the cigarette. Her fur coat falls open, revealing a tight shirt underneath, her nipples pointed and at attention in the cold. She takes a step and each breast jiggles minutely. How long, he thinks, since there was a woman down in the tunnels? As she pulls furiously on the cigarette he notices that the whites of her eyes are rolling around in her head. He keeps himself pinned to the dark, and when she starts to move he blows her a kiss.

She steps from the shaft of blue light into long darkness and into light again and then into an even further blackness, where all he can see is the outline of her figure as she moves, hugged into her coat. The tunnel is like a doubtful church, letting in light at strategic points and leaving the rest in shadows. A dog barks above a grate and the woman stops, looks up, takes out a small mirror, and wipes a hand across her cheeks—she must be crying—and he imagines the mascara stains darkening her face.

He slithers along behind her on the same side of the tracks.

The woman walks in the hard-packed dirt. Her high heels leave tracks. Treefrog wipes his hand across a runny nose and then lifts his head at the sound of a noise. Two pinpoints of light appear in the distance: the upstate train. He darts a look at the woman ahead of him. She has her head down as she walks. Treefrog's heart jumps. The sound of the train grows louder, and suddenly his throat feels dry.

"Don't," he whispers. "Don't."

She lifts her head and stares long and hard as the headlights bear down. She moves nearer to the tracks. The train horn blasts loud and sparks flare from the underside of the carriage and the noise is deafening and he thinks that she is going to stand in front of the train—to clutch it to her chest like a massive bullet—and he shouts, *"Don't!"* but the shout is drowned by the howl of the engine. He covers his eyes, and when he looks again she is simply standing by the track, staring up at the windows, letting the Amtrak rifle past.

He sits on the ground and puts his hand to his heart and closes his eyes and says aloud to nobody, "Thank you, thank you."

She moves on once more in the tremendous cold. Treefrog follows behind at a safe distance, all the way down to the cubicles at 95th Street. The cubicles—concrete bunkers once used by the railway workers—are set in a long row.

She doesn't even flinch when Faraday comes out from his solitary cell and stares at her. Faraday, in his filthy black suit, lets out a low whistle and she ignores it, swings her handbag like a weapon.

"Hey, honey," says Faraday.

"I ain't your honey."

"You sure look like it."

"Fuck you."

Her voice is high and shrill and uneven, and Treefrog is sure she is sobbing.

"Yes, please," says Faraday. "Fuck me please."

And then she steps through the orchard of garbage outside the cubicle where Dean the Trash Man lives. Light spills in behind her and she goes tiptoeing past the mounds of human feces and the torn magazines and the empty containers and the hypodermic needles with blobs of blood at their tips like poppies erupting in a field—in her black high heels she moves like a dark, long-legged bird—past the broken bottles and rat droppings and a baby carriage and smashed TVs and squashed cans and discarded cardboard boxes and shattered jars and orange peels and crack vials and a single teddy bear with both its eyes missing, its belly nibbled by rats. She keeps on going among all the leftovers of human ruin.

Dean comes out of his cubicle when she passes. He wears a rescued pince-nez and shoves it to his eyes and watches her go. Dean licks his lips, and there is a smile on his face as if he might one day collect her too.

An old piece of newspaper catches on her foot and wraps around her ankle, and she carries the page for about twenty yards. Treefrog—hidden way back in the shadows—thinks of headlines sweeping down into her ankles and being carried the length of the tunnels forever, but she kicks off the paper and reels on toward Elijah's place. She must have been here before, thinks Treefrog, the way she moves, the way she never looks over her shoulder.

She stops outside Elijah's cubicle where the ground is clean and free of rubbish. Papa Love has planted a tiny tree in the hard-packed dirt, and she rubs her hands along the brown deadness of its branches. Catching her breath, she stands in the shaft of light and then shouts, "Elijah! Hey, Elijah!"

She looks up and down the row of concrete cubicles.

"Elijah!" she shouts again.

Treefrog can tell she's crying, and he wants to stretch out and touch her, but as he steps out of the shadows Elijah emerges from his cubicle. He rubs his eyes and looks across the tracks to where she stands by the tree. Treefrog tucks himself away in the dark once more.

Elijah steps across the tracks and takes the woman in his arms, and she collapses into his shoulder and sobs. She pulls back the hood of Elijah's sweatshirt and rubs her fingers over the scar on his face. Elijah shoulders her to his cubicle, kicks the door open. It swings drunkenly on one hinge.

Treefrog sits outside and waits.

After an hour Elijah comes out of the cubicle and pisses against the wall like a dog marking his territory. He punches his arms toward the roof of the tunnel in delight. Treefrog turns and walks back down the tunnel to his solitary nest. He takes out the photograph of Dancesca and his daughter, throws the photo up and down in the air, catching it with both hands before it hits the dirt floor.

Chilblains. Hands so big from the cold and damp they feel like they could burst their gloves.

He will find out later that her name is Angela. She was living in another tunnel, downtown, between Second Avenue and Broadway–Lafayette, a subway station, a hundred yards from the platform, with trains going past every few minutes, no light from grills, all noise: a vicious tunnel, the most vicious of tunnels, the worst in Manhattan.

She was there for six months, sleeping on a rain-bloated mattress. Vials were crumpled into pieces in the pockets of her jeans. One night she fell asleep on the mattress in a walled-off hole by the edge of the tracks, no more than five feet from the trains. The noise had become nothing; it was like the sound of her own rhythmic breathing. She sucked down the steel dust that hung in the air. While she was sleeping four men with bicycle chains came down from the Broadway-Lafayette end. They kicked her awake and dragged her up by the hair. She'd never seen them before. She screamed and one of them shoved a sock in her mouth. They ripped her T-shirt and wrapped her arms with the bike chains, tightened them so they left a bracelet of oil on her wrists, bent her over, and took their turns. They whispered a world of obscenities in her ear.

When Angela gagged, they took out the sock and vomit streamed out after it, but they kept on going. She remained silent after that. One of them licked his tongue at her lobe and stole a gold earring with his teeth. He leaned down in front of her with the little hoop of gold on his tongue. She didn't have the energy to spit in his face.

Bent on all fours, she pleaded for mercy, closing her eyes to make them anonymous. When they finally left they threw down fifty cents each and told her to buy some candy—a Mounds bar, they said—and they laughed all the way out of the tunnel.

Angela couldn't walk for two days. The mattress stank. She used a stuffed elephant for a pillow. Its pinkness was ribboned with blood. In the subway trains, commuters rushed by, shadows in the windows. She looked at the shadows and watched them go and reached up and twirled the one remaining hoop in her ear.

She was found by a man named Jigsaw, who said, "Shit, Angie, I'll kill the motherfuckers did this to you."

Jigsaw leaned down and held her real tight and he stank, but she let him hold her anyway. He had ropy arms. Later he bought her some hot coffee and a sandwich she couldn't eat. He stood in front of her with his tongue lolling around in his head—she called him Jigsaw because his mind had gone to pieces.

"Leave me alone, Jiggy."

"No."

"I don't want to talk to nobody."

"You'll die here like this, sister."

"That sounds nice."

"Shit, girl."

"I mean it, it sounds lovely, I'd like to die, it sounds like strawberries, it sounds delicious."

"You gone crazy, girl."

Jigsaw let Angela be and melted into the yellowy darkness— the tunnel punctuated with electric lights—and she came top-side through the emergency manhole, out onto a traffic island in the middle of Houston Street, stumbling along in the snow with her body parched and her head imploding. She sat weeping in a bus shelter until a teenager with a nose ring took pity. He put his arm around her shoulder and took her to a police station in the Bowery. She was surprised at his smell of aftershave. It was alien to her, deep and sweet and lengthy.

A cop brought her inside a small interrogation room with the brightest of desk lamps. The room was warm. She sat with her hands limp and asked for the desk lamp to be turned off; it was hurting her eyes. A second cop twisted the neck of the lamp and pointed it at the floor, and a yellow spot of light remained imprinted on her retinas. She couldn't sit for longer than five minutes on the chair. She tried to write a report, but the cops said she had been asking for it, that's what you get for being a whore, that's just the way it is, you were looking for it, sister, why're you wearing a miniskirt and thin little panties?

"I ain't a whore."

"Look, we're not stupid. You look like you're flossing your goddamn ass."

"Don't look at my ass."

"Don't worry."

"Don't look at my legs. I told you I ain't a whore."

"Uh-huh."

"I ain't! I'm a dancer."

"A dancer?"

"Yeah, you got a problem with that?"

"A dancer! Shake your thing for us."

"You're just motherfuckers, that's all."

"A dancer!"

She stuttered then and said, "I ain't a whore."

When she pushed open the door of the waiting room, the boy with the nose ring was gone, but the scent of him was still there; she hauled it down into her lungs. One of the cops followed her to the front of the station and said, "I believe ya, sister." And then he smiled and said he was sorry for what happened, that he'd make a trip down the tunnel, he'd write a report, she should come back the next day; and he gave her twenty dollars from his pocket. She hung her head, stuffed the money in her handbag, walked out of the station and through Greenwich Village in a daze, until she remembered her old friend Elijah living uptown, and she ducked down into the subway at Astor Place, changed at Grand Central, changed again at Times Square, came all the way to 72nd, walked down the road to Riverside Park and through the hole in the chicken-wire fence at the entrance of the railway tunnel, powdering herself with the rem-

nants of her crack vials as she went, poking her finger around
the containers. Then she came up the tunnel, stepping in her
black high heels. If, at that time, Treefrog had made a map of
the beats of his heart, the contours would have been so close
together the lines would almost have touched one another in
the steepest and finest of gradations.

Climbing back into his nest, Treefrog lies down with Castor at
his side. So many winter hours in the tunnel are spent in sleep.
Not an ounce of noise around him. From the bedside table he
takes out the last of his remaining ganja and rolls himself
a small joint, pinches it between thumb and forefinger, and
pulls hard.

Above his bed his socks hang from the clothesline, a long
multicolored line of neckties—blue ties, red ties, paisley ties,
torn ties, magenta ties, even one from Gucci—all strung together
with a series of perfect knots. The ties loop from one end of the
dark nest to the other, sixteen altogether, each of them rescued
from garbage Dumpsters. In a few places the line is nailed to the
top of the tunnel so it doesn't bow to the ground too much.
Treefrog takes off his shoes and hangs his socks on the clothesline. The socks are stuffed with sweat. After an hour they begin
to ice over, and it looks to him as if another man's feet are dangling in midair.

"Heyyo," he says, "heyyo."

He moves to the back cave with the candle and reaches up to
the shelf where he keeps his maps. He has hundreds of small
graphs and one giant map on a sheet of art paper, carefully
rolled and precisely tied with a shoelace. Treefrog spreads a
plastic bag on the floor so the paper doesn't get covered in

muck. He opens the shoelace and unrolls the map. The one thing he hates is having to use the eraser, but it is necessary when he gets a new reading. Here, the bedside table, rising up to a plateau. A long butte for his mattress. Circular mounds for the rise in the dirt floor. A cave for the Gulag. All elevations marked in tiny increments. Delicately he scrubs out a contour and widens it for a new reading he made of the cave wall this morning after the woman's visit; he may have been wrong, his hands were trembling after he saw her.

He bites the top of his glove to unfreeze his fingers, brings blood to them, works for hours, then falls asleep. When a rat tiptoes across his genitals he wakes and is disgusted to find that he has left a bootprint on the edge of his map.

Moving out from the back cave, Treefrog wipes sleep from his eyes and sits on the side of his bed.

In a giant plastic bag he keeps all the leaves from fall.

The leaves are brown and brittle to the touch, though their outside edges are a little damp where they have started to mulch. Treefrog rubs them between his gloved palms, crumples a few in his fingers, and sprinkles them equally around the fire pit—a ring of rocks with a dome of old ashes in the middle. He tears a yellowed *New York Times* into thin strips and curls them around the leaves. Near the bedside table—one leg supported by books but the whole table still a little drunken—he reaches for his pile of kindling.

He breaks eight little twigs in his fingers, makes a tepee of them around the newspaper, and lays some bigger twigs above them.

When the fire is lit and leaping, Treefrog reaches into the Gulag and unwraps some ham from its aluminum foil. He rips up one of the slices for Castor, tears it into nice little chunks—

just enough to keep her happy and enough to keep her hungry. He pours a small amount of milk in a pan and puts the pan on a grill above the flames. Prometheus Treefrog, the fire stealer! Come down, lovely eagle, and consume my liver for eternity!

He touches the pan with his right thumb and then his left, sits back against the mattress, and waits.

As the milk begins to heat he strokes Castor, fingers a knot of mud from under her belly, throws the mud from hand to hand. She keeps her head cocked toward the pan, and when the bubbles begin to appear Treefrog pours the milk into a small bowl.

Castor laps at the milk delicately, noses over to the plate of ham, and sniffs around.

"Good girl," he says, "good girl."

Treefrog reaches for his bottle of gin. He drinks deep, then carefully cracks two eggs into a pan. A long hair from his beard drops and he picks it off the unbroken yoke with his right finger, imitates the movement with his left. He lays a slice of cheese over the eggs to melt. Treefrog eats his breakfast on the catwalk, using a hubcap for a plate. Looking along the tunnel, he remembers the way the woman had stepped near to the rails. She was so lovely, in her fur coat and red miniskirt. Gorgeous legs, long legs, magazine legs. She reminded him so much of Dancesca. Treefrog smiles and lets some bread soften against his tongue.

A church on Park Avenue. Christmas. A choir sang. They entered together. They had never been in a Catholic church before, but they liked the singing; it drew them in. Dancesca adjusted her hair. He held Lenora in the crook of his arm. The child was six months old. It was 1976. She still only fit between the length of his hand and his elbow. He leaned down and kissed the child's forehead. His hair was short and he had no beard. He opened the zipper of his ski jacket, and then he touched Dancesca's wrist. She nodded. They went to a back pew. The singing was lofty and beautiful. The priest was drinking from a chalice of wine. The choir sang on. Around them the pews began to empty. The people were walking toward the altar. He and Dancesca looked at each other, suddenly nervous, unsure of the ceremony. They followed the line toward the altar and began to imitate those around them. He put out his tongue, and the bread was placed gently by the priest. The priest touched Lenora on the forehead and smiled. Walking back down along the aisle, he could feel the strange wafer soften and stick to the roof of his mouth. He reached in with his forefinger and scraped a little of the bread off. A tiny piece remained on his finger. He placed the sliver in his child's mouth. An old woman in a head scarf stared at him, eyes wide. He could feel his cheeks suddenly flush. He had done something wrong, he didn't know what. For the rest of the service he kept his head bowed and pulled his child close, cradled her. When the service was finished they walked, head-hung, embarrassed, out from the church, but when they were far enough away, up Park Avenue, Dancesca burst out laughing and the sound of it erupted around him. At a row of parking meters, he handed Dancesca the child. He stood up on a meter—it was his trick—balancing on just one foot. He felt wonderful and ridiculous and alive. He could still taste the bread in his mouth. They walked to their apartment together, turned the key in the door, stood by the heater, put their arms around each other, and kissed, their sleeping child sandwiched between them.

. . .

When noon threatens, Treefrog rises from bed and switches a red coffee can from hand to frozen hand. There is no water left in his yellow canister, so he drops all the way to the gravel and saunters along between the two railway tracks.

Far down the tunnel, he passes the cubicles. An array of graffiti spiders its way across their doors. ELIJAH IS KING. SAILORS AT SEA. GLAUCON WAS HERE, '87. FUCK YOU. On Faraday's door, beneath the suspended toilet seat, are the words ALL I WANT TO DO IS SIT ON MY ASS AND FART AND THINK OF DANTE.

Treefrog stops and blows a kiss to Elijah's door, where the woman must still be sleeping.

Under 94th Street there is a giant kitchen area with a campfire grill in the center. MOCKINGBIRD DON'T SING. LLCOOLJ. TROGLODYTES! I THINK, THEREFORE I AMBLE. WE ARE NOT MILITIA. NY SUCKS. An overcoat is hung out to dry on a long steel cable. The area is all darkness, punctuated by the beams of light coming from the grills. The shafts bear down, blue and white and gray, upon the graffiti and the murals that Papa Love has painted on the tunnel walls. The murals are spread out every hundred yards or so, rats running under the faces of Martin Luther King; John F. Kennedy; Miriam Makeba; Mona Lisa with a penis in her mouth; Huey Newton being crucified beside two white thieves, Nixon and Johnson. There is a petroglyph of a bison with USDA BEEF written on the side. Someone has drawn giant pink udders on it.

Fields of cans and bottles and needles are strewn beneath the paintings.

Pulling the overcoat collar up around his neck, Treefrog goes through a hundred yards of tunnel, past the cubicles and shacks.

He can tell the time of day by the angle of the light shaft—that and the trains.

He reaches the metal stairs and climbs up to the gate, fourteen steps and always fourteen. Dean's shopping cart is tied to the gate with a length of barbed wire—four tiny teddy bears are wound around the side mesh of the cart, along with the Star-Spangled Banner, mudstrewn. Four dented Pepsi cans sit in the bottom of the cart, but Treefrog decides to leave them alone; no need to cause trouble for just twenty cents.

He peers out the gate, through the lacy ironwork, to the embankment covered in a foot-high drift of snow. All is silent, few cars even on the curve off the West Side Highway. There are often crashes on the curve, and he likes to remove the hubcaps from the wrecks before the tow trucks take them away.

Treefrog hunkers down on the metal steps, shoves the empty coffee can through the gaps in the gate, and scoops up some snow and packs it down with his gloved fists: right first, then left.

Below the fresh coating of snow he comes upon hard ice. He should spread water on his catwalk and it would ice over and then nobody would come calling to his nest for sure, they would slip and fall and snap their necks and he would be left in peace forever.

He shoves the can of snow into his overcoat pocket and returns along the tunnel, climbs up on the catwalk—he knows he will never fall; he can even do it on tiptoe—and, in his nest, begins to light another fire. Almost out of wood and leaves, he uses mostly newspaper.

The flames rise up quickly.

He dumps the snow into a blackened pot and chooses an herbal teabag from the Gulag. The Gulag is four feet in the air and one foot deep into the tunnel wall above his bed, built in his second year underground. It took him weeks to chisel out and smooth down perfectly flat. He laid down a little steel toaster tray in the center, so the food wouldn't get rock dust in it, and hung a red bandanna in front for a door. He hammered nails in the wall and then meticulously filed the nails down into spikes, so that if rats jumped up and tried to steal the food they would rip their feet to bits on the sharp points. He has never seen a rat make the leap, so mostly he uses the spikes to hang his socks from.

He leaves the pot over the fire, gets back in his sleeping bag, listens to the sibilant wind whistling along from the south end, waits for the gray snow of Manhattan to boil. So slowly time passes, he thinks, if it passes at all.

On Broadway in the evening, when the snow has briefly relented, he walks along with a bag full of cans and spies her, sitting under the awning of Symphony Space.

With an outstretched arm she holds a tall stack of perhaps twenty paper coffee cups. The top coffee cup almost bows in supplication to the street. He laughs at the sight and listens as she says to passersby, "Spare some change and I'll dance at your wedding!"

Even when nobody gives her money and her body slumps to the ground and her arm becomes tired and her feet are splayed and her eyes are glazed and the edges of her mouth are carved into two deep sorrowful furrows, she continued to smile and say, "Spare some change and I'll dance at your wedding!"

He listens at the door until he is sure that Elijah is not around: easy to tell, since the radio is not playing and Elijah always insists on noise—even when he's sleeping.

Treefrog toes his way forward, waits, knocks, and hears her moan.

"Heyyo."

A long silence and a ruffle of blankets, and he nudges his feet against the door and raps on the wood again. Another moan, but he can tell she's shifting in the bed.

"Get out."

"It's me."

"Who?"

"Treefrog."

"Who are you?"

"Just me."

"Get out."

"Hey, where's Elijah? When's he back?"

"Don't touch me."

"I won't touch you. Got a smoke?"

"No."

"Is today Wednesday or Thursday?"

"Get out."

"It's Friday, ain't it?"

He enters, and she is flat on a mattress in the fabulous dark; he can't even make out her shape. Electricity must be out. He flicks the lighter with one hand, then the other, holds it over where he knows the bed to be. She puts her arm across her eyes and says, "Get out!"

He can tell that she's been crying, her upper lip sucked in against her teeth, her fists clenched, her eyes red.

She looks like a sad sandwich between five sets of blankets.

Shoving the lighter into his pocket, he sits down in the darkness on a wicker chair by the bed, puts his feet on a shattered television set with a fist hole in its glass, and listens to her rummage under the blankets. The chair has two short legs, so he rocks it diagonally.

"What's your name?"

"Don't hurt me."

"I won't hurt you. What's your name?"

After a long silence she says, "Angie."

"There's a song about that."

"If Elijah finds someone here he'll kill me."

"I just wanted to say hello."

"You said it. Now get out."

"You look just like somebody."

"Get out, I said."

"I just want a cigarette."

"I have a knife," she says. "If you come any closer, I'll kill you."

"Saw you this morning," he says. "And I saw you up there on Broadway, too. With the coffee cups. I like that. A big long line of coffee cups. Never seen that before."

"Out!"

"You look just like a friend of mine. I thought you were her. Hey. Why you crying?"

"I ain't crying. Shut up and get out."

"What's wrong with the juice?" he asks.

"The what?"

"What happened the electric?"

"Elijah'll kill you if you don't get out. He said don't let nobody in here."

"You'll have to get Faraday to fix the electric."

"He that ugly white motherfucker in the suit?" she asks.

"Yeah. Connects everyone up. From the light poles topside. Runs the cable down. Even goes to the other tunnels. He can pirate it off the third rail. Sometimes he steps the electric down with transformers. He's a genius with the juice."

"Elijah's gonna kill him too. He whistled at me. Say, what's your name again?"

"Treefrog."

"That's the weirdest goddamn name I ever heard in my life."

"I play the harmonica."

"That don't explain nothing."

"Everyone else calls me that. I don't call me that. I don't like it."

He hears her pull the blankets high around her neck. "Motherfuck," she says, "it's cold." There's a scuffle in the background and she sits up urgently. "What's that?"

"A rat."

"I hate rats."

"You should get a cat."

She shivers. "Elijah don't like cats."

"You want some more blankets?"

"Yeah."

"I got some extra," says Treefrog. "Back in my place. Gimme a smoke first. A smoke for a blanket for the barter man."

"I don't got none."

"I saw you smoking this morning."

"You promise you'll give me a blanket?"

"Yeah."

He feels a cigarette land in his lap and he searches in his overcoat for a lighter, snaps it aflame, pulls the smoke down deep into his lungs, continues rocking the chair diagonally in the darkness.

"Thanks, babe."

"Don't call me that."

"Thanks, Angela."

"It's Angie."

"I like Angela better."

"You're an asshole," she says. "Motherfuck, it's cold. Ain't it cold? You ain't cold? I'm cold."

He rises up from the wicker chair. "Don't go nowhere," he says. "I'm gonna get you a blanket."

He goes to the door and looks across the tunnel to the fading light from the grill. "It's snowing," he says, after a moment.

"I know it's goddamn snowing."

"I like it when it snows. The way it comes down through the grates. You seen it?"

"Man, you're crazy. It's cold. Snow is cold, that's what it is. It's cold. That's all. Cold. This is hell. This is a cold, mother-fucking hell."

"A heaven of hell," he says.

"What you talking about now, asshole?"

"Nothing."

He walks down the tunnel, beating his arms around himself to stave off the wind that howls down from the southern end. In his nest, he finds his extra blankets in huge blue plastic bags beside his books and maps.

Angela, he thinks, as he walks back down toward the cubicle, carrying a blanket for her. A nice name. Six letters. Good symmetry. Angela.

He sees her at the tunnel gate one evening, so stoned that her eyes roll around in their sockets. She tugs him by the sleeve and whispers to him that she used to dance in a club in Dayton, Ohio.

"A little shithole there, outside of town," she says. "I used to do my face with the nicest makeup. There was two platforms.

One girl on each. One night I was onstage and I look up and see my father coming in, you know; he sits himself at a table at the back of the club. My goddamn father! He orders himself a beer and then goes to giving the waitress a hard time 'cause he paid five dollars and only got a plastic glass. Sitting there, just staring up at me while I was dancing. I was scared, Treefy. I thought he was gonna get up there on the stage and hit me like he always done. I wasn't dancing, hardly, I was so scared. All these men were booing and hissing from a table. And then I look down, and my father, he's gone changed the angle of his chair; he's looking at the other platform, at the other girl. Licking his lips. So then I decided. I danced the finest dance I ever done in my life. I swear all heads were turned at me, excepting him. He's just drinking and staring at the other girl and never once looks at me. And when I go out in the parking lot he's waiting for me and he's drunk, and he says, Girl—I'm twenty-two and he's still calling me Girl—and then he asks the name of the other dancer and I says, Cindy. And he says, Thanks. And then he leaves in his old gray Plymouth and leans out the window and says to me, That Cindy girl sure can dance. That's what he said to me. That Cindy girl sure is a dancer."

He dreams that night that she is standing in his liver. A red-brown wall rises in front of her. She has been given digging instructions by Con O'Leary, Rhubarb Vannucci, Sean Power, and Nathan Walker.

She knows how to stand with widespread feet, one behind the other, and how to use all the economy of her body. She chunks away at the wall of his liver, scooping and bucketing out the sickness and disease, so delicate with her shovel that he doesn't feel a thing. Angela scrapes all the residue from him, and when a spot is clean she leans across and kisses it, and it sends a shiver through the rest of his body. All the filth comes away at her feet and she buckets it out of his liver, and when she has the gland completely clean, when the buckets are empty, when he is cured, they dance around his liver together in an ecstatic twirl, their eyes closed, round and round and round, Angela with her colorful beads bobbing in her hair. Then there is a sucking sound and they are blown upward through his body and out his mouth and she stands in front of him, smiling, all the bile gone, even from beneath her fingernails, and she reaches out and touches him softly, moves along his chest, plucking at his hairs, and her fingers go down further to where she opens his fly with spectacular delicacy; there's not an ounce of pain in his liver, it's a beautiful dream. Every now and then a dream can be impeccable in the tunnel.

chapter 6

1932–45

Rhubarb Vannucci and Sean Power set up a pigeon coop on the roof of Vannucci's Lower East Side tenement building, a wooden coop with two sliding doors and a chicken-wire roof. There have been some recent robberies, so Vannucci has dipped his pigeons in vats of bright dye bought from a clothing factory. He soaks every part of the pigeons except their heads. Even the underside of the wings sucks up the dye. The birds flap, rudely orange, through the sky. Anyone in the neighborhood can instantly point out a Vannucci pigeon. They look like winging orange peels breaking the skies of Manhattan.

Sean Power decides to paint his birds bright blue. The shed feathers make a fabulous collage on the rooftop.

On a July morning the two men challenge each other to a pigeon race. They make a bet of a dollar each.

Nathan Walker and Eleanor O'Leary have agreed to carry the pigeons over the Brooklyn Bridge and release them on the far side of the river. They weave along on bicycles. Eleanor's hair flows in a stream behind her. Walker balances the pigeon cases on his bicycle basket. They move in strange tandem; there is a quality of waltz to the journey. Whenever she can, Eleanor directs her bicycle along a length of shadow, keeping the tires within its width. Walker plays the game of avoiding the same shadows. He watches as she takes both hands off the bars and stretches her arms wide, tottering slightly but still keeping her bicycle true to the long lines of dark.

When they reach the far side of the bridge, Eleanor leans her bike against Walker's. They spread a blanket on the concrete to share a picnic before they release the birds: a bottle of Coca-Cola, a bar of chocolate, some bread with cheddar cheese.

Eleanor touches Walker's wrist, points at the pigeons in the cages—one orange and one blue—and they both laugh.

Halfway through the picnic, a passing pedestrian spits in Walker's face and shouts at Eleanor, "Nigger lover!"

She thumbs her nose at the pedestrian and Walker wipes the spit away with a handkerchief. He drops the handkerchief off the bridge toward the water. They watch it spiral away. He says nothing, but they pack the last of the picnic back into the basket, take out two jars of paint, and later they release the pigeons into the air.

The couple pedal furiously back across the bridge, watching the pigeons vying for the lead.

Walker is way out in front, the empty cages still balanced on the front of the bike. "Wait for me!" shouts Eleanor. The pigeons disappear in the sky.

When the two cyclists arrive back at Vannucci's home, both

of the gambling men are furious. In their hands each holds a pigeon that has been newly painted, half orange, half blue.

They are fighting over which one belongs to whom and who is the rightful owner of the two dollars. Walker and Eleanor stand on the tenement rooftop, doubled over with laughter.

The two men give the couple strange glances, then tuck the multicolored pigeons back into the coop.

"Frig me," says Power.

"What is frig?" asks Vannucci.

"A frig is . . ."

And then Power, too, starts to chuckle.

"A frig," he says, winking at Walker, "a frig is somewheres ya keep things cool."

Eleanor places a picture of her mother and father on her bedside table. It was taken at a summer carnival in Brooklyn in the early years of the century, a Ferris wheel in the background static against the sky like a cheap bracelet. Con O'Leary has the beginnings of a mustache smudged above his lip. Maura's dress is buttoned high at her neck, but the third and fourth buttons have popped open, unnoticed, revealing cleavage. They are standing by the strong-arm machine. The bell on the machine is at the very top—where it says STRONGMAN EXTRAORDINARY!—and Eleanor is sure that her father is the one who has just slammed down the hammer. He is smiling, his belly is full and proud, and his cheeks are puffed out. Eleanor likes to think of him in that same position when she takes the subway out on weekday mornings to the Brooklyn Heights haberdashery where she works. She salutes her father's sleeping form as she travels back and forth underneath the river. She doesn't think of him as agonized or frozen in a strange ascension—rather,

he is upright, proud, standing by some muck-bed strong-arm
machine, held in tableau, grinning.

Familiar and trembling, they meet in darkness. One evening on
a park bench she asks Walker to comb her hair. He steps
behind the bench. Her hair is heavy, pendant. When he is finished, she turns and kneels on the wooden slats and leans
toward him. In his hands he can still feel the weight of her hair.
She says his name out loud: Nathan. He looks at her, and it
seems to him that her voice bends back the nearby grasses.

Eighteen years after the blowout, Nathan Walker emerges from
a railway freight tunnel on the West Side of Manhattan.

Quick clouds cast shadows, and the streets are thatched with
ribbons of sunlight. There is a spring in his step, although he
has been digging all day. Working the railway tunnel is easier
than working underwater, although just as dangerous, men
dying when boxes of dynamite explode in their fingers, their
bodies ripped apart and their thumbs blown so high they could
be hitching a lift to heaven. At the age of thirty-seven Walker's
body has changed a little, just a slight slide out at the waist and a
new scar above his left eye from a Great Depression riot when a
policemen mashed a billy club into his head. He'd emerged
from a diner one night into a dark sea of faces. The protesters
carried placards. They were shouting about job losses and low
wages. Walker had gone alongside the protesters silently and
stoically. His wages had been cut too—the tunnels were full of
desperate men ready to work, and he kept his job only because
Sean Power was head of the union. He had moved with the flow
of eyes. Screaming was heard further down the street, and then

the billy club came from behind. It landed first in the soft part of his skull and then whipped around to his forehead, smashing against his eye. He caught a fleeting glimpse of the cop before he went down, and then there were horse hooves all around him. A hoof landed on his groin. Pain shot through him. Winded, Walker crawled across the street and lay under the awning of a cigar shop, feeling the blood run past his lips. At the hospital he had to wait five hours for the stitches—the doctor pried open the scab with brusque fingers—and the suture was done drunkenly, leaving a wormlike wiggle through Walker's eyebrow.

He strolls way uptown, along the landfill by Riverside Drive, past the shanties, then east toward a shop full of tuxedos.

A bell sounds at the shop door and a small black man with granite-colored hair comes from behind a curtain, a pencil at his ear. He looks down at the mud on Walker's boots, gives a derisory eye-flick at his filthy overalls and the red hat strung under his chin, and goes immediately to a row of cheap rentals, but Walker directs the clerk to the expensive rack. Under a faint yellow light he tries on a large black jacket with a shiny velvet collar. It is so long unused there is a mothball in the pocket, but it's the only one left in his size, since there's a dance in Harlem that night and a skein of men has been in and out of the shop all day. Walker counts out money for the suit rental and a new shirt.

At home he washes his body in the porcelain sink and tries on the frilly white shirt. The buttons seem tiny and foreign. Arthritis has already begun to nibble at his hands. Walker can predict a rainy day by the pain in his fingertips. He doesn't button the neck of his shirt but lets the bow tie cover the gap.

He can't help chuckling at the way the shirt frills rumple at his chin, at how exceedingly white the cloth is. "You are so god-damn handsome, Nathan Walker!" he says to the dusty mirror, and then he leaps across the room in delight and nervousness, swinging around a broken stovepipe, his knees protesting at the sudden violence of dance, a silver cross bouncing at his neck.

The cross was bought for two dollars from a woman down-stairs, a fortune-teller who always wears a long red dress and two feathers in her hair. She tells the future by the pattern of spit that tobacco makes in a spittoon. Men, and women too, lean across the metal cup and spit into it, the men in big gobs, the women in shy dribbles. She stares down into the tobacco grains and prescribes remedies for future despair. Everybody is due despair in their lives, she says, and therefore everybody needs a remedy—it's a fact of life and it only costs two dollars to cure, a guaranteed bargain.

The cross, she has told Walker, will keep his heart from fer-rying its way into his mouth when he is nervous. He must wear it against his skin all day long, no matter what.

Walker stands by the piano that has been given to him as a gift. A white ribbon has been tied around the instrument, so he doesn't open the lid. He touches the smooth ribbon, and then he rubs his fingers along the piano lid, drags a stool across, and sits—in underpants and white shirt and silver cross—pretending to play, running his fingers through the air, inventing ragtime, until he gets so sweaty he takes off the shirt. He rubs his lips together for a tune and his music grows louder and louder until he hears a foot stomping on the ceiling above him and a roar: "Shut up already, down there!"

The following day he and Eleanor are turned away from four restaurants and refused admittance to a cinema despite their clothes. On the streets people mutter about them. Cars slow down and taunts are hurled. At home, in the apartment on 131st Street, Walker must bend his body to duck under the doorframe. Eleanor puts her hand in his jacket pocket as he carries her over the threshold.

Her waist is wren-thin and adolescent, and he whispers that he could carry ten of her and she says, "Don't you even think about it, I'm the only one of me you're ever going to get."

She takes the mothball from his pocket and shakes her head in amusement, thumping him playfully on the chest. The long white taffeta of her wedding dress swishes as she walks down the corridor to the common bathroom. She flushes the mothball down the toilet.

"Get ready for me," she shouts along the corridor over the gurgle of water.

"I'm ready, hon."

Back in the room, she latches the door. She has translated her face by removing her makeup. Just seventeen, she looks even younger. Walker is out of the jacket and standing by the piano, motioning for her to play. She shakes her head, no, and drags him away from it, onto the single bed, where they fall in a rehearsal of many nights of dreams.

"Ready my foot," she says, and her hands disappear inside his shirt, around to his back, and she pulls him very close.

They move like two chiaroscurists above the covers, black and white, white and black, then sleep under foreheads wet with sweat. They lie on their sides, arms around each other, one hip a hill of bony pink, the other muscular brown. Eleanor wakes and kisses the scar above Nathan's eye. The clock on the wall cuckoos for eight o'clock in the evening. Desire lies on her tongue like morning breath, and she wakes him with a playful jab to the stomach.

"I love you."

"I love you too," he grunts.

"Don't fall back asleep."

He opens his eyes. "Did y'all ever see a crane dance?"

"No."

"One foot first, then the other."

"Show me."

"Sandhill cranes," he says. "Like this. I saw them all the time in Georgia."

She laughs as he rises from the bed and dances on the mattress.

Later, there is a loud knock at the door. Walker, in his underpants, ritually bends his head at the doorframe. He scratches his belly as his eyes adjust.

Vannucci, Power, and the fortune-teller stand, grinning, with four bottles of champagne in their hands. The fortune-teller breezes in, clicking across the floor in gold lamé heels, her butterfly sleeves hanging down. Power limps after her, his teeth already pulling at the champagne cork.

Vannucci's balding head peeps around the open frame, then backs away, embarrassed.

But the fortune-teller sits on the bed beside Eleanor and pulls back the covers to reveal the girl's white toes. Eleanor flushes and draws her foot back. The fortune-teller chuckles and grabs again.

Walker, leaning against the piano, struggles his way into a pair of trousers, one foot in the air, while Power tries to push him over and spray champagne down his underwear.

Only Vannucci waits outside the door until the couple is fully dressed, and then the party begins, the handle on the Victrola wound up ferociously by the red-faced Italian. He stands above the machine as the needle travels over the grooves. It gives out solitary, beautiful notes. He smiles at the rhythm, clicks his fingers, drains a glass. Power puts an empty bottle to his lips and imitates a trumpet with it. The fortune-teller lifts her dress way up high to reveal two very red garters and seamed stockings. She scissor-kicks toward the ceiling, singing with the music, the songs slowly dropping down from her throat toward her hips, where they swivel.

"You're a classy dame," says Power.

"Thank you, sugar. You been at the laudanum, then?"

"Why's that?"

"Either that or you're drunk."

"No I ain't."

"Then why ain't you dancin'?"

"You just said the word."

"He's drunk as a stewbum!"

"No I ain't!"

A hush descends when Maura O'Leary appears at the door. Still in mourning black, hair in a bun, lace at her neck, she says she hasn't come to stay. She sighs and looks around the room, sees the piano in the corner topped with bottles and a lit cigar propped over the edge, smoke curling up from it.

"Well, well, well," she says.

"Ma'am?"

"No more ma'am. No need to call me ma'am."

"Yessum," says Walker.

"Maura is easiest. Call me Maura."

"Yessum. Yes."

She sighs. "I never thought I'd see a day like this, never thought I'd see anything like it."

"Me neither."

"I'm not saying it's the best thing."

From the far side of the room Sean Power belches and says, "Nothing wrong with it."

"I didn't ask you," says Maura.

"And ya didn't not ask me, neither."

"I mean," she says, "in some places it's not legal."

"Not New York," says Power.

Maura touches the lace at her neck, fingers it for a long time. "In some places you go to jail. In some places they'll kill you."

"Illegal don't mean it's not right."

"Well, that's true," says Maura.

"So we agree?" says Power.

"Perhaps we'll agree to disagree."

"I knew we'd agree on something," mutters Power.

"Shut up, Sean!" says Walker. "Let the lady say what she has to say."

A silence permeates the room. Power slugs at the bottle of champagne and passes it to Vannucci, who doesn't drink. The fortune-teller goes to the window, looks out.

"We love each other, Mom," says Eleanor eventually.

"It's not always enough."

"It's enough for us."

"You're young."

"Walker here ain't exactly sprung chicken!" says Power.

Looking around again, Maura says, "And I don't know how Con would feel about this either, but I guess I'll just have to wait for heaven and see then. I'm not so sure he'd be happy. I'm not so sure I'm happy. I'm not so sure anybody's happy."

"I'm happy!" shouts Power.

Walker darts a look at his friend, then shifts his stance. "We ain't out to make you unhappy, ma'am."

"You gotta remember," she says, "it'll be hard times for you even when it's good times."

"We know that. Thank you, ma'am. Maura."

"Well. I said what I wanted."

"Thank you."

"Now I'd like a little drink, please."

"Forgetting my manners," says Walker.

Maura wets her lips at the edge of a glass of champagne. "Good luck to you both, I suppose." Putting down the glass, she turns to leave, but at the door she hangs her head and says, "Maybe you'll be good together. Maybe you'll be okay."

"You think she means it?" asks Walker, when the door is closed.

"Of course she does," says Eleanor. "She gave us the piano, didn't she?"

"She's a fine woman. The finest of fine women."

"All right, then," says Power, swinging his cane. "Let's dance!"

"You the dancingest cripple I ever seen!" says the fortune-teller, moving away from the window, swirling her hips.

"You bet ya."

And then Power roars, "Let the jelly hit the fan, boys!"

The group raises a toast to long life and happiness, and, to the beat of Sean Power's imaginary trumpet, the newly married couple flaps a crazy dance, all arms and legs, on top of the piano late into the night. Walker winks at Eleanor as he stands on one foot and stretches out his arms.

A series of bricks greet them through the bedroom window, leaving shards of glass on the floor and a hole in the frame until they simply just tape up a sheet of plastic to slap in the wind. One of the bricks is wrapped in a note that reads NO PENGUINS ALLOWED. Another says SILKS OUT. Another says, simply, NO.

Walker pays for the damage to the windows and rents an

apartment higher up, unreachable from the street by stone or rock. He knows it would be much worse elsewhere; in other parts of the city they would end up dead. He feels as if he has exiled himself to the air, but he knows there is safety for Eleanor in the exile.

Marriage has brought to him the things that it marries: temperance and bitterness, love and disaffection, fecundity and bareness, longitude and its own startling finality. So he leaves the stone throwers alone and drags everything upstairs to the new apartment, even the piano.

It is a larger room, the sunlight exposing gaps in the wooden floorboards, yellow wallpaper peeling off the walls, iron-colored water stains around the kitchen sink. They still share a toilet with other tenants. The floorboards of the corridor creak when they walk toward it.

Eleanor throws her toothbrush out one morning when she leaves it at the sink by mistake. She has seen legions of cockroaches crawling around the bathroom.

Next door to them lives a cornet player, and his deep notes sound out at all hours of the night. He plays with a truncated rhythm, waking up at the weirdest times. And in the morning when they walk past his room he hisses at them through the gap under the door: Penguins, he says, fucking penguins. Eleanor has developed a special walk through the apartment—she calls it the Antarctic Shuffle—and she laughs when she does it: her feet flatfooted and her ass sticking out, her elbows tucked in by her waist, and her hands flapping out at her side. But late at night she curls up in bed and cries at the thought of slices of glass landing on their bed, ripping open their naked flesh. And so Walker tells her things that help her sleep, things he invents and remembers and, by remembering, invents.

. . .

"I weren't much more than a shirttail, see, and I wanted to make myself a gator-skin wallet. I'd seen lots of boys at school with wallets from gators. So I told my momma. She had herself a shotgun and I asked her for a loan of it. I said I was gonna shoot myself a gator so's I could make that wallet. And she said, Y'all can't shoot a gator, I done told you that before, Nathan; it ain't right to hurt nothing.

And I says, Momma, it's no different'n a cow. So she looks at me all Momma-like and smiles. No different'n a cow! she says.

Big ol' voice. She had a big ol' voice right up till she died.

Anyways. Next day she takes me out in the canoe, and I'm the one paddling. Right over near a place called Cow Island. We wait a long time by the swamp, her and me, and all I could see was gator eyes. And this one gator, he's lying in the mud, all quiet like. Then this heron flies low over the water and lands nearby. The gator just ups and swishes his tail and knocks the heron clean dead. Eats it up. And so Momma, she turns to me and says, Well then, son, y'all ever seen a cow do *that*?"

On Sunday mornings they walk together to a Southern Baptist service in a basement by Saint Nicholas Square. If the streets are quiet they walk hand in hand. But if they hear a car come behind them, or a window opening, or voices around a corner, they unclasp and part like two rivers. Eleanor likes to arrive at the service a little late so the great lift of gospel music greets her when she pushes open the door. She feels comfortable here. The preacher's voice goes up and down, a wild landscape of vowels and consonants. Sometimes he punches his hands toward the ceiling, and after services he kisses all the women on the cheek, even Eleanor.

On a late spring morning she is baptized in a tub of cold water near the basement stairs. The choir, in white tunics trimmed with gold, stands around and sings. The preacher rolls up his sleeves. A chorus of hallelujahs is raised when he dunks Eleanor in the bath. Embarrassed by the white dress against her skin—the wetness exposes her girdle—she folds her arms across her breasts, but the preacher whispers, "You look like an angel, pull back them wings." She sits up in the tub and laughs. The choir rings out in song again, and afterward the congregation munches on potato salad and well-cut sandwiches.

She and Walker stroll home in the heat, and her dress is almost dry by the time she turns the key in the door.

In the Catholic church downtown where she used to go there were dark mutterings from the white people in the pews, even though Walker never went there with her. The priest grew red-faced and shook his finger at her, all resentment and narrow eyes and acrimony. He banned her from the services when Eleanor suggested to him that Jesus was, more likely than not, much darker than He was ever allowed to look on the cross.

She sits on the fire escape, hidden from view. She pulls down one shoulder strap of her summer dress and holds her face up to the sun in the vainest of hopes for something near equivalence with her husband. Earlier, at a shop on 125th Street, the owner wouldn't allow her to try on a hat. He curled up his lip in disgust. He said he'd heard about her, that anyone who lived with niggers became a nigger themselves. He said he didn't want any nigger hair in his hats. Bad for business. The words

COLUM MCCANN / 100

foamed at the edge of his mouth, and he tightened his eyes. "You can buy one," he said, "but you can't try it on."

Eleanor placed the hat on the counter silently and went home to sit on the fire escape.

Now, turning her face to the hot sun, she drops the second strap on her dress. Below the fire escape, rows of boys sit on crates and shine shoes as the summer sun hammers down.

Walker can only chuckle at the sight of her burnt skin. "It won't do no good for what's in your belly," he tells her.

He rubs cream on her chafed back and across her neck.

"Bet it's a boy," he says.

"What makes you think that, hon?"

"The fortune-teller told me."

Eleanor laughs. "A boy by tobacco spit."

"And a good load of it, too!"

"You really think it's a boy?"

"It don't matter to me none," says Walker. "It can be a kangaroo for all I care."

"Hopping all over Harlem."

"Hopping and skipping and dancing."

"Y'ever get that feeling?" she asks as he rubs her shoulders. "That feeling that when you walk down the street their eyes are ripping you up? You know? When you walk past and you feel like they've just sliced you? Like they've got these razor blades in their eyes."

"Welcome to the real world, hon."

"All of us are supposed to be created in the image of God."

"Maybe so, hon, but even God's gotta take a shit every now and then. Even God's gotta wipe His ass like the rest of us."

"Nathan! That's sacrilege."

"No less true, sacrilegious or not."

"You know what?" she says, after a moment. "That man in the shop wouldn't let me try on a hat."

"Holy Name! That's only the tip of the iceberg. It gets worse. It gets to be a routine. It gets so's you think it's normal. It gets so you think God is just shittin' on down every minute of the day. Like He's gone and got Himself a bad case of diarrhea. Like it's just raining on down from His ass."

"Nathan!"

"Well, it's just the truth. Y'all ever heard that song? Bill Broonzy."

And he sings: Lord, I'm so lowdown, baby, I declare I'm looking up at down.

He stops. "That's us, baby, looking up at down."

She unwinds a thread from the bottom of her dress, wraps it around her finger, and then snaps it off. "I want my child to be able to buy hats," she says.

"He can buy all the hats he wants. He can even borrow mine."

"Come here," she says.

"What?"

"Kiss me."

Walker leans to kiss her, and with her forefinger, she smudges some of the cream on his nose. "No son of mine is gonna wear that thing," she whispers. "No daughter neither. It's horrendous."

"I believe even God Hisself got one of these hats."

"Listen to you!"

Two months later Clarence Walker is born at home, greeted by a string of rosary beads. Eleanor allows the Catholic ritual for her mother's sake.

Maura O'Leary is the midwife. Lately she has allowed the gray hair to amass on her head. She is fifty-one years old and has only three months left to live; already her lungs seem to have migrated from her chest, weighted down with so much phlegm. She carries a number of large handkerchiefs and, embarrassed, she drops the phlegm into them, closing the cloth as if sealing a vital letter. Almost blind, her eyeglasses have acrobatic twists of plastic at the edges and thick lenses between them. Yet Maura's sickness has given her a strength and a quiet tolerance—she will die in a fit of coughing in a hospital bed, screaming at the nurses that her son-in-law should be allowed to come to the bedside. The nurses will say no, they cannot fathom a Negro at any white woman's dying bed. She will rant and rave in the immaculate bedsheets, and she will die with a whispered curse on her lips for the nurses.

But, right now, she wipes a washcloth across her daughter's brow and says, "He's a fine strap of a child, girl, a fine young strap."

Ancestry steps through Clarence in colorful swaths—he has light cinnamon-colored skin and tufts of rude red hair on his head.

The women take turns holding him until Nathan Walker comes into the room. Walker winks at his wife as he places the red hat on the boy's head.

"Don't do that!" says Eleanor, sitting up in bed.

"What?"

"Take that thing off his head!"

Laughing, he removes the hat, wraps the baby in a sweater, and bears him proudly down the street in his arms—past vendors of pig's knuckles and rice, past women eating tania roots on doorsteps, past boys playing stickball in a vacant gray lot, past bored men in caps leaning against light poles. On a corner he waves to some well-dressed men who are signing up soldiers for the struggle in Ethiopia. Nearby, four men look up from their game of dominoes, and Walker grins at them. They smile back. On an outside stoop of a brownstone he nods to a young girl whose voice is in mourning for the fields of Alabama.

"Sing on," he tells her.

Further along the street a yellow Cadillac overtakes a low-slung Packard. A man leans out the Packard window and stares as Walker goes by. Walker is aware of all the whispers but he swings his body, big and threatening in the sunlight, all the way down to the corner shop, where he browses in the aisles for a long time, buys two bunches of nasturtiums to bring home for the ladies. A five-dollar bill is pulled crinkled from his overalls. The shopowner, Ration Rollins, tugs at a shirtsleeve garter and doesn't even look in Walker's eyes. He lays the change down on the counter and turns away, blowing air from his bottom lip up to his gray hair. With his back turned, Rollins starts arranging cigarettes that need no arrangement.

"And a block of ice," says Walker. He throws the change on the counter and adds, "To cool yourself down."

He tucks the flowers under one arm, the baby in the other, and leaves the shop with his head thrown back in laughter. He whispers to the baby, "Clarence Walker, you are so goddamn handsome!"

But behind some conspiratorial windows he is indicted for carrying something that doesn't rightly belong to him: most red-haired nigger child I've ever seen.

Two more children follow in '36 and '37, both girls, Deirdre and Maxine. Eleanor fits the girls in a pram, and the boy walks beside her, holding her hand. They go to the park: soiled swans on a small brown lake; a seller of chestnuts; a man in a bow tie proclaiming the love and scholarship of Marcus Garvey; a row of schoolgirls, amazed, bent over the baby carriage; other mothers smiling at Eleanor, coming over to ruffle the strange texture of the children's hair. But Eleanor sometimes feels uncomfortable. Mostly it is the whites—the cops and the shop-owners—who stare at her. At times she finds shade, sits under a tree in the park for hours. Or decides to walk with the kids late in the evening, in the approaching darkness, a head scarf on. She is most fully at ease in these moments of aloneness.

As night falls on Harlem, she closes the curtains and climbs into bed beside Walker while their children sleep. She runs her fingers along his tired shoulder blades.

Two nights a month the fortune-teller looks after the babies and Eleanor joins Walker at Loews Seventh Avenue theater, a cinema for Coloreds. Her husband arrives early—after clocking off from the tunnels—and Eleanor tiptoes down the steps to find him. When she gets to Walker's row of seats, she puts her finger to the lips of an old black man, who stares at her, aston-ished, as she moves past. The old man touches her hand and smiles. "Go on ahead, ma'am."

She returns his smile, shoves her way along the row toward her husband.

Darkness hides them, an illicit love affair being made out of their own marriage.

They sit rigidly until the lights are turned off and the music sounds out. Then they drape their jackets over the seats and melt down into the soft red velvet. Walker rubs his wife's wed-ding ring finger, lifts her hand, tongues along her knuckles. The titles flash away from the screen; it is 1939 and Don Ameche is stepping out in the film *Swanee River*. Walker whispers that one day he will take his four-year-old son down there, to the country of his own youth. He wants the boy to know what it feels like to take a boat through swamp water, to skim under trees of hanging moss, to turn a corner and avoid a sleeping alligator, to come, amazed, upon a flock of dancing cranes. When he speaks of Georgia, Walker sounds as if he has swallowed its rivers and mud in gulps. Eleanor lets the dream seep out of him. She's aware that if the child was taken south, both father and son might just end up like the Spanish moss, swinging from the limb of a tree. In Tennessee recently they lynched a man by hammering nails between the bones in his wrists and feet, nailed him to a bough of a tree, just like Jesus, except Jesus at least had the dignity of a solar eclipse and there probably weren't any buzzards in Jerusalem to eat the swinging carcass.

"You should go," she says, not meaning it, saying it only for the sake of his brief pleasure.

"Georgia," he says, as if it's her name.

Eleanor takes the head scarf off and her hair falls and she lets Walker's breath caress her ear, his tongue against her lobe, and she closes her eyes to the images on the screen: *Howilovya, howilovya, my dear ol' Swanee.*

They sink down in their seats and, instead of their bodies, they send their minds out to roam.

"We had a canoe, see. And the swamp had all these tall cypress trees what y'all never see in New York. They blocked out most of the light. And I went out looking for Spanish moss. Paddling away. It was nice out there. Quiet. Dark. Lots of water lilies and tree stumps and all. Sometimes I'd be paddling along and I'd turn that paddle and it was like some hand just came out of the water and turned me. Front end swinging and back staying the same. And sometimes you'd be feeling like you was spinning in the center of the world. Flipping the paddle sideways and pushing against the flow.

Anyways, I weren't much beyond ten years of age. I stood in the center of that boat, feet even spaced, and reached up to take the moss from the trees. Filled the back of the canoe. Then the boat'd drift past the tree and I'd kneel down on the wooden slats, take the canoe in a circle. I had good arms for a kid. I coulda stood under the same cypress all day long and grabbed all the moss I wanted, but I liked that game. Return. Collection. Return. Collection. I'd go home at night and lumber that moss up the road in sacks. Y'all's grandmomma, she'd dry the plants for weeks in the sun, hang them from the top of our porch. Then she'd take old shirts and make pillowcases from them, stuff the cases with moss.

When I lied awake at night I could put my nose to the pillow and smell the swamp and, Lord, if it didn't move with me in my dreams.

That summer I found myself the skull of a gator shored up between two fallen logs. It musta died and been washed down-river. In that part of the swamp, there was all these trees been shattered by lightning and wild muscadines and vultures sitting on the branches, flapping they wings and getting rid of lice and insects like they do. Now don't be scared, 'cause it wasn't scary. The boat rocked in the water. The sun was going down. I made a circle and went on back, leaned over the side of the boat, picked up that skull, poked it a few times to see if there be any cottonmouths sleeping in it. Then I grabbed that skull and threw it to the back of the boat, where it landed and looked like it was grinning. Then I paddled like hell. The skitters were out and they was biting. I lit a branch with lots of resin at the top, went through the swamp, holding the branch. Lord, it was beautiful. But when I got home, was your grandmomma ever mad! She was waiting on the porch, a switch in her hand. I tried to go on past her, but she went grabbed me by the back of my shirt, told me to bend over, and then whupped me good. At the dinner table she told me to wipe the grin off my face, that a boy when he's whupped should act like a whupped boy. But ya see, while I was in my boat, I'd gone shoved moss in the back of my pants. So I didn't feel a thing!

That night, she came into my bedroom. The skull of the gator was sat on my bed. She stood looking at it. She smiled her big smile. And then she reached underneath her apron and took out some moss.

Y'all left this in the outhouse, she said to me.

And then she just left me there, with that big load of moss, scratching my head. That was your grandmomma; she was a fine woman.

Now y'all's grandpa, I didn't know him much—he went to heaven when I was a little boy—but, story is, he could go underwater and hypnotize a gator. The gator'd be just lying there in the sun. And he'd swim underneath the water and stroke the belly of the gator, and that gator would get sleepy like the sleepiest little boy. And sometimes he put his hat on the sleepy gator's head, and soon everyone'd go off to sleep together all hush hush hush, right off to sleep like the sleepiest little boy."

Walker carves his children's initials on his shovel and carries it down to Riverside Park with him. He doesn't dig anymore, just puts the finishing touches on the grouting of the railway tunnel—a high, wide tunnel meant for freight trains—but he keeps the shovel with him as a reminder of the ability of miracles.

Eleanor gets an afternoon shift in a defense plant. Sometimes she brings home a couple of bullets for Walker's favorite trick. He tells the children the history of the trick, and the history of it exaggerates itself. But, when Walker demonstrates, he is too slim and the bullets keep falling out of his navel, delighting the kids.

Three years older than the century—too old to fight—Walker collects rubber tires and scrap steel for the war effort. He goes around the neighborhood and roars, "Victory scrap! Victory scrap!" He hangs a homemade flag for the 369th Regiment out his window and tells stories to his son about the first Colored pilots to wing their way over the beachheads in Anzio. His hands, though bitten by rheumatism, make great sweeping motions in the air as he talks of the airmen and their fabulous planes. When the 369th returns there is a party in Harlem, and bunting flaps with bravado over the streets. Trumpets are blown. Ticker tape whitens the pavements and shouts ring loud. Walker leans out of his window and sees his son dance through the collected tires, feet stepping quickly, pure motion. He remains at the window for much of the evening, watching his son, all love, all pride, all fatherly envy for his youth.

chapter 7

we have all been
here before

*H*e thinks about inviting Angela up to his place, but a couple of years ago, in his second summer underground, he brought a girl to his nest and she froze with vertigo. A leg either side of the narrow catwalk, she sat and wept. Runnels through her makeup. He had to wrap his arms around her and then guide her down the catwalk like a stubborn mule. She wore tight black jeans and a pink tank top shorn off at the rib cage showing a silver earring protruding from her belly button. Halfway along the beam she froze again, glanced down at the tracks, and screamed.

Treefrog looked at her and was reminded of the idea of wild animals caught in traps; he wondered if she would bite her own heart out and limp away lopsided.

After an hour of coaxing he lifted her to the ground. She leaned against him, trembling. A run of blood appeared at her teeth where she had chewed her upper lip. He didn't want to touch her after that, though he'd paid twenty-five dollars up front and he'd been waiting for months for a girl, saved up all his extra money. He hadn't had a woman since Dancesca, back in the good days, the best of days. When the girl was gone— when she left the tunnel and was far away, back on the streets— he crawled along and put his nose close to the beam and sniffed the catwalk and breathed her in and she smelled good.

The warmth of the library on 42nd Street and the vast staircases and the many-bulbed chandeliers and the strangeness of electric light and the pleasure of a shit over porcelain in the second-floor bathroom, though the toilet paper is cheap and a little rough to the touch. At the basin, Treefrog lets the hot water cleanse his hands and face. He feels good walking through the corridors, past the showcases of books and into the study rooms, sometimes closing his eyes just for practice, never bumping into people. Books everywhere, fabulous books, even engineering journals, which he sometimes steals, but it's too cold today to think of acquisitions.

Instead, Treefrog makes his way to the third floor, where he fills in a slip for a tunnel-building book—he knows the author and call number by heart. He waits in the long pew until the number flashes on the screen above his head.

"Thank you, friend," he says to the young man who hands him the book.

The third floor is always warmest. He takes a seat in the center of the giant reading room, opens the book, but doesn't read it, just leans back in his chair, warms his hands under the table lamp, and stares up at the fabulous universe of the ceiling, the faded clouds, the cherubs, the flowers, the vines, the rosettes, the acanthus leaves. He takes off his blue wool cap, lets his hair fall around him, counts the panels in the ceiling, their perfect symmetry. Great men must have put together the ceiling once, carving the intricacies, using tiny scalpels to add the twists to the cornices, chiseling form out of wood with slow and brutal patience, using the mathematic skill in their hands to animate their work. He tells himself that he would like to make a map of the ceiling, re-create it on graph paper.

An Asian girl, too polite to move away from the opposite side of the desk, looks up when he takes off his coat. He knows that he smells and he wants to tell the girl, I have my pride, Sister Asia.

He shuffles in the puddle of melt at his feet, looking furtively at her from under his hair.

Treefrog has seen men in the library take out their penises and flail them beneath the table—not homeless men, either— fumbling first with their flies and then delicately letting their members flop out. They look down as if they're about to speak into a microphone and then they change their gaze, stare intently into books as they begin to stroke themselves, so adept that the rest of their bodies hardly even quake. Once he saw a businessman licking semen off his hand—he caught Treefrog's eye as he licked and grinned. Treefrog had a pair of scissors in his pocket. He fingered it gently, held it up, and the businessman scurried out of the library.

He clamps his arms down and closes tight on his armpits to trap the scent of his body, puts his hands between his knees. Sister Asia is so lovely: her blue blouse is buttoned high and her spectacles are gold and her eyes are brown and she has a full red mouth with a glisten of Vaseline over dry lips. He lifts his head and smiles at her, but she stares into her book, adjusts her eyeglasses on her nose. Perhaps she caught a whiff of him when he leaned across.

Maybe he should pay a visit to the welfare hotel off Riverside, just breeze his way up the stairs to the bathroom. Scrub himself down to nothing, maybe even shave his long beard, then slash at his reflection in the mirror: black man white man red man brown man American.

His laces open, his feet unswelling in the shoes, the gloves relaxing around his fingers, his hat not quite so tight around his head.

Down the stairs and out through the revolving door, opening his overcoat to show the security guard that he has no books. He feels the weight of a spud wrench in his pocket.

It's dark now and Treefrog huddles under the portico, counting out his money. Eighteen dollars forty-seven cents, and he drops one of the pennies to the snow to make the total an even forty-six. He walks down the steps and sticks out his gloved hands to capture a few snowflakes. One of these days the snow will stop and he will be able to sell some of his books up on Broadway, make a few dollars, perhaps enough for a little more ganja from Faraday to see himself through.

Past the statues of the lions, hooded with white, along Fifth Avenue onto 42nd Street, into Bryant Park.

Some poor bum is lying under a green bench, not even shivering; maybe he's dead. The moon up above him like the face of a bloated drunk. Treefrog hunkers down beside the man. "Heyyo," he whispers loudly. Not a stir. "Heyyo." He lifts up

the end of the blanket and begins to unlace the man's shoes.
Leather, and no holes either. Pity they aren't a size nine. The
shoe comes off easily, and the man just rolls a little on his side.
All the topside bums are stupid enough to keep their money
under the insoles of their shoes. Treefrog lifts up the sweaty
flap. Goddamn, just five dollars. He puts it to his nose and
smells. Enough for another small bottle. Robin Treefrog Hood.
Steal from the poor to give to the poor to give to the liver.

He leaves the shoe half dangling on the bum's foot. At the
edge of the park he throws three pebbles at the man, hits him
with the third, wakes him. The man jumps up and looks around,
but Treefrog disappears behind the bushes and hops over the
wall. Just wake the poor fool so that he doesn't get his feet frost-
bitten. Sorry, brother. Won't do it again. That's a promise. But
there was probably twenty dollars in the other shoe anyway.

Out of Bryant Park. Along toward the Times Square subway.
Down the iced piss-slick steps of the station. He vaults the turnstile. Why pay to enter the corridors of your own house?

Lifting the edge of his wool cap and folding it an inch above his
ears, he shuffles on the platform among the commuters; they are
swollen with shopping bags. Treefrog watches as an old woman
sniffs at the air and tightens her grip on her handbag. She has
gray hair, dark skin, muck-brown eyes. The bones in her face
look like they could rattle. Her coat is thin at the elbows. Clutching the handbag, her fingers are long and slender and worked.
She sniffs the air again, her lips trembling slightly, and her hand
tightens its hold on her purse. He has seen this happen often
enough to let it slide by. But there is something about her: the
coat, the eyes, the fingers. And all at once he would like to reach

out to her. He would like to say, Please. He would like to tell her something very ordinary. Treefrog reaches into his pocket, and his fingers crumple the stolen five-dollar bill. The old lady flicks another quick look at him, and then she puts the sleeve of her coat to her nose. She flips the handbag around to the other side of her body. He breathes hard. Begins to rock, ever so minutely. His knees bend, buckle, unbuckle. She looks again. She takes one step. He wants to say, No. She takes another step. He stops his rocking, watches her. She tries to be nonchalant as she steps away, but her movement is flagrant. He says aloud, "Please." She pretends she doesn't hear him. He says again, "Please." She moves out of sight, is swallowed behind pillars. He closes his eyes. When the train is gone, Treefrog remains alone on the platform. He opens his eyes, tightens his fist on the five-dollar bill, and then walks up the stairs in the solitary abandonment of rush hour. From warmth to cold, he thinks, cold to warmth.

Burma Road. Sheets of steam from the underground pipes. Treefrog moves through the metropolis of cloud. The face of the woman in the subway station follows him. The pipes are thick and gray and hot to the touch. Sodium lights on the wall emit blueness, giving the steam the color of a new bruise. He pushes his hands through the air, and even the air is hot. He has only been down here once before, in this weedlot of steel, four floors beneath Grand Central, the heart of the heart of the city. The ceilings are low, the corridors narrow, the floor dripworn from the steam pipes. It is called Burma Road because of the heat—the words are scrawled in graffiti at the rictus of the steam tunnels. He knows full well that men and women live down here and he must be careful. He is a pinchbeck arrival among them, a man who still lives in some modicum of light. He has seen them, the truly damned. They live crouched under platforms strewn with clothes, or high on steel girders, or in hidden cubbyholes, or buried underneath broken pipes. Wounded men and women living in their lazaret of hopelessness. There are seven floors of tunnels altogether—and he has heard of murders and stabbings down here. But Treefrog is comfortable now in his shame, and he walks with small broken strides.

He opens his overcoats as he goes. Reaching up to touch his beard, he feels the droplets of water that have settled themselves upon it.

The corridor of Burma Road widens where the pipes meet— thin tubes in the air and thicker larger ones low to the ground— all of them hissing and moaning like some aberrant hospital.

A huge wide emptiness seeps into Treefrog's stomach, and he feels the eyes of that old woman still following him, carving their way through him. His footsteps are loud and echoing. He swipes at sounds in the air. Rapping his knuckles on a pipe, he can hear the vibration, the movement of the noise through water, through steam, through air, maybe all the way up into the city. He comes to the end of the corridor and scales down a metal ladder beyond the CAUTION: OFFICIAL PERSONNEL ONLY sign. The ladder is slippy with wetness but he takes it easily, jumps the final three rungs. He stands in a larger room twelve feet below, where dozens of pipes meet and flow. The steam billows out and forms great clouds that hang and then disperse and drip down toward the ground.

The first time he came here he was with Elijah, who was stealing copper from the tunnel wires. Elijah had stood under the pipes, with steam around his feet, and then he disappeared and left Treefrog alone. It was as if he had vanished into the steam. It took Treefrog half a day to make his way out through the labyrinth, and the domed ceiling of Grand Central had greeted him like a sunrise.

Now Treefrog stands and stares at the room. Water falls down from the filthy pipes like fabulous rain suddenly gracious. Machinery groans. Electric light leaks in and is then arrested so that it paints the outside of the steam.

He takes off his clothes, boots first, then his coats, his jeans, his shirts, his underwear, and moves naked into the sodium-blue clouds. Water drips hot on his skin. He wishes he had soap and shampoo. It is only when he reaches up to his hair that he realizes he has left his blue hat on. He tosses it out of the steam. It is the first time he has been fully naked in ages. The water welts his skin, and he throws his head back and lets the drips wedge themselves down around his closed eyelids, the lovely viciousness of the way the drops thump their heat into him. "Fuck!" he shouts. "Fuck!" He rubs at himself with ferociousness, cleaning his toes, the back of his heel, his shins, bringing his hands upward along his calves and thighs. His penis and testicles are already raw from the heat of the water but he keeps on going, ferreting away in his navel, his ass, his armpits, rubbing the burning water over his chest, the heat pounding down on him, ecstasy, hypnosis, swiping his hands through the steam until he sees her. At first she looks like a shop-window dummy, but then she moves minutely and peers in, still holding her handbag. She allows herself a little embarrassed chuckle as she wipes the vapor away from her wrinkled face. She looks at him and steps forward, fully clothed, into the torrid mist. She sniffs at the air and nods now with approval. Treefrog cups his hands over himself and hangs his head down to his chest, the carnival shape moving around him. There is sudden laughter and

Treefrog joins in. His forehead creases and his mouth opens so wide that he can feel the steam burning at his throat and he keeps on laughing. He reaches out to take the hand of the vision and she comes forward until he notices that—right at the edge of the clouds—something real, something human, is staring at him, no movement except for the flickering whites of the eyes.

Treefrog steps out of the steam. He hears a rustling movement, the slap of shoes. He follows the figure, moving quickly now. He hears the sound of heavy breathing. Treefrog reaches the ladder, scales it. The curious shape is already running down along Burma Road, disappearing, laughing out loud. Treefrog remains on the ladder. "Fuck!" he shouts. He knows that his clothes and boots will be gone, so he doesn't even check, just watches the fading form. But—when the figure is gone—Treefrog descends to the room, and his clothes are still there, even the money in the pockets of his jeans. He looks back at the ladder and wedges his knuckles into his eye sockets and steps back into the steam once more. The subway woman has vanished, and there's nothing else to do but wash himself clean.

When Lenora was a baby he would bathe her in the kitchen sink. He would fold a towel and place it beneath her head. Her feet would kick a little and warm water would splash out. He'd dampen a cloth, soften it with soap, and rub it over her. She would cry out until he took a jug of water and poured it from a height. Dancesca sometimes helped him. When they were finished they would swaddle the child in a towel that had been specially warmed over a radiator. Later, they'd gently rock Lenora in their laps while the television flared in the background.

. . .

The wet hat chills his head as he emerges onto 42nd Street in the night. He decides to walk all the way uptown, searching the garbage for cans and bottles as he goes. The snow has stopped but the streets are bright with whiteness. He wears his sunglasses. Not many people drinking sodas in wintertime, but he collects enough bottles to redeem them for two dollars and forty cents. Combining all his money, he buys himself a couple of cans of ravioli and the largest bottle of gin he can afford.

He passes the empty playground, the ghosts of mothers and children ranged around it. He tips up his sunglasses. Lenora, girl, how are you and what is it like being alive and would I enjoy it?

He climbs over a railing and down the embankment through the drifts of snow.

Ice on the tunnel gate. Treefrog gets down on his hands and knees, goes headfirst through the gap, and twists his body around, brings his legs through, sits on the metal platform, holding his breath. Always a moment of fear. Maybe somebody waiting for him just inside the gate. A man with only one shoe, missing five dollars. Or a kid waiting to fling a bottle of gasoline with a lit rag in the top. Or a cop with a gun. Everything stands in the purest blackness so that he can hardly even see his palm in front of his face. And then there's a slow coming together of tunnel and light shafts, and he can see through the shadows. He listens for movement, and the fear sits back down in his belly and rests in his liver.

No one in sight. He sweeps his hair under his hat and reaches for his shopping bag, the bottle clinking against the ravioli cans. He takes off his gloves and places each one between the bottle and the cans to deaden the clinking, so he won't have to share if anybody hears him.

Treefrog makes his way soundlessly down the metal stairs. All quiet on the western front. He stops outside Angela and Elijah's cubicle and puts his ear to the door, hears them sucking their way down into a crack pipe, the slow pull and the ecstatic exhalation and then a few giggles as they move together under their mangy blankets.

He thinks of Elijah's hand unbuttoning Angela's shirt, moving slowly along her dark skin, the slow rise of nipple between Elijah's fingers, then the slide of his hand under her breast, down along her stomach, a meander of finger around her belly button, tracing her bony hip, massaging it, caressing it, belonging to it, the slow draw across her hipbone, feeling her moistness even in the freezing cold, his fingernails sliding into the warm layers of her body, Angela lying back in the blankets, blissful, moaning, her eyelids shut tight, Elijah suspended on the scent of her, leaning down and breathing into her ear, Angela's fingernails dragging along his back, making rivulets in his skin, and the movement of their breathing, fast fast fast fast, a wild thrust from each of them, until it is all crushed into long segments of breathing, slow slow slow slow, and then the two of them might lie there in anticipation of more.

Treefrog stands by the door until he hears the pipe sucked on again and—bending over at the hip a few times to calm his erection—he goes carefully along with the bag, past the row of cubicles and the giant communal area and the shacks.

Only Dean is out, his campfire burning, yellow hair up in spikes and his hunting jacket tight around him. He stares at nothing, not even looking at the fire like any normal man would do. Dean once bit out a man's tongue in a lovers' quarrel. Ever since then he's been going around with the other man's life in his mouth. Sometimes he roars about a lawn not being cut in Connecticut, the edges of flowerbeds being way too grassy, needing to be clipped. Or the china dishes having spaghetti stains on them. Or the credit card bills not being paid.

As he goes past, Treefrog gives a quick wave, but Dean just looks into the distance. A young boy lumbers out of Dean's lean-to, beside the pile of garbage. The boy and Dean sit beside each other. Dean runs a finger along the inside of the boy's thigh, and then suddenly they are standing and meshed together beside the fire—the boy is so small that his head only reaches Dean's chest—and they are locked together in embrace by the light of the fire. Treefrog can see the boy nibbling at Dean's neck and the slide of Dean's hand to the small of the boy's back.

Treefrog shivers.

Another hundred yards and he's home. Before he climbs he imitates the turning of a key in the door, shouting upward to his nest, "Honey, I'm home!"

Treefrog slips the shopping back under his coat, ties the handles of the bag to his belt loop, and climbs the catwalk, careful with the bottle. He lights some candles and places the bag on the bed beside Castor, who is curled up by the pillow. Reaching to the shelf by the Gulag, he takes down a can opener and sighs. "I'll dance at your wedding, I'll dance at your wedding."

In the morning he practices a loop shot against the wall, and the pink handball goes high in the air, rebounds down off the stalactite, and lands perfectly for his right hand, then left. He feels good, energized, almost clean after yesterday's shower. He closes his fist for an underhand shot, and the ball barrels out from the Melting Clock. The ritual continues until warmth floods through him. Along one part of the tunnel wall he sees a fat sheet of ice insinuating itself into existence, the drops of water coming from an overflow pipe topside as if to say, We have all been here before.

"Heyyo."
"Shit."
"Hey, Angela. Up here. Turn."
"Where?"
"Heyyo."
"Goddamn. It's you."
"It's me. Where you goin'?"
"Nowhere," she says. "What you doin' up there?"
"The presidential suite. I'm putting mints on my pillows."
"You got any more blankets? Our goddamn electric's still out. Heaters ain't working. Elijah's gone looking for that guy Edison."
"Faraday."
"Same difference."
"You wanna come up?" asks Treefrog. "I got a fire going."
"No way. If Elijah saw me up there, he'd rip your head off and shit down your throat. He says that to me all the time. He says he'll rip my—"
"Elijah won't see us. He's left the wilderness and been fed by ravens and gone off in a whirlwind."
"Huh?"

"Nothing," says Treefrog. "You kill those rats yet?"

"No. I . . ." She hesitates and scratches at the side of her face. "I like the fat one," she says. "She's cute. She wouldn't hurt nobody. She's pregnant."

Angela stands by the tracks, wrapped in a blanket, caught in a stream of topside light with her face tilted up, sad and beautiful.

Treefrog says to her, "You should get Papa Love to make a painting of you."

"Who?"

"The guy in the shack down by the cubicles. With all the drawings on it. He never comes out except sometimes when he wants to. You should get him to make a painting of you."

"I don't want no painting," she says, but then her face brightens. "Say, has he got a heater?"

"Yeah, but he don't answer the door."

"Shit. Where the goddamn hell is Edison?"

"Taking a dirt nap."

"Huh?"

"Edison's dead. He's the man made the first phonograph. He's the man gave us music. He's the man gave us light. Edison kicked it sixty years ago. Faraday's his name."

"He's a motherfucker."

Treefrog laughs.

"I had a warm house once," says Angela, stamping her feet on the tunnel gravel, looking up at Treefrog, perched twenty feet up on his catwalk.

"It had a wraparound porch and a feeder for birds," she says, "and it was bright as all get out. There was trees outside, and sometimes we went climbing in the branches. I hate New York. It's cold. Ain't you cold?"

"You're high, ain't you?"

She ignores him. "It was cold in Iowa but we had a stovepipe, and my father, he broke it off and smashed it in my momma's face. Left a big dent in her cheekbone. That's what happened to the stovepipe. Big dent in the stovepipe too, after he smashed it in the wall 'cause he was sorry. Then he did it again. I hate him. He always said he'd take me to see the sea, but he never did. He just did the stovepipe thing. The doctor gave her an eyepatch. She dropped it in a well. Ever been married?"

"Yeah."

"What's her name?"

"Dancesca."

"Did you hit her?"

"No."

"You're a liar. I know you're a liar."

"No I ain't."

"Ever been beaten?" asks Angela after a moment. "You get used to it; it's like breathing. It's like breathing underwater."

And for some reason he thinks she's smiling, though her back is turned now and all he can see is her hunched figure wrapped in the blanket.

"Angela," he says. "Turn around. Let me see you."

"I bet you beat her until she couldn't even walk no more."

"No I didn't."

"I bet you got a blue washcloth and wrapped it on your fist so the bruises wouldn't show."

"Shut up."

"I bet you took a yellow pencil and stuck it in her ear and turned it around and around till the lead snapped and went into her brain."

"Shut up."

COLUM MCCANN / 124

"I know you did."

He shifts on the catwalk. "I had a wife and child," he says. "I never hit them."

"Sure sure sure."

"She left me."

"Sure she did."

"They both left me."

"Yeah yeah yeah. You ain't got my sympathy."

And for a moment he is back in the playground near 97th Street and it is four years ago and he is with his daughter and she is on the cusp of puberty. It is a summer's day and he is guiding her on the swing—she is too old for swings and her legs are too long so she tucks them underneath the small wooden platform but kicks them out when she rises high. He must push with both hands and she shouts with joy; this is the moment that Lenora loves the most, but she will not love it for very much longer. He pushes her in the high center of her back but one hand slips and she is in a tight T-shirt, she has been growing taller in recent months and there is not much money for clothes, he has lost his job, he has lost control of his hands, he is pushing her at the armpits now and still she is moving with joy on the swing and his fingers by mistake touch the soft swell of new flesh, with just one hand, and his head is thumping and he must equalize the pressure and his fingers stretch out and gently touch the other side of her body, and there is a shoot of something like electricity to him, and he is trembling, but it feels so soft, so lovely, it eases him for a second, all the time he is pushing her and she doesn't even notice, his hands are at her armpits and he wishes he could lift his history out of her, his daughter, he is touching her and he will touch her again and he will be found out and he will come down the tunnel and he will try to murder his hands in shame.

"They left me," says Treefrog.

Angela turns around and points up at him. "I bet you had a blue washcloth. I bet you had a yellow pencil. I bet you knocked their eyes back in their heads."

"No I didn't."

"I bet you twisted their arms behind their heads. I don't got no sympathy for you. You're only looking for a knock. That's what you're looking for. A knock. You want a knock? Go goddamn knock yourself."

"Angela," he says.

"You're just like the rest. I don't got no sympathy for you, no way. I hope you fall. I hope you fall down a goddamn well. You should cut your beard. And your hair. Then fall down a well. Get an eyepatch."

A vision of Lenora again flashes across his mind.

"I didn't hurt her," he says.

"Bullshit," says Angela, the word elongated into something almost lyrical.

Treefrog buries his head in his hands for a while and then he stands and moves along the catwalk with his arms outstretched. He disappears into the rear of his cave, knocking over the piss bottles at the end of his mattress. He reaches out to the rickety bedside table and rummages in the broken drawer. The smell of piss rises up from where the bottles have leaked across the floor. He rifles through the clothes—some of his old hand-drawn maps on graph paper are crumpled up among them—and he scatters them around until he finds a thermal shirt. He tucks it into his overcoat, stumbles over his mattress in the dark, swings his way down the two catwalks, and lands—knees bent—in front of Angela.

She crouches and shields her eyes. "Leave me alone, motherfucker!"

"Here."

"Don't hurt me, don't hurt me, don't hurt me!"

He shoves the thermal shirt toward her. Angela takes her arm away from her eyes and looks at him and says, "Wow."

"It'll keep you warm," says Treefrog.

"Thanks."

"Put it on."

"Now?"

"Yeah."

"You just wanna see me naked. I seen the way you narrowed your eyes. I seen it, man."

"Shut up, okay? Just put it on."

She looks at him, shy and circumspect. "Turn away."

He turns and sees a clump of snow fall through the metal grill on the other side of the tunnel. She drapes the fur coat over his shoulder and when he turns around Angela is smiling, with her arms behind her head and her elbows out, like a movie star—she has put the thermal shirt over three or four blouses—but still he imagines her nipples erect in the cold and he wants to touch her, but he doesn't, he can't, he won't.

"I didn't hurt nobody."

"I believe you, Treefy."

"You do?" he says, with sudden surprise.

"Yeah, 'course I believe you."

"Thanks."

And then Angela reaches for the fur coat and says, "Ain't I cute?"

"Yeah," he says, and he puts his arms around her.

"You smell, man."

"I had a shower yesterday. In Grand Central. In the steam tunnel. You should come down there with me sometime. The water's hot."

Further up the tunnel they hear a rattling at the gate.

Angela's eyes open, wide and startled. She unlocks herself from Treefrog's embrace. "Elijah!" she says.

In one swift motion Treefrog has his fingers in the handhold, and within seconds he is up in his nest. Angela puts her fur coat on, tightens it, and scuttles along the tunnel. In the distance Treefrog watches Elijah emerge through a shaft of light, carrying a heater, shouting, "Faraday! Hey, Faraday! Yo. Where the fuck is Faraday?"

chapter 8

1950–55

Walker has timed it perfectly. Just before the sun rises over the roofs of 131st Street and shines through the window, his arm is raised and it shades his eyes. It is good exercise; his muscles beginning to give even more to rheumatism, the disease of tunnel men. He keeps his arm up until the sun hits the crossbeam in the window, and then he is given relief for two and a half minutes exactly.

A shadow supplied, a shadow lost, and the forearm is lifted as the sun rises further.

Walker likes the sofa, even though he's confined to it two hours a day, by pain, not desire. It has shaped itself to the contours of his body, and it gives him a view of a street maddened in recent years by motorcars. He perches on a history of coins dropped beneath the cushions, and sometimes, when he wants chewing tobacco, he reaches in under the cushion, grabs a few dimes, and drops them down to his children, who, when not at school, sit on the steps below. The coins land noisily and his children scramble, then make their way down to the store.

The stylus of the record player tumbles across an old jazz record: Louis Armstrong. The pulse of the man. The gorgeous rhythm. The syncopated slide. Walker moves his head to the beat, and the silver cross sways gently against his neck. When the record finishes he stands up from the sofa to break the cramp in his knees and stretches wide, bending the pain from his fingers. Carefully he places the needle in a groove just beyond a scratch in the vinyl. Last week the needle began to skip, but the jabs were so terrible in his knees that he just let it sound over and over and over again at the point of a shrill trumpet note—it got to the stage where he didn't even hear it anymore, he was back underneath the river, he was digging, his friends were around him, it was the compressor sounding out— until Eleanor came home and repositioned the needle.

She wants to buy a new copy of the record, but money is tight these days. He is long finished in the tunnels; there is no more need for diggers. Most of the family's money comes from her job in a clothing factory—the wages are low, the hours are long. Walker has begun to do some of the housework, and the room is bright and tidy, partitioned by a curtain that hangs from the ceiling. Walker's shovel hangs above the fireplace. On the mantelpiece, a row of photographs. By the kitchen, five chairs are ranged around a small table. There are three beds: a double for themselves, a double for the two girls, a single for Clarence. Walker made the single bed himself, strung the rope between poles, frapped and crisscrossed until taut and strong.

On the days when his fingers don't give up the ghost, Walker makes furniture to sell at a street stall: chairs, shelves, bedside tables. He gives credit to those who can't pay up front. Days and days are spent on each intricately carved piece. Afterward he has to immerse his numb hands in warm water for relief.

Walker lets the music roam in him and shuffles to the stove to put on the kettle. Eleanor has taught him the art of making tea, the necessity of warming the pot first, drying it out, carefully apportioning the leaves, letting them stew for a minute or two. He uses a tea cosy, a foreign thing, inherited from Maura O'Leary. Walker has even acquired a taste for milk in his tea. He lingers over the saucepan, then puts a plate on it so the water boils faster. He has had to learn these little tricks of middle-aged domesticity. Like making the beds and folding the sheets back over the blankets. Or hailing the milk wagon with a high whistle from the window. Or adding a touch of vinegar to the mop water. There is no refrigerator, but Walker bought a plastic icebox from a World War Two veteran who claimed it would work as well as anything.

Bending down, he takes out the milk but it has already begun to thicken, so he shakes it with violence and pain shoots through his arm and shoulder. He is generous with the milk. It won't last much longer. He watches the way it whirls through the dark tea.

As he sips at the drink, he prepares for Eleanor's return, laying the cosy over the pot, putting a cube of sugar on a spoon, arranging it neatly on the counter so that all she will have to do is pour and stir. The slowness of these days. It's almost as if he doesn't inhabit his body but hovers somewhere beyond it, a wheel of energy watching himself beginning to break down. He likes to remain perfectly still sometimes, just standing in the kitchen with his body bent in such a way that he can no longer feel any pain. The doctor has said it will only get worse. It will gnaw at his elbows, slip into his hips. Walker was given medicine but it ran out after a month, cost too much, and the drugstore won't give him credit.

He tries to recall his mother in Georgia. There was a plant she used to counter the rheumatism, but Walker can't remember the name of it.

Standing by the stove, again removed, again hovering, Walker watches himself as a boy, guiding a canoe through the black swamps, alongside cypress trees stumped by lightning. He imitates the remembered swerve of the paddle, then shuffles across the room, through the whirling motes of dust in the sunlight, to the record player.

He hates to stop the great Daniel Louis Armstrong in midflight, but it's better than continually rising from the couch. His hands tremble when he lifts the lid of the record player and positions the needle at the beginning. On the couch, he stretches out his feet and extends his neck to see down the street, but there is little to see, just the slide of women out from the Laundromat, a pawnshop sign flickering, and a few young men gathered around a fire hydrant, holding cigarettes, exhaling to the sky, the smoke curling out flaccidly above their heads. Three prostitutes in tight pants totter back and forth around the corner, trading insults with the men.

Walker lies back gently and blows on his tea, even though it's already cool. The afternoon withers away.

Fastened to the skipping music, he falls asleep, and when he wakes his three teenage children are standing in front of him, home from school, laughing, having tilted the tea cosy comically upon his head.

. . .

Below them, in a room thick with marijuana smoke, Hoofer McAuliffe, a car mechanic, can be heard at all hours of the night. A tough man, his face is mutilated—one of his nostrils was bitten away in a fight, leaving his nose ruined and scabbed. McAuliffe brings whores to his room late in the evening. He guides them gently by the arm. The smell of reefer drifts up the stairs. Great gollops of laughter rise up through the floorboards. Loud slaps are heard and then the lowest of whimpers. The women slink from the room, shy and high and beaten.

One morning, as Walker accompanies his daughters downstairs on their way to school—past the rich graffiti on the stairwell wall—Hoofer McAuliffe lets a long lecherous tongue hang out from the gap in his half-open door. Walker pushes the door open and stands in front of him.

"I wouldn't touch it anyways," says McAuliffe. "Mixed pussy's bad for a man."

Walker slams McAuliffe up against the wall, shoves his knee into his crotch, presses his fingers in his throat, and watches McAuliffe slide to the floor beneath him, gasping for breath, eyes wide and white, his one nostril flaring. The morning sun concentrates the smoke in the room, makes it glide through the air. Walker counts to ten and then squeezes McAuliffe's neck one last time and whispers, "Don't ever look at my girls that way, hear me? Don't ever even turn a head to them. You listening to me? You listening?"

McAuliffe nods and wriggles his head free, stumbles across the room, opens his window, and gulps down air. Walker turns around to find Clarence in the doorway, staring at him, schoolbooks in his hand.

"Y'all go to school right now and forget your eyes," says Walker. "Forget everything y'ever saw."

His son nods and leaves, going down the staircase slowly, books tucked under his arm.

Walker spends the rest of the day in his apartment, nursing his aching hands in ice.

On better days he rides the subway trains and looks at the curves of the tunnel walls. He stands in the front car next to the driver and stares through the window, face propped close to the glass. He shades the top of his head with newspaper to reduce the glare.

The tunnels greet him with magnificent speed. He can spot the mistakes: the too-sudden curve where an engineer miscalculated, an area likely to be flooded in the rains, a switch placed in the wrong part of the tracks. He wishes to be back down underneath, digging. To feel again the fluidity of his shovel. One, two, three, strike, return. He even made an application to become a sniffer—to walk through the subway tunnels and check for gas leaks or fires or dead animals—but the application was turned down, like all the other job applications he makes.

Still, he loves the tunnels, moving from the darkness into the bright yellow light of the stations, the slow roll into blackness once more, the screech of steel on steel, the workers shining flashlights, the elation of being slammed along on a midmorning express, commuters shuffling their feet on platforms as he whizzes by.

On weekends he takes Clarence with him and is greeted with stares from passengers looking at the curious paler skin of his teenage child. Clarence is tall enough to have to bend at the window to see along the tunnels. He has the beginnings of a mustache around his lips but is still too embarrassed to start shaving. He stands in silence, looking out the window, his father's hand on his shoulder.

Sometimes Walker rides all the way downtown and meets up with Vannucci and Power on the Manhattan side of the water.

The men race their pigeons back and forth across the East River. Vannucci has taken on new colors for his birds: red and white and green. In a moment of drunkenness, Power has drawn fifty tiny blue stars on one of his favorite pigeons. The men sit at the waterside and share bottles—Kentucky bourbon and grappa—palming them around in sweat-wrinkled brown bags.

As they wait for the pigeons to return, the men remember themselves when young, diving down into the alcohol with happiness and regret.

"Pass me the slop!" shouts Power. "Gotta keep on sloppin'. Sloppin' till the end of time."

" 'Member the time me and El dunked them pigeons?" says Walker.

"I shoulda kicked your ugly black ass."

"Those were the days, huh?" says Walker.

"Weren't they just? How's that fortune-teller of yours, Nathan?"

"She says y'all'll be sloppin' till the end of time."

"Fine by me, buddy." Power claps his hands. "I bet that woman could suck the chrome off my fender."

"Excepting you don't have a car!"

"That's exactly right."

"What is the meaning, the chrome?" asks Vannucci.

"Ask your wife, Ruby. And Ruby—"

"What?"

"Don't forget to ask her about the custard."

"I do not understand."

"Pass me the bottle and I'll show ya!"

One afternoon they take the subway under the East River. They sit in the front carriage and ask the driver to stop the train for a moment. The driver curls his upper lip and shakes his head. "No." "Come on, bud." "No." "A dollar?" "No." "Dollar and a half?" "No." "A thick jaw?" "Come on, you guys, quit kiddin', I said no."

And then Power flashes his union card, along with a pair of dollar bills. The driver nods and the train comes to a halt. They crowd into the driver's cabin and spread open the sports page of the newspaper. Power leans out the window and reads Con O'Leary the baseball reports: It is June 1950 and the Brooklyn Dodgers have just gone into first place in the National League by beating the Cincinnati Reds 8–2 at Ebbets Field, Gil Hodges landing a grand slam homer in the upper deck in the third inning. "Yessir, Mister Big Gil himself," says Power. And then Walker leans over the top of his colleague and says, "And ol' Jackie Robinson got a double, buddyblue."

The driver grows nervous and mashes his hands together as the men shout other scores at the ceiling of the tunnel.

The afternoon surrenders control to the bottles. They switch trains back and forth between the two stations, and they grow loud and raucous until they are kicked off a train and Power shouts, "You can't kick us off, we're the Resurrection Men!"

Eleanor stands in the doorway and leans her head against the frame. Halfway across the room toward her, Walker sees that she is weeping. And then he realizes that Eleanor doesn't want to cross the threshold, as if something has pinned her there.

"I was sitting in the warehouse, Nathan. Sewing the hem on a pair of trousers. We all sit in a big long line, the Singer machines in front of us. I don't know what happened to me, Nathan. It was terrible. He was coming from school. He had his report card. He got himself an A in science. I guess he just wanted to tell me that. I guess he just wanted to tell his momma that he was doing good in school. And the other women, Nathan, they don't know a thing about me. All they know is that I live uptown. They don't even know where uptown. They don't know anything about you or the kids. It's just that—well, it's just—I don't know what it is. I'm not ashamed. It ain't that. I suppose I just didn't want them to know about me. Just to keep us all safe, you know?"

"Take it easy, El."

" 'Member I told you that the boss's name is O'Leary? Well, I told him—when I first got the job—I told him my maiden name is O'Leary too. I didn't say nothing about being a Walker. And, seeing how I'm an O'Leary, he's nice to me, doesn't shout at me if I spend too long at coffee break and all, seeing how I'm Irish. He likes me—not in that way—but he likes me. Anyway, I'm sewing the hem on those trousers when I look up and there's our Clarence up at the door of the warehouse. He's pointing at me. I put my head down, Nathan, I don't know why. I was trembling. I pretended I was concentrating on the hem, being very careful with it. I could hear the footsteps. They're the loudest footsteps I ever heard. And when I looked up again, they were both standing in front of me."

"Don't cry, hon."

"And O'Leary says to me, 'This here boy says that he wants to see his momma.' "

"Oh, no."

"I don't know what happened to me. All of a sudden I let go of the trousers and the hem zigzagged across. You wouldn't believe how quiet that place was. Everyone was looking at me, all the other seamstresses, silent as could be. I just said, 'Pardon me?' And the boss he says, 'This here boy says that he wants to see his mother.' Real insistent, the boss, he's real insistent. And I just let out this nervous giggle, Nathan, I'm just sitting there giving a nervous giggle. And I said, 'Oh, that's just a term of speech, I know his momma very well.' "

"Oh, El. You didn't? You couldn't have."

"I'm sorry. I'm sorry."

"Oh, Eleanor."

"And O'Leary was staring at me and his eyes all wide. And Clarence he's just staring too. Clarence has got this report card in his hand. I looked at the boss and I said it again, 'It's just a term of speech, you know how people talk.' And Clarence, he's got this look on his face like the whole world has just tumbled in on him. Like something went in and just collapsed his face right down. He says to me, 'Momma.' I think I'm gonna hear that word forever, the way he said it. Momma. Momma. Momma. Like it's just the most important thing he ever said. But I just looked around the warehouse and everybody was staring at me. 'His momma is a friend of mine, his momma lives local to me'— that's what I said. And O'Leary, he takes Clarence by the scruff of the neck. 'What're you wasting this lady's time for?' he says. And Clarence says, 'I just wanted to tell her that I got an A in science.' And O'Leary he swells up real big like and he coughs and he looks around the warehouse. 'An A in science!' he shouts. 'It musta been in evolution!' "

"The sonofabitch."

"And Clarence was there and he was crying."

"I can't believe it, El."

"He's got these big tears coming down his face. And he says to me again, 'Momma.' And I didn't say a word to him. I just didn't say a word. I didn't even say well done. Well done for the A in science. I was just dumbstruck and I didn't mean it, I didn't mean to be that way; it just happened to me, Nathan, I swear I didn't mean it; oh, God in heaven, believe me that I never meant to ignore him like that. I just sat there and watched O'Leary drag Clarence out of the warehouse, and I've never felt a sorrier thing ever in my life. I turned and looked at the other seamstresses and—oh, God, Nathan, I just got up and I pushed my way past O'Leary and grabbed my coat and ran and went to look for Clarence. But he was nowhere around. I looked and looked but he was gone. I know I've lost my job, but I don't care. I just ran and ran but I couldn't find him."

"Where is he now?"

"I don't know."

"Enough crying, woman."

"Can you go find him for me, Nathan? Please? Can you explain it to him? For me?"

"I don't reckon, El, I can explain a thing like that."

"I never meant to ignore him."

"I'll say this one thing and I'll say it one time—it's the ugliest goddamn thing I ever heard in my life."

"Oh, please."

"It's ugly, El. Pure goddamn ugly."

"I swear to God I'll never ever ever do a thing like that again in my life. It's just sometimes, sometimes, sometimes things happen to us and we don't know why. Just say that to him. Please. Say I don't know what happened to me. Say that I could never be sorrier than what I am. Tell him I love him. Tell him it's the truth. It's the truth, I swear it."

"Well, I'd say that's your job, El."

"Nathan."

"No."

"Please. Just explain it to him for me."

"No! When you quit crying you can explain it to him your own self. I'll go find him and you can explain it. That's your cross to carry. It's mine too, I suppose, but you're the one gotta do the mending."

Clarence says nothing as Eleanor puts her arms around him. The young man leaves his head on his mother's shoulder, all the time staring beyond her into some unfathomable distance.

And, that evening, Walker too turns his face away from her as they lie in bed. She isolates her grief by shoving it in a pillow. But as the weeks go by, she moves toward him and puts her knees into the crook of his, her chest against his spine, breathes warm and frightened on his neck. She remains—spooned against him—until Walker gathers the courage to turn and awkwardly touch her hair.

In the weeks before Clarence leaves for army training camp in Virginia, his godfather, Rhubarb Vannucci, teaches him about dynamite, how and where to strap it, how deep to go with bore holes, where to put the charges if you want to get rid of evidence:

a body, a horse, a tree trunk. The classes are held on Vannucci's rooftop. The old Italian is meticulous in his instruction, kneeling down on a piece of cardboard, using his finger to carve out imaginary maps on the ground.

Vannucci keeps having to take Clarence's face in his hands to stop the young man's eyes from straying to the colored pigeons and the feathers arrayed on the ground.

"*Ascoltami!*" he says.

"Sir?"

"Listen me!"

All the important words are given in his own language: *carica, explosivo, spoletta detonante, una valvola.* He traces out diagrams—how to dig a proper tunnel, defuse a booby trap, deal with the spoons that hold the springs back in a grenade. He tells Clarence to always carry an extra boot lace, that they come in handy. Look carefully for the dummy fuse. Teach your brow not to ooze sweat. Never let your fingers tremble, even when you're not working. Learn to hum a single tune while defusing, it'll keep your mind from wandering.

At the end of one lesson he says, "And tell your father I gotta the custard."

Clarence comes home and relays the message. "Rhubarb said he got the custard, whatever the hell that means."

Walker, by the stove, slaps his thigh in delight. He goes across the room and whispers to his wife, and she berates him with a gentle slap on the wrist.

Clarence rolls his eyes to heaven. Embarrassed by his parents being in the same room, Clarence sleeps huddled outside on the fire escape. At night he hears them move toward each other, tentatively, when they think everyone else is sleeping, a movement in the bedsheets, curious muffles, a rustling together of their bodies, and there is nothing Clarence hates more than that sound.

He wants to be part of a bomb disposal unit, but they sign him up as a cook instead. He is seventeen. A photograph is taken of him; the hair, no longer tinged with red, doesn't clash with his military uniform. The freckles have faded from his cheeks. He is white-toothed and grinning, but despite the grin, the eyes are deep and brown and serious, like two very carefully blown-out holes in his head.

Eleanor takes the photograph to the store and tells Ration Rollins that if he doesn't put it up she'll give her custom to another store down the street. Ration tapes the photograph up on his cash register, along with the pictures of all the other local men who have gone to Korea to fight. Their faces obscure the numbers that rise up on the glass window of the register. One dollar fifty-six cents. Five dollars thirty-four. Sixteen cents. The edge of Clarence's face covers the square where the pennies roll.

Each night Walker and his wife make their way down to the grocery store to watch the television news. Eleanor remains silent at the back, by a freezer full of ice cream, fidgeting with a special prayer card encased in plastic. Walker stands beside her, but they still don't touch in public. From the television set, Eisenhower looks down at them sternly. They search for their son's face in the rows of tired men walking along hot dusty roads. They imagine helicopters flapping in over the paddy fields of the dead, row upon row of men and rice.

Back in their apartment, Eleanor writes long letters. The writing is neat and minuscule:

> *How are you over there? We hope you are well and keeping your handsome head down. We are all doing fine. We miss you sorely. I especially miss you sorely. Your father is making plenty of furniture. The girls are growing up you wouldn't believe how much. Deirdre met a musician and he tuned our piano. It sounds good. Maxine sang a Mary Lou Williams song. One night we went to the Metropole and heard Henry Red Allen blowing his brass in his suit and tie.* Whamp! Whamp! *He's the funniest thing. Everybody is asking for you especially some pretty girls who saw your photo down in Ration Rollins's place. You wouldn't believe it, but Ration has been very nice to us these days. He asks about you every day, and he even gave us some free tea. Imagine that. We were in the store and heard someone say they eat dogs over there in Korea. That's not true is it? Your sister Maxine says* Woof Woof! *And your father says stay away from the hind end. Just use some barbecue sauce he says!*

She uses a sharpener to keep the lead tip of the pencil alert. The shavings fall down around Walker's outstretched feet.

> *The sad news from these parts is that your father's old friend Sean Power passed away. At least he had a good number of years to him. Cirrhosis of the liver is what took him. Rhubarb put a bottle of bourbon in his*

coffin for the journey. We all of us got to go sometime, but it was sad. Your father said a prayer at the service. Everyone got drunk and singing at the wake. Someone asked your father if he was a waiter. They said go get a glass of whiskey for me, boy. And then they was all saying things about him. Boy this. Boy that. There was nearly a fight, but there wasn't. Rhubarb told them all to shut up. I told your father he has got to keep his mouth zipped, but you know him. At the end of the evening your father and Rhubarb sat around in the corner and talked about old times.

I can't tell you how much I think of old times, Clarence. Old times are on my mind ever since you left.

One thing I got to say, Clarence, and I have to say this again—it has been on my heart and it is so heavy I can hardly bear it—I never meant it that day when you got the A in science. I just don't know what happened. I'll carry it to my own grave I suppose. I've never felt more ashamed and I want you to know that. I carry it in me like the world's heaviest thing. I'm not asking for forgiveness. I just want you to understand. I think understanding is more important than forgiveness. So please understand. Sometimes it just weighs the whole of me to the ground so much I feel like I'm bending over when I walk.

Eleanor always uses the same line at the end of each letter:

Like we said, you keep your handsome head down, Clarence, and come back to us in one piece and don't go making us spill the river with tears.

On the evening that the war officially ends in stalemate, they receive a letter from Clarence to say that he will remain on in the demilitarized zone. He should be home shortly. He hints that he has met a girl at the army base: she is a nurse's aide and she has painted a bowl of grits on the front of his cook's helmet. The letters arrive monthly—one of them even comes when Clarence is on R&R in Japan. Eleanor keeps the stamps in a special envelope.

And then one afternoon, in the late summer, they receive another letter. They open it with their heads hung penitently. They already know from a two-week-old telegram that Clarence has been injured. A knife rolls slowly through the top lip of the envelope. Walker feels a bead of sweat roll down his spine. He uncurls the sheet of paper very slowly and hands it to Eleanor to read.

She throws her arms around him in simultaneous relief and grief when she reads the letter. The letter has been dictated by Clarence to the nurse's aide. It takes a moment for Eleanor's eyes to adjust to the handwriting.

Dear Mom and Pa,

I am alive and well. I was hit by a mine when I went out walking. We had just clocked off from the canteen, a buddy and me. We were south of Pusan, just going for a walk in the forest at the bottom of the mountain. It must have been a trip wire. I should have listened more carefully to Rhubarb. My buddy, he lost both his legs. Some of the shrapnel hit me in the eyeball and I lost my eye. I'm sitting here trying to be brave about it, but hell. Anyway, the nurses here have been looking after me good, especially that girl Louisa I told you about. She's right here, scrib-

bling down every word I say. Well, almost every word! She's from Chippewa country out West. She's been treating me special. She even went found me a gramophone and some 45s of old Rex Stewart so I can listen to him blow that horn. The radio stations here aren't so good—all you get is Nat King Cole and all. But I get to listen to old Rex. Just lie here in bed and let him play. My injury doesn't hurt much. Sometimes it's hard looking only through one eye, but I reckon I'll get used to it. Don't let that river spill over because I'm as good as can be expected. You know that bowl of grits that I told you about—Louisa painted it for me—well, I think that's about the funniest thing in the world. I'm looking forward to you-all meeting Louisa. We are good friends. Well, more than good friends to tell you the truth. And you know what? I understand that day, now, I understand that day, Mom, in the warehouse when you said you didn't know me. In the Army you learn not to know yourself at all. And I got to thinking. And I know what you're saying. So I understand and I forgive you, Mom. Well now, I don't want you to get getting weepy, so I'm going to sign off. One thing is, though, we been thinking about getting a discharge, going back to New York, Louisa and me, start a little business, I don't know what. Maybe even get married, how about that! Something so we can all go get a big apartment and live together and be happy and no more spilling of rivers for any of us.

The letter is signed: *Clarence W. and Louisa Turiver.* Beneath that, a P.S.: *I have a feeling that something will grow*

in the forest where my eyeball is. And beneath that another P.S.:
No jokes about the eyepatch please!

Eighteen months later, in 1955, Walker and Eleanor peep around
the curtain separating them from their daughters, slip outside
into the corridor—noise of thumping fists coming up the stairs
from Hoofer McAuliffe's place—and walk along, floorboards
creaking under their feet, to the shared bathroom. Eleanor
puts a finger to Walker's lips to stop him from laughing. The
walls are yellow and smudged with handprints. The tiles on the
floor are black and cracked. Eleanor scrubs the basin and wipes
the side of it with toilet paper, making the sink immaculate, so
that when she shunts up and sits up on the porcelain and lifts
her nightdress to take him inside, she feels clean and young,
although she's thirty-eight years along and her body has begun
perambulating downward.

"How're your knees?" she asks when Walker stands on his
toes and his back arches.

A vagabond breeze comes through the small open window,
leaving the bathroom cool. She undoes the clips at the back of
her hair, reaches to touch his hip.

"How're your knees, honey?" Eleanor asks again.

"Still there, Grandma," says Walker, rocking on the balls of
his toes, biting his lower lip with his teeth to block out the
laughter.

She jabs him in the chest. "Don't Grandma me. I'm not a
grandma just yet."

They remain there, making love, and Walker will remember
this forever: the clean sink, the yellow walls, the handprints, the
lifted nightdress, the portent of a moth careening wildly below
the bare lightbulb.

chapter 9

back down under where you belong

*S*ounds of scuffling feet, and Treefrog knows there are people at the tunnel gate. Maybe some kids who have come to play Burn the Mole. Or Elijah and Angela making love again, screaming in their ecstasy and dejection. Or Dean with a bundle of boys at his hip. The voices carry, and then someone says very loudly, "Shut up, assholes."

Flashlights illuminate the tunnel.

Treefrog climbs out of bed and puts on his overcoat, shoves his feet into his boots. He blows out all the Sabbath candles. Perfect darkness. Out on the catwalk, he tucks his overcoat beneath him, sits, leaves his legs dangling over. He sees the beams from the flashlights catch on the snow falling through the ceiling grate and he hears a voice: "Well, fuck me running backwards."

Eight of them, some in plain clothes.

They bunch close together. The clips on their holsters have been undone. Gloved hands on their guns. They lean into radios as if telling immortal secrets. Their flashlights move frantically, catching on the dead tree planted under one of the grills, moving up and onto the murals and the same voice intoning again: "Fuck me with a bar stool, boys, they even got themselves a tree over here, fuck me."

"Fuck you," whispers Treefrog, "fuck you."

The cops move along the side of the tracks and Treefrog says a little louder, though not loud enough for them to hear, "Oink, oink."

He pulls his legs up and makes sure he is shrouded and unseen. The last time the cops came down a murdered man had been found under 103rd Street. Nobody knew him; he died with his penis erect, a necklace of bullets on his chest. Dean found the man first and nicknamed him the Boner and the cops came down, running in the darkness like Keystone fools, waving their guns at shadows. They lined everyone up against the wall—"Up against the wall, motherfuckers!"—and frisked them for weapons. There was an argument over who would search Treefrog's nest; they were scared of the climb. Eventually they brought down a ladder. Although he stole a map that Treefrog had been creating, one of the cops tried to get Treefrog to go to a city shelter. "You live like an animal! You should get some help, man, you're living like a goddamn rat!" But Treefrog stood impassive with his long hair around his eyes and then began chuckling. The cop slapped him with the back of his hand and told him to take the smirk off his face or he'd end up like the dead man.

"What? With a boner?" Treefrog said.

And the cop said, "Shut your mouth, man."

They were down in the tunnel for two days, but nobody found out who the dead man was, or why he was murdered, or even if he had murdered himself.

Treefrog watches as they come to the row of cubicles and stand outside Elijah and Angela's place. Some light leaks out from the cubicle. The cops spread back in twos, some of them crouching down by the tracks with their guns out. *"Po-lice! Come out! Po-lice!"* Treefrog wonders if Elijah and Angela are sucking a pipe. *"Po-lice!"*

One of the cops steps forward and kicks the door, and suddenly Elijah comes out of the cubicle with his arms above his head, Angela behind, pulling her fur coat over the thermal shirt, shouting, "We didn't do nothing, we didn't do nothing!"

"Take it easy," says a cop.

"Don't touch me!" shouts Angela. "Don't touch me, don't touch me!"

"Stand still!"

"Leave us alone, we ain't got no drugs."

"Shut the fuck up, lady, okay?"

"We ain't got nothing. We was sleeping!"

"Hey, somebody shut that bitch up, will you?"

"Who you calling bitch, motherfucker?" says Elijah.

"Jesus wept," says a cop.

"You guys know it's illegal to be down here?"

"I lost the key to my penthouse."

"Funny funny."

"Forgot the mortgage payment too."

"I told you they all crazies down here, what did I tell you? I told you, didn't I tell you? Moles! They're crazy."

"Fuck you," says Elijah. "I ain't a mole."

"Why you living underground then, mole?"

"Enough!" shouts one of the cops. "You all know James Francis Bedford?"

Silence in the tunnel. Treefrog sees one of the cops go across the tracks to the dead tree and look up to the roof, with snow falling down around him in the circle of his flashlight, the cop shaking his head in amazement.

"You all ever heard of James Francis Bedford?"

"Pardon me?"

"Don't fuck with me, answer my goddamn question!"

"Never heard of him."

Treefrog watches as Elijah and Angela stand shivering in the cold. A flashlight swings and captures Dean's face as he slips out from his shack. He shades his eyes with his arm. Papa Love pulls back the curtain on his cubicle door.

"Another couple of moles here!"

Papa Love stands silent, outside his shack, his gray dreadlocks slack on his shoulders. Dean bravadoes up to the cops and pulls the flap of his hunting cap up off his ears.

"You know James Francis Bedford?" says a cop.

"Who?"

"Watch my lips. James. Francis. Bedford."

"Never heard of him."

"White guy. Six one. Scar on his chest. Tattoo here."

"What about him?" says Dean.

"Found him dead yesterday. Heard he lived down here."

"Shit," says Elijah. "Someone died?"

The cop shines the flashlight in Elijah's eyes. "Six hundred volts. Electricity went right through the top of his head. Splattered him around a little."

"Damn," says Dean. "That's Faraday."

"Who's Faraday?" asks the cop.

"What's wrong with Faraday?" says Angela.

"James Francis Bedford," says the cop.

"Goddamn. That's Faraday. That's his nickname."

"White guy?"

"Yeah," says Dean.

The cop lifts his hand in the air. "About yay tall."

"Yeah."

"Tattoo of a circuit board here."

"He's dead?"

"As a doornail, buddy."

"They killed Faraday!" screams Angela.

"You don't even know who Faraday is," says Elijah.

"They killed him, killed him, killed him!" She begins sobbing into the sleeve of her coat. "I liked Faraday! I liked him!"

"Where did he live?" asks a cop.

"Why you wanna know?" says Elijah.

"His family wants his stuff."

"His family?"

"Yeah, you know, brothers, sisters, aunts, uncles. Come on, no fucking around. Hey you! Dipshit! Where did he live?"

"There."

Dean points out Faraday's cubicle.

"He lived in that piece of shit?"

"That's his house."

"Goddamn. What's the toilet seat for?"

"A doorbell."

"I'll be fucked."

One of the cops jimmies open the lock, and the door to Faraday's place swings open. They step inside and later emerge with a crate filled with a bundle of papers.

"Nothing in there excepting some books," says a cop.

"You all know who James Francis Bedford was?"

"He was Faraday."

"He used to be a cop."

"Faraday? A cop?"

"He was good people," says the cop. "Had himself an accident once. Lost his nerve. Shot someone. Never recovered. His family asked me to come down get his stuff. Good people, Bedford's family. They was all good people. Even Bedford was good people once. Before he came down here."

Treefrog jumps down from the catwalk and walks soundlessly through the tunnel gravel until a cop pins him with a beam of light.

"Shit, we got moles everywhere!"

They gather together outside the cubicle—Elijah, Angela, Dean, Papa Love, Treefrog—and watch the cops comb through Faraday's shack.

"What they looking for?"

"Fucked if I know. A gun, maybe."

"Motherfuckers," whispers Angela.

"They prob'ly killed him," says Elijah.

"You really think Faraday was a cop?"

"No way."

"You think he shot someone once?"

"Maybe."

"He owes me twenty bucks!" says Dean.

"Shut up, man."

"Hey!" says Dean to the cops. "Leave Faraday's shit alone! He owes me twenty bucks! Leave it alone! That's mine!"

"Finders keepers," whispers Angela. "They woke me first. I keep Faraday's shit."

"I'll slap you, you bitch," says Dean.

"Elijah!" she shouts. "Elijah!"

But when she turns around, Elijah is not listening. He has pulled down the hood of his sweatshirt, scrunched up his eyebrows, and tilted his face sideways. Then he scratches his head and says aloud, "Faraday? Faraday had a family?"

Faraday—they hear later—had gone fishing for electricity way downtown in the Second Avenue tunnel. He went to help someone hook up a transformer, but on the way he found a fishing rod in a Bowery dumpster. He was sprung after snorting heroin and wanted to test the rod out. Whisking it through the air, Faraday descended through the emergency manhole cover into the Second Avenue tunnel. He stood at the edge of the tracks and played riverbank with the darkness, whisked the rod like a dream above his head. The little fly hook at the end of the line went spinning out and down toward the tracks, then came up again and jiggled in the air as Faraday lassooed the rod back over his shoulder. It happened in an instant: he stumbled and fell across the tracks and touched his hand against the third rail. The current sucked him in and his body went lengthwise against the metal, and the fishing rod completed the circuit. He must have been a corpse of wild blue sparks. Every fluid in his body boiled first, all the blood and water and semen and alcohol boiling down to nothing. Six hundred volts of direct current blew a hole in the top of his head. The cops had to turn the electricity off before they could peel him from the rail. They placed a bit of his brain in a blue plastic bag, one of the cops puking up at the sight, and the people who lived in the tunnel stood around, staring, saying nothing, although one of them later ran off with the rod—Angela was sure it must have been

Jigsaw—saying there were beautiful rainbow trout to be found in the puddles under the platforms, the most fabulous rainbow trout ever seen in the city.

Treefrog unloops the clothesline, takes down a dark necktie, and beats it against the wall to free it of tunnel dust. The dust slips through the candlelight and descends lazily, landing on the spider limbs of wax at the base of the candles. The tie emerges black, with a pattern of red squirrels. He has forgotten how to fix a knot and so he simply loops it under the collar of a filthy flannel shirt. He tries to run a comb through his hair, but it is too long and matted and twisted. He shoves an extra T-shirt into his overcoat pocket to use as a balaclava later, if necessary. Reaching into his bedside table drawer, he takes a sample bottle of aftershave, stolen once from a drugstore, and dabs a little high on his cheeks. It smells nauseating to him. He completes the blind ritual through his nest, touching everything with both hands, finally laying his hands on the speedometer.

While waiting for the others, Treefrog plays handball against the Melting Clock to warm himself. He is down to one handball and will have to buy another soon in case he loses it.

When Angela, Dean, and Elijah arrive he lifts up his beard and shows them the tie. They laugh at the sight of him— "Mister Treefrog Rockefeller!" says Angela—so he wraps it around his forehead and the four of them leave the tunnel together. Papa Love has decided not to go. They shove themselves through the gap in the gate and leave footprints in the snow on the steep hill up toward the park. Angela squeals as the snow touches her feet. She and Elijah are soaring on what they have smoked, and she has drenched her mouth with lipstick, looking vaguely beautiful and gaudy.

Treefrog has to walk the hill four times to get an even number of steps, touching his hand against the icy trunks of the crab-apple trees each time as he goes.

"You're a goddamn loon," shouts Angela.

He jumps the fence and catches up with the others as they walk past the playground by 97th. A shiver runs through him as he watches a mother launching a child on a swing, the child's feet swinging through the air. He tips his sunglasses on his head and waves goodbye to Lenora.

Between West End and Broadway, they stop at the Salvation Army store for Angela to get a scarf. She emerges with an extra pair of socks tucked under her fur coat, saying, "I think I'm about frozen."

She pulls the socks high on her legs and steps back into her lopsided heels.

On the subway train to Brooklyn, Treefrog sits alone at the far end of the car. The others stay by the door, looking at their reflections in the dark glass. Treefrog tucks himself away in the corner seat, reaches for his Hohner, and plays softly.

In a Brooklyn diner, under a neon sign for Boar's Head ham, the cook is so perfect at cracking eggs that he does it with his eyes closed. Treefrog's head bobs in approval. The cook pierces the shell with one long fingernail and flips the contents out with ease, two eggs side by side.

The yolk doesn't break or spill. Hands and spatula are held over the hot grill.

Treefrog, still wearing his tie on his forehead, rubs a bill between his fingers while he watches the cook; he got the money at Faraday's funeral. They had been late for the mass, but a deacon told them where the interment would be. They walked to the nearby cemetery. The dead man's father saw them approaching halfway through the service. He came over, shuffling on a cane, and offered them each ten dollars to stay away, saying "Please" as if the weight of his world depended on it. Behind him, at the graveside, the rest of the family watched. A woman—it must have been Faraday's mother—kept dabbing at her eyes with a long black scarf. Dean demanded twenty dollars apiece, and Faraday's father looked at him long and sad. Dean shrugged. Faraday's father reached into his pocket and took out a wad of bills from an envelope meant for the priest. The old man removed one glove and, with shaking hands, passed around the twenty-dollar bills.

By the time he got to Treefrog he had only a ten and one five left, but Treefrog said, "That's okay, Mister Bedford."

Faraday's father looked at him and for an instant his eyes brightened, but then he said, "Just don't come near the graveside, okay?"

He turned his back and walked away like a man unburdened.

The four of them watched the rest of the service from a distant gravestone.

"There goes Faraday," said Elijah, as the coffin was lowered.

"His name ain't Faraday," said Angela.

"It's Faraday to me."

"I shoulda got forty bucks!" said Dean. "He owed me twenty! The sonofabitch never paid!"

"Man, look at that coffin," whispered Angela. "Them gold handles. Goddamn. He's stylin'."

"He's stylin' down." Elijah laughed.

"I bet he was rich," said Dean.

"No less dead if he was rich or not," said Treefrog.

He swivels a little on the stool at the counter, and the money is warm now in his hands.

Watching the cook, Treefrog brings the bills to his nose and smells them. Then he folds the ten-dollar bill down until it is tiny. He checks out all the pockets in his overcoat for a good hiding place. The red lining of his coat is full of holes, but he finds a good place for the bill and punctures it with three pins to make sure he doesn't lose it. He chuckles to see the pin go through the eye of a dead President.

The cook flips the eggs in the air and they somersault onto a bun. Laying two slices of bacon across the eggs, he winks at Treefrog.

Perhaps he will give the cook a tip for the show. He hasn't tipped anyone in years, but he suddenly feels huge and magnanimous. When the plate is set down on the counter, Treefrog takes off his tie, puts it in his pocket, spins the plate twice, licks each of his fingers, and lingers over the food like a man in love.

A thumbnail of moon in the sky and the snow has briefly relented. He shoehorns himself through the gate and climbs up to his nest, carrying two bottles.

From his overcoat he drops a pile of branches and splintered wood—on the walk home he found the wood beneath the overpass, the stash belonging to some topside bum living under the bridge at 96th Street. The wood was wrapped in a blanket, kept dry. No accounting for the stupidities of the ones who live topside, some of them warming themselves over steam grates, gusts of hot wind cooking the undersides of their bodies, the top half of them frozen, always rolling over like absurd pieces of toast.

Treefrog uses his Swiss Army knife to chop some of the wood into kindling, makes a tiny lean-to of twigs, and tears a newspaper into strips. He squats over the small fire, his overcoat lifted and his ass just above the flame.

He remains perched until the heat seeps through him, and then he throws on a few larger twigs and a black plastic bag to help the fire take quicker. As the flames jump, he goes over to his bed and lies down with his arms behind his head like a bored teenager. The smoke drifts across the tunnel and out through the grate on the opposite side.

He kicks at the end of the blanket and sees some pellets of rat shit somersault in the air. He whistles for Castor—"Here, girl, here, girl"—but she doesn't come.

Opening the first bottle of gin, he sticks a dirty straw into the neck and drinks and then fumbles under his jeans and his thermal long johns, cupping his hand down by his crotch to catch the warmth.

When the first bottle is finished he stares up at nothing. In the tunnel all is quiet. He takes the harmonica out of his pocket, but it is cold and he decides not to warm it. The train from upstate blasts its way through the tunnel, and, feeling drunk, he rises when he hears the sound of someone whistling in the distance. He looks down along the tunnel at Papa Love emerging from his shack.

Treefrog leans far out on the catwalk to get a better view.

Middle-aged and dreadlocked, Papa Love is swathed in clothes, only his face and fingers exposed, but he moves with fluidity. He puts wood on the fire opposite his shack and carefully arranges cans of spray paint on some old wicker chairs. Moving with slow grace, Papa Love lines the cans of paint up one by one and flaps his arms in the cold. Along the side of his shack, on top of the boards, are the words THERE IS NO SELF TO BE DISCOVERED, ONLY A SELF TO BE CREATED. Beneath this, a collage of yellow lines and a Confederate flag in African liberation colors.

Treefrog has seldom seen Papa Love go topside, except to get food and paint. The old artist still keeps a bank account from his days as a high school art teacher—he first came down to the tunnels after his lover was hit by a bullet. It was a simple drive-by; the killers were high on amphetamines. His lover was whisked to a Manhattan hospital, but the red line of the heart machine bleeped and bottomed out. Papa Love had seen lots of men die in Vietnam, but he wasn't prepared to watch his lover go that way. He began walking after his lover died, walked the length and breadth of the city, slept on the steps of a church, and then one summer he decided to strap his heart to a cardboard box. He found the cardboard at the bottom of a doorstep on Riverside Drive, and he carried it under his arm down into the tunnels, and he strapped his aorta on one side and his pulmonary on the other, and he tied them both very neatly together, and he strapped all his veins longways down the cardboard, and he strapped all his arteries in the opposite direction, and he weaved them together with a muscle of his heart and he felt as if his blood were exploding and he lay down on the brown sprawl and looked along the length of the dark tunnel and saw a rat moving over the tracks, and he chuckled in grief and said to himself, I have strapped my heart to a cardboard box.

That was Papa Love's first painting—a self-portrait of his heart tied around a sheet of cardboard—and people mistook it for a love heart and gave him his nickname, and he never corrected them.

Once, years ago, a gallery dealer came along the tunnel and woke Papa Love, said he wanted the artist to do some work topside. Papa Love had drawn another self-portrait—as a coffee percolator, the slow downward drip of dark flesh. The gallery owner wanted him to do it on canvas. Papa Love said no and the gallery owner left the tunnel hurriedly, beads of sweat at his brow in the cold, so scared that his legs almost whipped out from underneath him. Dean brushed against the man and palmed the wallet from his pocket. It was the only time that anyone ever saw Papa Love angry. He smashed Dean's blond head against the wall and went running topside with the gallery man's wallet. When he came back to the tunnel he was panting, screaming for Dean, but Dean had run off. In revenge Papa Love drew Dean's portrait under a churchlike series of grills beneath 86th, and he wrote the word PEDOPHILE in giant letters, though later that same day he felt guilty and scrubbed the letters out, left the painting, and Dean took it as a compliment, his portrait on the tunnel wall.

From a distance, Treefrog sees that a huge area of the tunnel wall—directly across from Papa Love's shack, lit by the fire—has already been primed with white paint, a perfect rectangle outlined in black.

Papa Love steps up to it and stacks four crates on top of each other to use as a ladder. He covers his mouth and nose with a red bandanna, so as not to suck the paint fumes down. An old pair of battered spectacles is placed comically over the bandanna. He stands on the crates and shakes a can of paint. Treefrog can hear the metal marble bouncing inside. Papa Love stretches out his arms and, with sudden violence, sweeps in toward the wall, moving his arms through a giant arc.

A mist of air issues from the top of the bandanna as he steps off the crates—they begin to collapse like a house of cards—and his body travels through the darkness as if on a rope, and the paint strikes the wall as the artist travels, a big half-circular sweep; and then, almost as quickly, Papa Love is on the ground by the campfire, rubbing at his knees with the pain of having hit the tunnel floor.

He steps back, nods at the wall, and begins to restack the crates. Standing up on the curious ladder once again, Papa Love falls in toward the wall and, in another perfect arc, sprays over the half circle a second time. His gray hair swings as he flies. The paint covers every inch of the first sweep. He lands by the campfire and then rubs his hands vigorously against the cold. He spreads the crates out, stands wide-footed—he could be the ghost of Nathan Walker; he could be digging—takes another can of paint, and jets two moons underneath the half circle. Each time he steps back he warms his fingers over the fire.

Treefrog drops down from the catwalk and moves further up the tunnel, stands in the shadows, watching.

Papa Love bends and draws a long straight tube emerging from the half circle. A series of striations are drawn across the tube. The center of the mural is sprayed yellow and then tinged at the edges with a cloud of red. Papa Love works furiously, the cans scattered around him on the ground. He stops every few minutes to ignite his hands with campfire warmth, then stepping upward, haunts the wall with colors using long sweeps of his arm, zeroing in afterward to draw lines emerging from the top of the circle.

The portrait on the tunnel wall grows and a giant lightbulb appears, ten feet high. Papa Love stands by the fire and works at the nozzle of a spray can with his knife. In the high center of the lightbulb he draws two furred lines and, underneath them, ovals tinged with blue. Treefrog realizes that the old artist has drawn a pair of eyes within the lightbulb.

Papa Love uses a paintbrush to draw circuit boards for pupils. Using only one crate now, a long swatch of nose appears

beneath the eyes and then a mouth set into half a grin. Some
stubble is drawn at the bottom of the bulb.

Papa Love steps back and admires his work, hands in his
dungarees.

"Heyyo," says Treefrog, stepping forward.

"You go to the funeral?"

"Yeah, we got paid. Faraday's father gave me fifteen bucks to
stay away. Rest of them got twenty."

"Bullshit."

"First funeral I ever got paid for."

"I'm too old for funerals now," says Papa Love.

Treefrog points at the mural. "It's Faraday, huh?"

"Gonna be. Maybe. Ain't fully finished yet."

"He's looking good."

"A brother in the spine," says Papa Love.

Treefrog shuffles in the gravel. "There's a grave inside all of
us." And then he is embarrassed by what he has said, and he
mumbles, "You think it's ever gonna stop snowing?"

Papa Love shrugs.

"You think Faraday did it on purpose?" asks Treefrog.

"I doubt it. But at least he went the way he probably
would've liked. I mean, that's what he probably wanted."

"Hey," says Treefrog. "If you were to draw a picture of me,
what'd you draw?"

"Man, I only draw dead people."

"You drew yourself. And Dean."

"Dead people and people I want dead."

"Oh." Treefrog pauses for a long time. "Say, what about
Miriam Makeba?"

"I been wishing she was dead too," says Papa Love.

"Why's that?"

"So she could come on down here and join me."

Treefrog laughs.

Papa Love turns to his mural. "You like it?" he asks.

"Yeah, man, 'course I like it. Old Faraday, man. Damn. Hate to see him go."

"Brother's in the blood."

Papa Love shakes another can of paint.

"You seen that Angela girl yet?" asks Treefrog.

"Yeah," says Papa Love. "Sister's living with Elijah."

"Man, you should draw her."

"Last time I saw her, seemed like she was breathing pretty good."

"Yeah, but you should draw her anyway," says Treefrog.

He slaps Papa Love on the shoulder as the old man sets to work on Faraday's chin.

In his notebook Treefrog writes, *Back down under the earth where you belong. Back down under the earth where you belong.* Each letter is like a perfect mirror of the one that has gone before, his handwriting tiny and crisp and replicate. He could make a map of those words, beginning at the *B* and ending at the *g*—where all beginning begins and ends—and they would make the strangest of upground and belowground topographies. And then he writes: *Angela.* Two *A*'s, one at each end. Nice, that. A good name. Lovely. An elaborate pencil mark at the end, a tail fin.

chapter 10

1955–64

A massive blue Buick with an exaggerated tail fin cruises the neighborhood. The driver hangs his arm out the left-hand side window, an open bottle of whiskey held at his crotch. He wears sunglasses and a shirt patterned with playing cards, open at the neck to the jack of clubs. In his breast pocket a small bag of marijuana dents the cloth.

Hoofer McAuliffe steers with his knees, one hand tapping the dashboard and the fingers of the other drumming on the outside panel of the door. As he drives, he leans out the window to look at his brand-new set of whitewall tires, almost hypnotizing himself with their swirl. He takes his hand from the dashboard to grab the whiskey bottle and drinks long and deep. Whiskey streams down his chin, dribbling in the stubble. The car travels slowly, twenty-five miles an hour.

On the street's far corner, McAuliffe notices some boys out playing with a fire hydrant. Huge jets of water stream across the road. The boys are laughing as they soak each passing vehicle, and one of the kids is pointing at McAuliffe's car. The boys punch each other with delight, the fists sliding off one another's wet shoulders.

McAuliffe pulls his arm in from the window, and in the quick movement of winding up the handle his whiskey bottle tumbles to the floor. He curses loud into the steering wheel and bends down to grab the bottle. He jerks the wheel and turns the car across three lanes of traffic, away from the boys. A checkered taxicab behind him blares its horn. Hoofer McAuliffe rights himself in the seat, all concentration. A man on a bicycle—salmoning his way against the traffic—swerves to avoid the Buick.

McAuliffe slams the brake for an instant, but the boys across the street have directed the hydrant water toward him, a giant fountain making an arc in the air, and he pumps down on the accelerator once more.

The traffic light is red and the accelerator goes deeper to the floor and the engine whines.

He doesn't see the woman on the crosswalk carrying the large laundry bags in her arms. She is looking over her shoulder and chuckling at the boys anointing the street with water. A roar hits her ears—"*Watccchit laidyyyy!*"—and she whips around, too late. The Buick crumples the woman at the hip and she is in the air, flying, half somersaulting, clothespins tumbling out of her dress pocket, her thin frame smashing against the windshield, making a spiderweb of glass, her body rolling up onto the roof, denting the metal, her green dress billowing, the street silent but for the patter of water and the screech of tires.

Her bag of laundry—cloth diapers and baby clothes—gets pinned to the front of the car. She is flung to the rear, her outstretched arm slapping against the beautiful tail fin.

She flies beyond, slamming her head on the pavement with such a thump that it is the only sound the passersby will later remember, the full dullness of her head against concrete and then the sight of a clothespin soaking up blood, other pins strewn around the street.

The Buick smashes into a mailbox—pinning the bag of laundry against it—and careens out, comes to a halt, sashayed across two lanes.

Hoofer McAuliffe is out of his car, ripping at the buttons on his shirt so that it falls open and the patterned playing cards roam to his hips. He runs back and forth between the car and the woman, beating at his head with his fists. Across the street somebody uses a wrench to turn the hydrant off. McAuliffe's moans grow louder and he sinks down at the front of his car, on his knees, fingering the massive dents in the hood of his Buick.

It is fifteen minutes before Clarence comes running home, shouting, "Momma's been hit by a car!"

Walker lunges from his seat and his leg hits against the record player and another scratch etches its way across the vinyl and the needle keeps skipping, skipping, skipping as father and son run for the door. Clarence helps shoulder his father down the stairs.

At the street corner Hoofer McAuliffe is rubbing his fingers over the dent in his car and he shouts at Walker, "It weren't me! The light was green! She jumped out in front of me! See!" And he points at the imprint of her body in the hood and, beneath his breath, says, "Bitch jumped out in front of me."

The crowd grows silent as Walker kneels on the ground and

takes Eleanor's head in his hands. The way Eleanor's hair would touch him in moments of pleasure, like when they hunkered together over a letter and she would sweep her head sideways, the unruly red strands touching his face. Or when she drew the curtain across as the children slept and slipped in beside him in the double bed, hair mashed against the pillow. Or on the bicycle before they were married, taking her long tresses and, from the crossbar, swinging them around and giving him a red mustache, joking, "That's what our kids'll look like!" There were long strands of her hair left in the sink when she washed it and, as his own started to gradually peel away from his head, she would take the strands and place them on his forehead, all laughter. Brushing Deirdre's, Maxine's—but never enough to remove the kinks and curls. She told their daughters to be proud of the curls. The way he broke a jam jar against the wall when she came home with her locks shorn short. Eighteen months later the locks were there, long again. And once, when he mopped the floor, she came home and was so amazed that she bent her body at the waist and walked crabways across the room and let her hair trail over his work, saying that she trusted him every inch of the way. "Look!" She giggled when she got to the opposite side of the room. "Not a bit of dirt in my hair! You're the best mopper I've ever seen in my life!"

Walker takes off his shirt and cushions his wife's head, then stands and slowly walks over to the Buick. Tears streaming down his face, he smashes his fist down on the hood until it is collandered with ridges and hollows.

Later that evening, Hoofer McAuliffe is on the street, casually pointing out the dents in his vehicle. The clothes and diapers that Eleanor had been washing for her grandson have already been picked up from the ground.

. . .

He removes the metal head from the shovel at the foot of the door and leaves a note upon it.

> *I might be gone for a while, Pa. Please look after Louisa and the baby for me. I'll be in the place you told me about when you were young. Don't tell nobody. I'll be back when the clouds clear.*

Tucking the shaft of wood into the inside of his overcoat, Clarence picks up his cardboard suitcase, goes down the stairs two at a time, melds into the 4 A.M. darkness, rain slanting yellow in the streetlights of Harlem.

The feel of the wood in his hands and the way it crushes the skull, like opening up a cantaloupe with a single blow. McAuliffe slumps down against the fender of his smashed-up Buick. Clarence pounds again with the handle of the shovel. Some blood jets out and hits the corner of his eyepatch. He says to the corpse, "We forget we have blood till it comes from us, motherfucker."

As he rounds a corner, running at full speed, a whistle is blown and he is knocked backward with a police nightstick. But the adrenaline is huge and unstoppable in him, and he rises from the ground with the shovel handle swinging. There is a mighty strength in his aim at the white cop's jaw.

Hoofer McAuliffe and the white cop, in their sudden silence, are left with the unbelieving looks of men searching for the beat of their own gone hearts.

. . .

Clarence rocks between the cars of a southbound train. Adrenaline still shoots through his twenty-three-year-old heart. A cooling wind brings him relief, the heat unbearable in the rear of the train. He props his sinewy arms between the carriages and goes with the sway. Looking down at the bloodstains on his shoes, Clarence spits on each, smears the blood on the back of his dungarees.

It is morning and the world is heating up already as the train whips out of a tunnel and merges into the gray and green of New Jersey: two boys fighting on a heap of coal, ravaged cars on cinder blocks at the edge of pasturelands, warehouses, a church steeple reaching up in the distance.

The conductor takes his ticket. "Georgia?" he asks.

Clarence doesn't reply.

"Change in Washington."

Clarence stares at the railway man's badge.

"Hey," says the conductor, staring into Clarence's face. "The words 'Yes sir' mean anything to you?"

No reply.

"Hey, uppity nigger, I'm talking to you."

After a silence, he leans into Clarence's face. "You goddamn sumbitches, all of y'all. You listening to me? You're a goddamn uppity sumbitch. Understand?"

And in his weariness the young man says, "Yessir."

When the conductor leaves, Clarence leans against the carriage, puts his cheek to the cool of the metal. He could fall right now, land on the tracks and lie there, snakelike, and wait for the segmentation of his body, let the wheels chop him into the tiniest of pieces, let his head travel a mile from his feet, slice his heart into two pumping pieces, scatter his toes to the different winds.

Looking down at the spinning gravel at his feet, Clarence imagines his mother coming home with the laundry as she was supposed to do. In the vision, she sits on the sofa beside her grandson and jokingly puts a finger in the child's belly button. Then she goes back across the room to the kitchen, where she removes the cosy from the pot and pours herself a cup of tea. She drops the sugar cube in and lets the spoon whirl and says, "Ahhh, now that's the medicine." She brings the steaming cup across the room and sits on the edge of the chair and, smelling of tea leaves, she leans over her grandson and says, "He's the cutest thing I've ever seen."

Clarence lets the vision drift with the miles—grain elevators, smoke from slag heaps, whitewashed farmhouses.

He reaches Brookwood Station in Atlanta the following day, wanders way beyond Peachtree Street. The city is a conundrum of highways and overpasses. Sapped of all energy, he stumbles along, feet slapping languidly through puddles. On the outskirts of the city, a new concrete ramp reaches out into empty air. Men work on the ramp, dangling on ropes in midair. He watches their antics in the rain, then raises his head, sees the sun break out behind dolorous clouds.

In the afternoon he finds a Laundromat off Hunter Street, and the dark-skinned manager lets Clarence sit in the bathroom in his underwear until his clothes are ready. There is a newspaper on the floor. He picks it up. On the front page there is a report of a fourteen-year-old lynched in Greenwood, Mississippi, for whistling at a white woman. Maybe the boy whistled and maybe he didn't. Maybe his body is still whistling. Maybe he will whistle forever. The face stares out at him from the newspaper, and Clarence's hands shake.

After an hour the Laundromat manager hands his clothes around the door. Clarence finds the blood stains have left small copper patches on his dungarees. Dressed, he gazes long and hard at himself in a cracked mirror, then wanders across the street to a barbershop where a red-and-white pole swirls merrily. He gets his hair shorn down to the scalp and the black barber says to him, "There ya go, bud, good as new."

Clarence looks at himself in the barber's mirror. "Shave me," he says.

The hot wet towel is placed on his neck and the cream is lathered on. The razor feels cool against his throat. He imagines it going deeper and deeper into his neck, right down to the tendons and the veins and beyond—when the veins are open and deep, his baby boy will swim down into his bloodstream, his groin, his brain, his heart.

The towel grows cool as the razor slides.

"Even better'n new," says the barber, scraping the side of the razor on the hip pocket of his apron. Clarence leaves a small tip and wanders on, looking at his reflection in shop windows, seeing a person he doesn't want to be.

Later that week, in the main post office on Forsyth Street, he searches for his own face on the WANTED posters but sees only the eyes of other men, all of them dark and grim, expectant of death. He walks the city streets of Atlanta, weeping.

Four policemen stand in Walker's room as he sits holding Louisa's hand. Louisa is shaking. She hugs her baby high, hiding a milk stain on her dress. Maxine and Deirdre lie sobbing on the beds.

"So," says one of the cops, "where d'you think he might go?"

"No idea."

"He won't get too far with one messy eye. Not too many men running around with eye patches. You listening, Walker?"

"Mister Walker to y'all."

"Where is he?"

Walker looks at the ceiling and remembers himself in the canoe when young, moving beneath the cypress trees that blocked out most of the summer light, reaching up to grab Spanish moss, his gnarled paddle making long swishes in the water, a silence to his movement, a quiet intent, a slight twist of the wrist at the end of each stroke to redirect the canoe, the paddle barely making a splash, bending himself into the work of repetition, the moss coming away softly in his fingers, the Okefenokee screaming around him.

The cop leans over and stares in Walker's face. "We need you to tell us where you think your son might go. He's in a high heap of shit."

"Is he now?"

"We can help him."

"I bet you can."

"You're asking for it, old man."

Walker remembers rounding a corner, holding a flaming branch with the resin burning, seeing a huge sweep of white in the night air, a whole flock, and a solitary sentinel at the edge of the swamp, not moving.

"If you find out, you better tell us. It's for his own good."

"Sure it is," says Walker.

"Don't get smart with me, old man."

A poisoned silence floats through the room.

"Where the hell is he?"

"I'd say he's probably done made his way to California. He was always talking about California. Ain't that right, Louisa?"

"That's right," she says.

"Little town by the name of Mendicino, I believe. He was always talking about Mendicino. Don't know what it is attracted him there. But he was always yapping on about Mendicino. Sun and waves. He was partial to the idea of sun and waves."

"Gonna get himself a suntan, was he?"

"I'm not rightly sure he needs a suntan."

"California?"

"That's where he'll be."

The cop moves toward the door. "I know you're lying."

"Don't hurt him," says Walker. "If you hurt him I'll hurt you back. That's a promise."

"I'd say that's a threat."

"Don't hurt him," Walker says again. "Please don't hurt him."

Three weeks after the cops' visit, Walker borrows fifty dollars from Rhubarb Vannucci and takes a train down to Atlanta, where the police have found Clarence.

Walker bends his big frame into the heat, finds himself sipping at a water fountain marked Colored. Trees are in blossom all over the city. Febrile grackles sing out loudly on the branches. Women in pastel hats shade their faces from car fumes. Just outside the train station, he sees a young boy shining shoes. The boy looks up at him and smiles. Walker tries hard to remember where he has seen the boy before, but can't.

He walks, swinging his shoulders solidly, unwilling to telegraph his grief.

Mosquitoes seem to gather in prayer outside the window of his hotel room. The heat is unbearable, and he opens the window. The insects swarm in, congregate around him. He squashes a few of the mosquitoes, and a little smudge of blood is left on his fingers. A welt swells up beneath his eye. Standing at the window, his sight is fuzzy: trees make shapes and a bar sign blurs. He leaves the hotel and goes across to the bar, orders a shot of whiskey. A sultry jazz singer looks at him from a stage, moves a pink tongue around her lips salaciously. Walker all of a sudden remembers the face of the boy shining shoes at the train station and realizes that he might have been looking at himself when young. He puts his face into the cups of his hands, knocks over the full whiskey, shoves his way out into the night.

Staggering across the street, he claps a flying moth. He flicks the remnants of dust off the palms of his hands. A threadlike antenna remains on his palm and he blows it off, remembering another moth in a different room months ago.

In the morning he wakes to birdsong and makes his way to the mortuary. Not even the hands of the morticians can disguise the beating Clarence must have received, his jaw slopped sideways, his cheekbones bloated blue with bruises, a new eyepatch over an even deeper wound in the socket. The police tell him that Clarence was shot dead while trying to escape through a junkyard on the outskirts of the city. Clarence, they say, robbed a liquor store at knifepoint and ran into the yard to take cover, was shot as he slipped on oil drums. The knife was recovered at the scene, and Clarence's pockets were stuffed with money.

"That's what happens to a cop killer," they say.

Walker stares at his son's accusers.

"You know," says one of the cops, "I got myself one of your kind in my family tree." He gouges at his teeth with a toothpick. "Just a swinging away from the highest branch."

Walker's eyes are misty with tears. He fights them back, bites his lip.

When he returns to his hotel room he falls on the dirty sheets, lets the evening's mosquitoes rave around him. He doesn't even flinch as they bite. He thinks for a moment about revisiting the Okefenokee of his boyhood but decides against it. When he boards the train to New York his face is puffy with red welts. A conductor shoves him toward the rear carriage. From the train window he watches the landscape of America flow by.

Back home, he sleeps in Clarence's bed. Then he moves across and arranges the pillows beside the ghost of his wife. All three of them lie down together. The pulse of Louis Armstrong sounds out from the record player, the notes moving tenderly through his torment.

On a pale weekday he buries Clarence, laying him beside Eleanor in a Bronx graveyard. His daughters and Louisa stand behind him.

Walker kneels at the stone but doesn't say any prayers. Prayers strike him as flaccid things now—useless supplications curling out only as far as the throats of men before falling back down into their stomachs. Spiritual regurgitation. He ignores the nearby gravediggers, who stand fat and complacent over the freshly dug hole. Walker takes a shovel, throws the first clodful over his son's coffin. He steps back and gathers his daughters in his arms, and they walk together to a waiting car.

He has hired the car to drive his family home. The girls clamber in, but Walker decides to go alone. Dull gray birds escort him as he walks through the Bronx all the way across the bridge to his street in Harlem—a five-hour walk—where he tells himself that he will strap his body to the sofa, elbow on the armrest, for the rest of his years. Even the idea of revenge strikes him as hollow.

Walker stares at the ceiling, his body a dark room of nothingness, empty, vacant. He recognizes the necessity of sorrow—if sorrow fades, so too does memory. He keeps the sorrow alive for the sake of memory, evoking Eleanor's movements, rehearsing them in his brain. His head spins through their gymnastics of love. Small shocks of remembered bliss. He aggregates the beauty of their lives together, weighs it in his fingers. Even the dullest moments over teacups are replayed in his mind. He does the same with the memory of Clarence, then combines them, wife and son standing together at the piano, where he talks to them.

"Eleanor," he whispers, "you're looking good."

"Hey, Clar, go get your momma her hairbrush."

"I've never seen you look so fine, honey."

"Thank you, son," he says, reaching for a hairbrush that isn't there. "Give us a moment together, your momma and me."

And, after a silence, "He's growing up like a flower, ain't he, El?"

The days go by with a vicious lethargy. Even light is slow to fade. The future feels postponed by an eternal present. Walker develops a horror of time. He turns the clock face against the wall. The only day he recognizes is Sunday, because of the sight of churchgoers out the window. He resents their white teeth, their joy, the comfortable tuck of Bibles under their arms. As they walk, the gospel music seems already to be rising in them, the way they move on the tips of their toes. They will go to church and lift their voices to some useless heaven. A unified song of self-deception. God only exists in happiness, he thinks, or at least in the promise of happiness.

Walker turns his Bible spine in against the wall, bricks it in with other books, unread. Let them go on down to their ridiculous churches. Let them sing to their ceilings. You won't find me beseeching no Jesus. I'm finished with all that.

He doesn't move to the record player, just lets himself sink down into the folds of the couch. Beside him, a spittoon grows full and brown with chewing tobacco. He spits out a decayed tooth one morning, thinks nothing of it. He shoves aside plates of food. His daughters and Louisa bring him cups of tea that grow cold at his elbow. The window is shut to the sounds of the street. Walker mutters invectively to himself. Over the weeks, he grows wasted and haggard, and huge bags develop under his eyes. The spittoon overflows and stains the armrest. He shoos the preacher away from the door and asks his daughters to tell Rhubarb Vannucci that he isn't home in case the Italian comes calling.

He hardly even looks at his grandson in the crib; the boy is just a meaningless blur of flesh.

At night, Louisa tries to get him to go down the hallway to the bath, to wash, but he becomes a brick in her hands and she gives up. He welcomes himself back to the sofa. "This is where I'll lie," he says. He might let his body melt into the cushions and stay there forgotten, like one of his dropped coins. He might reach down for the decayed parts of himself and throw them out the window to the ghost of Clarence below on the stoop: bits of arms, legs, fingers, and an eyeball as a currency for the gone.

He notices that his daughters have begun to stay out late at night, but he says nothing. Louisa remains in the apartment with him, bottles of tequila in a ring around her. The alcohol lies heavy on her breath. She spends her time fashioning ancestral beads to sell at a market. Between them there is a contagion of hush.

She has decided to call the baby Clarence Nathan, after his father and grandfather. But Walker dismissed the name with a wave of his arm, glad of the pain it brings him. "Call him whatever the hell y'all want."

Louisa works on a dream catcher, which she suspends above the boy's head. The dream catcher is made with twigs in the shape of a triangle, crisscrossed with yarn; a dogtooth and beads and a feather tied onto the threads.

"It'll catch his dreams," she says.

"They'll go nowhere else," says Walker.

"Don't be so bitter. I can't stand it."

"I'll be bitter if I goddamn want to."

"I'm leaving," she says.

"Leave. Take your bottles. Grab y'alls beads and strings and thread and wrap 'em around your bottles and make a goddamn raft for yourself."

She doesn't leave, and she watches him fade further into the couch. At times she cooks for him and works with great tenderness, even when she's drunk—baked chicken, rice and beans, cucumber sandwiches—yet she finds herself drinking more and more. She changes the size of the bottles she buys. They make a great bulge in the grocery bags where she tries to hide them. Sometimes she drops tequila in the food just so she can smell it as she leans over the stove.

And then one morning she emerges from the bathroom to hear Walker muttering to himself. She is surprised at the sound of his voice, clear and deep and lunatic.

"I bet he didn't even see them," he says. "I bet he didn't even see them."

"What's that?" she asks.

"Nothing."

"What did you say?"

"Nothing."

"See what?"

"See goddamn anything!" he shouts. "They shot him in a junkyard! He didn't get to see all the things I told him about! A goddamn crane! He didn't even get a chance to see a crane! That's what I wanted for him! Ever since he was born! I wanted him to see a crane dance! Don't look at me that way! Fuck you if you think that's stupid! Fuck you! I wanted him to see a crane! That's what I wanted! I never got the chance to show him even that!"

There is a querulous rising and falling in his chest as he gasps for air. Louisa puts a hand on his shoulder and he slaps it away, letting a dribble of tobacco run down his chin.

She moves to the kitchen and leaves him in silence, but then she turns around and stares at him and says, "I saw twenty-seven of them once."

Walker doesn't reply.

"Near the trailer house where my family lives in South Dakota."

He rocks gently on the couch.

"It was on the edge of a lake," she says. "One by one. And then the whole flock of them. On the edge of the mud. It was soft and they left their footprints. Then the sun came and baked them. The footprints were there for a whole season. I used to ride a bicycle in and out of them. I cried when the rain washed them away. My father slapped me because I wouldn't stop crying."

Louisa removes the spittoon, sits on the edge of the couch.

"They came back again the next season," she says, "but I thought I was too old for bicycles. Besides, my brother was using the tires for slingshots. There was no way I could ride it anymore even if I wanted to."

"Y'all never married, did ya?"

"We never got the chance."

"It means the baby's a bastard."

"Never say that again. You hear me? Don't call my son that."

"They beat Clarence to death," says Walker.

"I don't want to think about it. There's certain things you don't have to remember."

"And certain things ya do," says Walker. "They murdered my son. They put their-all's gun barrels right down into his eye. They made a grave of his head."

"Shut up!" she says. "Shut the hell up and listen! Twenty-seven cranes. It was the most beautiful thing in the world. Back and forth. Going up in the air, wings fully spread. Around and around and around."

Neither of them stir, but after a moment Walker shifts on the couch and says to her, "Do it then."

"What?"

"Show me."

"You're crazy."

"Please. Show me."

"Don't go crazy on me, Nathan."

"Go ahead," he says. "If y'all remember it so well, go ahead and do it yourself."

"Nathan."

"Do it!" he shouts.

Louisa lowers her head and pours herself a large glass of

tequila. She doesn't even wince as the alcohol hits the back of her throat. Looking at Walker, she hesitates for a moment. She closes her eyes momentarily. Then she smiles, almost derisively. She wipes her lips and puts one arm out and she chuckles and stops.

"Go on," says Walker.

She starts to move: the high cheekbones, the threaded hair, the white white teeth, a gray dress, no shoes, her brown toes lyrical on the worn carpet. Walker, embarrassed, turns his head slightly, but then returns the gaze as Louisa dances, hands outstretched, arms in a whirl, feet back and forth, the most primitive of movements, dissolving the boundaries of her body. Walker feels a throbbing at his temples, a stirring of something primeval within him, a slow spread of joy rising, fanning out, warming him, supplying his flesh with goose bumps. From the couch, he continues to stare. He knows that there is alcohol coursing through Louisa, but he allows himself to forget that; he lets the movement surround him, breathe him, become him, ancestral and gorgeous. And when Louisa starts to lose her breath, Walker rises awkwardly from the couch, reaches to take her hand, and she stops dancing. He touches the side of her face. She drops her chin to her chest. They are silent for a long time, and then he whispers to her with a smile, "Ya know, ya looked ridiculous dancing like that."

She puts her head on his shoulder, and together they break into a long laughter, goose bumps still rising on Walker's skin.

"There's something we gotta do," he says, later in the afternoon.

"What's that?" she asks.

"A family ritual."

"A ritual?"

He is surprised at himself, his movement, a strange supple-
ness appearing in his knees. He beckons Louisa across the room
with a crooked finger. Side by side, they bend over the crib,
holding the dream catcher away, and they rehearse the words
first, and say to the baby, "Clarence Nathan Walker, you are so
goddamn handsome!"

Years later, during a time of riots and flowers and dark fists
painted on walls, Walker and his grandson will sit together in
the basement church in Saint Nicholas Park where Eleanor was
once baptized. A new young preacher will be telling the story of
an ancient Hebrew king, Hezekiah. The church will be quiet.
Walker and the boy will sit with their thighs touching, unem-
barrassed by their closeness. It will be hot. They will pass a
handkerchief back and forth. The preacher will rattle on about
tolerance, the necessity of belief, the permanence of struggle.
    Grandson and grandfather will not really be listening to the
sermon until the preacher mentions an old tunnel.
    Walker will nudge his grandson with his elbow and say, "Hey."
    "What?"
    "Listen up."
Hezekiah, the preacher will say, wanted to create a tunnel
between two pools of water, Siloam and the Pool of Virgins. A
team of men started on the edge of each lake and vowed to
meet somewhere near the middle. Underground, the diggers
worked the tunnel along, further and further. They expected to
meet. But they miscalculated and the tunnels missed each
other. The men shouted in anger and disappointment and then
they were amazed—in their anger—to hear one another's faint
voices through the rock. Underground, the men changed direc-

tion. And so the tunnels moved again. Axes and shovels swung. The corridors of dirt bent and curved. The men followed the sound of the voices, still dull through the rock. And the voices grew louder and they moved closer until their pickaxes smashed against one another, creating sparks, and their voices met. The men swept back the rest of the rock and looked closely at one another's tired faces. Then they reached forward and touched one another to make sure they were real. The tunnel made a giant misshapen S but, after a while—although the men had failed at first—water began to flow between the two ancient pools.

chapter 11
the way God supposed

The winter sun berths itself in the sky for a day and begins to melt the snow, so that he can hear cars topside making their way sloppily through the slush. But in the tunnel the wind lashes along, carrying its insistent chill. Thirty-two days of snow and ice. The most brutal winter he has known. Treefrog pulls the hood of the sleeping bag around his head and lays a shirt over his face, the buttons icy at his nose.

Best to stay in bed the rest of the day, he thinks, but Castor comes up beside him and nuzzles her way under the shirt and he feels her rib cage hard against his face.

Still in his sleeping bag, Treefrog manages to get on a few extra shirts and his gloves, then hops out and takes some milk from the Gulag, the liquid frozen solid. He stabs open the box with his knife, and a cube of milk falls into the pan. Quickly, he heats it over a small fire. Castor laps at the feast and afterward jumps onto the mattress and curls up on the blankets, white fur almost phosphorescent in the dark. Treefrog takes an old thermometer from a box of hubcaps. He rises and gauges all over: by the stalactite, at the ice wall, on the train tracks, in his back cave, by Faraday's broken traffic light, in the Gulag, at the fire pit, and on the bedside table, where it reads only sixteen degrees Fahrenheit—cold, so goddamn cold.

Warming the thermometer with his breath until it hits an even eighteen, he stands and urinates painfully in a piss bottle.

Time to dump the bottles up above.

With Castor inside his shirt, Treefrog goes outside through the tunnel gate, where the bright light stings his eyes. He puts on his sunglasses and pours his name in the whiteness near the crab-apple trees, but there is not enough to finish off the words. He breaks an icy twig off a tree and carves the remaining letters.

Four and a half weeks of relentless ice and snow already. Maybe he should carve the days in notches by the Gulag.

He follows the bend of the highway, walks down to the green benches at the edge of the Hudson.

Ice still on the water and he wonders about his crane, how far it has gone toward the sea. Across the water, New Jersey catches the sunlight.

Angela sits, alone, on the bench. Snow is bellied up around her shoes.

"Heyyo," he says, but she doesn't reply.

She has spread a blue plastic bag beneath herself so her clothes don't soak up the wetness. Treefrog sits on the high back of the bench. He takes Castor and puts her in Angela's lap, and the cat curls up, contented, as she strokes it.

"Fine morning," Treefrog says, "fine morning."

"No it ain't," says Angela.

"What's up?"

"I wanna wash my hair."

"Let's go to my nest. I'll boil some water for you."

"No way, I ain't climbing up there." She pulls her scarf up around her neck. "How come it's so cold and the sun still shining?"

"Refraction," he says. "The sun bounces off the snow."

"Oh, yeah? You're so clever, ain't ya? The only thing bouncing off the snow is your bullshit." But after a moment she says, "You know what? When I lived in that house with the wraparound porch we had hot water all the time. It was red 'cause it had too much iron and I didn't like to wash my hair 'cause it made my hair stiff and I thought the color'd be funky, but now I wish I could wash my hair in that funky warm water, I'd wash my hair in that funky warm water all day long and night too."

"It'd be clean, then."

"It's clean now, motherfucker!"

"I'm only saying."

"And I'd wash it in the afternoon too if I had the time."

Treefrog adjusts the glasses. "Say. Where's Elijah?"

"Gone to get his SSI. Five hundred bucks a month."

"Man," says Treefrog. "He's got an address?"

"He's got a friend with an apartment and then they get the money and then they go to the candy store. I hope he keeps me some. He said he'll keep me some."

"That stuff's bad for you," he says.

She chuckles and looks away.

"Hey, Angela," he says. "You killed them rats yet?"

"I told you, the pregnant one is pregnant. She's called Skagerak."

"Huh?"

"Papa Love told me they's Norway rats and I asked him for

the name of a place in Norway, somewhere like the sea, and he told me Skagerak and Barents, so I called them Skagerak and Barents."

"You talked to Papa Love?"

"He was out putting the finishing touches on that guy Edison."

"Faraday."

"Yeah, yeah, yeah, whatever."

"And you asked him about rats?"

"Yeah."

"And you gave 'em names?"

"Yeah, what's it to you?"

"Now I heard it all."

"The girl rat is nice. She comes right up beside me. Someday she's gonna take the bread right outa my hands."

"Damn."

They sit in a long silence, him perched high on the back of the bench, watching the slumber of the water.

"The sea looks nice," she says.

"That's not the sea, that's the Hudson. The sea's down there."

She purses her lips as if about to kiss the air. "You know what? I always wanted to see the sea. When we were in Iowa, we had a car, Plymouth Volare, a dented piece of shit, you know, and me and my sisters'd be in the backseat, saying, *I see the sea and the sea sees me*. And my father'd say, We're going to the sea. But then we'd always run outa gas and he'd kick that dented piece of shit and he'd say, Just a minute. He'd go down the road to get gas—he had a gas can in the trunk—but he'd stop in a bar and that was it. And we'd be in the backseat, singing that stupid song, *I see the sea and the sea sees me*. Once we tried to walk home through the fields, but the cornstalks were way up above our heads and we was scared and went back to the car."

"Nothing stopping you from going now to see it, is there?"

"No. I s'pose."

"You should go see it," he says. "Take the train to Coney Island, it's nice out there."

He moves to sit down on the bench, tugs some of her plastic bag, plants himself beside her, but she looks away. "Hey," he says, surprised.

She shields her face. "Leave me alone."

"What happened?"

"Nothing."

"He hit you, didn't he?"

"I fell, goddammit, leave me alone."

"When did he hit you?"

"You're a pain in the ass, you know that? You're a pain in the ass bigger than any I ever seen. I'm sitting here getting some quiet, you come along, why the fuck don't you leave me alone, huh?"

"You should go to a shelter."

"Ever been in one of them places? They got women with smashed bones and bitten ears and gaps in theys teeth wide enough to drive a D-train through."

"Why do you stay with him?"

Angela reaches into her pocket and takes out an empty vial with an orange cap, and she twirls it in her hands and smiles.

"You should stay away from that shit."

"Yessir, Mister Treefrog Preacher, sir." She sighs. "Elijah didn't like me giving no name to my rats. Said it's stupid. Said he's gonna kill 'em. He's gonna get some rat poison and make 'em eat it. Maybe even get hisself a cat."

"He don't like cats."

"Now he likes 'em. They just animals like you and me."

And then Treefrog remembers how once, in springtime—back in the bad days, the worst days—he fell asleep with a piece of bread near his pillow. When he woke up, a rat had taken a small chunk from the top of his right ear. The blood ran down the side of his face and hardened in his beard. He chased the rat to the rear of the nest. There were small brown pellets of rodent shit all over the back of the cave. Treefrog rumbled around in the darkness, so disoriented that he scraped his ear against the wall, and then the cut was filled with black tunnel dust. He cleaned it out with water and gin for disinfectant, tore a strip from a white T-shirt for a bandage, wrapped it around his head and underneath his beard. For days his ear sent jabs of pain through him. He was afraid he might lose his balance. He kept on pinching at the other ear with his fingernail, even pierced the flesh once, but it wasn't a bad cut. He forgot to change the bandage and Papa Love called him Van Gogh for a while, but the nickname wore off when Treefrog's ear healed. A month later he caught the rat in a trap beneath his library shelf. It wriggled and squealed under the metal bar that had trapped its body. He bashed its head in with his spud wrench and it let out one last squeal. Treefrog brought the animal topside, dug a small hole in the weed lot down by the river, and buried the rat with great ceremony, just in case it was still using the slice of his ear to listen to the secrets of his mind and body.

"I know what you mean," he says.

"D'ya think it's gonna snow again?" Angela asks. And then she looks to the river. "You know what? I had an uncle, he used be able to tell the weather. He could tell a storm from a million miles. He'd stand out in them cornfields and say, A storm's coming. Or, Sun's coming. Or, Tornado's moving in. He looked like the weather. Had a face like the weather. Hey. You think I look like the weather, Treefy?"

"You look like sunshine."

"You're cute, Treefy. Excepting sunshine gives you cancer."

"You sure?"

"It's a known fact."

"Gimme a cigarette."

"Them too. Sunshine and cigarettes."

She flips the gold clasp on her handbag and delves deep, pulls out half a flattened cigarette, rolls it in her fingers to make it cylindrical once more. He lights it for her and she blows the smoke away from him, but the wind carries it back. She takes five furious puffs, then hands the cigarette to him and Treefrog holds it like a lover. A thought strikes him deep and hard when the smoke touches his lungs.

"I'd like to make a map of your face."

"What you talking about, a map of my face?"

"Just a map."

"Maps for driving with, motherfucker."

"Come on, let's go try it."

"Where?"

"My nest."

"I ain't climbing nowhere. You just want a knock."

"Knock knock."

"Who's there?"

"Treefrog."

"Treefrog who?"

"Treefrog screw you."

"That ain't even funny," she says.

"It weren't meant to be funny. Come on. I'll show you."

He passes the cigarette, and she drags hard even though the filter is burning. "Maps?" she says.

"I keep maps. Sometimes I make maps."

"What the hell you make maps for? It's not as if you're going anywheres."

In the darkness, beneath his nest—she will not climb—he closes his eyes and touches the side of her face. She shivers for a moment, but he lets his fingers rest until her body stops quaking and she relaxes and says, "This is stupid."

The movement of his fingers is slow and precise. He will trace a line across from ear to nose, a perfectly straight line; otherwise the translation will be inaccurate. He begins at the outer edge of her ear—he has removed his gloves for exactness, spat on his fingers to clean off the tunnel dust, dried them on his overcoat. He moves from the top of her ear to the under-hang of flesh, and he gauges the tiny distance along the top of his forefinger. The distance decided, Treefrog opens his eyes and reaches into his overcoat pocket for a piece of graph paper and a pencil. On the graph paper he draws two lines, one ver-tical, one horizontal, meeting at an axis, fixed and finite in the center of the paper. Elevation on the vertical, distance on the horizontal. He flicks the lighter with one hand, then the other, and marks the elevation of her ear, the tip and the underhang: two small dots of pencil on the graph paper.

He must be careful; the eraser is down to a stub, and he doesn't want to make a mistake. Closing his eyes once more, he feels his way along her ear—it is full of rumples and ridges—and she says, "Ohhhh."

The tunnel is achingly quiet, only the zip of cars above, a

sound so constant that it is swallowed. He remains with his fingers tentative at the center of her ear, near the well of her eardrum, and he can feel the nervousness tremble through her.

"I don't like you touching me there," Angela says, but he tells her that it will look like a miniature lake. Some other time, he thinks, he will begin from a different point, maybe at the lobe where the missing earring will make a sinkhole of sorts. Angela shifts and lights another cigarette. He doesn't want to feel her face while she smokes; he says it will give a false reading, the suck-in of cheeks when she draws on the filter. She smokes it down to the quick and then Treefrog crushes it underfoot.

He snaps his eyes shut and moves across the ear until his finger touches the side of her face at the soft point just at the top of her jawbone.

"You sure your fingers is clean?" she asks.

"Yeah," he whispers.

There is a tiny ridge at the bone and he marks it on his graph. Angela is quiet now, and she too closes her eyes. Treefrog pecks at the air with his head and he is sure that he can smell the lovely mustiness of her, but then she winces when he touches the bruise on the middle of her cheek—the topography of violence—and he tries to skim the very edge of her skin where it must be colored blue.

"That hurts."

"Sorry."

If she cries, he wonders, will he be able to stop the water with his fingers so that the tense molecules might be arrested for a single second, become forever a part of her face? But she doesn't cry, and his fingers move a little more quickly now, away from the bruise. Her skin makes a little bump toward the side of her nose where it flares out.

"You got a nice nose," he says to her, as his fingers begin the rise to a bone that feels as if it has been broken many times. He touches her nostril and comes to the very center of her face, smooths his fingers along her cheek.

"You done yet, asshole?"

"I have to do the other side."

"Why?"

" 'Cause you can't have half a face."

"What if Elijah sees us?"

"I'll make a map of his fist. It'll look like a ridge with a big knob on the end."

She chuckles.

"Stand still, goddammit."

Treefrog reaches up with the left hand and strokes her right ear, remembering the exact movements of his fingers on the opposite side of her face. It is vital that each hand do an equal amount of touching. His fingers move across her cheekbone—no bruises on this side—and with infinite tenderness he maps the geography of Angela. When he is done, he climbs up to his nest, brings down four blankets, and they sit in the tunnel by the Melting Clock mural. A train whizzes past not ten feet away. He joins the dots together on the graph paper, licking the lead end of the pencil so that the joining line is dark and prominent.

He works with great care, making sure that the lines are consistent, uniform, unwavering, that a gentle curve appears between dots, that the graph doesn't become jittery or messy. He never once uses the eraser. The lighter and the pencil are switched from hand to hand, his fingers shaking in the cold. Angela looks over his shoulder, her chin on his overcoat, saying, "This is about the stupidest thing I ever seen."

When Treefrog is finished, he holds the paper up and shows Angela the rise and curl of her face—the canyons and ridges and riverbeds and hanging valleys that she has become.

"Heyyo," he says to the paper.

"That's me?"

"There's your ears, that's your nose, that's your cheek."

"Looks bumpy."

"I can change the scale," says Treefrog.

"Do me a favor, Treefy?"

"Yeah."

"Get rid of the bruise there," she says.

He looks at her and smiles.

Scraping his fingernails along the top of the eraser to make sure it doesn't leave black smudges on the graph paper, he scrubs out the hillock where the bruise was. She kisses him on the cheek and softly says, "Doctor Treefrog."

"If I take readings of everywhere I could make a map of the rest of your face. I'd have all these contours and your face'd look like this." He draws a series of distorted circles. "Your nose'd be like this. And your ear'd be like this. And your lips, they'd be weird. Like this."

"Where d'ya learn to do this?"

"I taught myself. I been making maps for a long time."

"You ever do it for anyone else?"

"I did it for Dancesca."

"Who's she?"

"I told you about her. And Lenora too. My little girl."

"Where is she?"

"I don't know."

"Nobody knows where I is either," says Angela.

Walker sits by the window. The apartment has been remodeled to twice its former size, the landlord stung for housing violations. The view from the window has changed in recent years—the sunlight is blocked out by large housing projects that step their way across the city. Giant gray and brown buildings, they frown against the skyline. Washing flutters out from balconies. Boys chat through adjacent windows, using tin cans and string. Suicides are heard for the length of their screams.

Only Louisa and the boy remain in the apartment with him. Both Walker's daughters have left to get married, Deirdre to a steamfitter in the Texas oilfields, Maxine to a welder from Philadelphia. Slowly the girls have faded from his life. Photographs of their children sometimes arrive late, as if they've suddenly been born at the age of one or two. Walker often thinks of making a trip to see them, but it never happens; his bank account will not allow it.

Most of his time is spent sitting by the window, watching his ten-year-old grandson, Clarence Nathan, playing alone in an empty lot across the street.

Sometimes, in the apartment, Louisa dances. Walker turns the couch to face the center of the room, tightens a blanket over his legs, balances a teacup on the arm of the couch. Clarence Nathan also watches—his mother's arms stretched out to an unvoiced song and her feet going back and forth delicately as Walker's big guffaws mix in with the city's sirens. She tucks her head to her chest, as if into a wingpit. Lifts it up again. Arms moving up against a heavy air, she seems ready for the sky, a chimera of movement and geometry. But Walker has noticed changes in the rhythms in recent years. From his position on the soft cushions, he has seen Louisa's movements clang toward a certain jerkiness, a loss of control. Tall and long-legged, she has developed the look of something wounded. Her arms don't quite stretch out as they used to. Her feet are not as lyrical. Her breathing is jerky. The primitive rawness is less than it once was, and she has lost something in the way she spins; there is often a temporary stumble on the lip of the carpet, as if her fluidity has siphoned itself down into the tequila, where Louisa searches for it. A bottle and a half a day. In the morning she stumbles out of bed and goes straight to the cupboard, doesn't even wince at the first sip. She loves to peel the labels halfway off, scraping them with her fingernails. Sometimes she hides in the bathroom for hours, comes out with the bottle empty.

Louisa wears a row of seashells at her neck, strung together on a piece of white twine. The shells jangle when she moves. She always says she feels a little dizzy, that a doctor has given her pills to help cure the problem. She swallows the pills in handfuls and they keep her awake for long stretches. She goes to late-night clubs, arrives home frenzied, her hair unthreading as she tosses in the single bed beside her son. In the afternoons, she wakes only to give a cursory kiss to the boy, then falls back silent on the bed.

A litany of men calls at the door and Walker has noticed—with a thickening sense of shame—the rise of her skirts high on her thighs.

Things have begun to go missing from the apartment: a vase, a soupspoon, a picture frame but not the picture.

"Y'all seen Clarence's frame?" Walker asks her. "He looks mighty naked without it."

"Haven't seen it anywhere," she says.

"Wouldn't happen to be in the pawnshop?"

" 'Course not. What you think I am, a thief?"

"Take it easy, girl. Y'all know I don't think that."

"You saying I soaked his frame?"

" 'Course not," says Walker. "I'm sorry. Just shooting my mouth off. Don't mind me."

"After all I do around here? Cook and clean. Keep you near your grandson. You know, I could live anywhere I want. And you tell me I'm a thief?"

"I was just wondering about the frame."

"Well, don't wonder."

"Hey," says Walker after a moment, "d'y'all ever think about what might be growing in the place of Clarence's eyeball?"

"What?"

"His eyeball. I mean, what sort of plant? In Korea. I mean, that's what he said long ago, wasn't it? That something might grow there in that place."

"You got a fever or something, Nathan? I've no idea what you're talking about. All I hear from you these days is things that don't make any goddamn sense."

"Don't cuss in front of the boy."

"I'll curse if I want."

"Sometimes I think it may be a big American oak."

"No such thing as an American oak," she says.

"Or a chestnut tree or something."

"No chestnuts in Korea."

"Maybe a maple."

She turns away. "I'm going out for a while."

"Where you going to now?"

"Just out."

"Watch that skirt don't disappear altogether. You'll be whistling down the street. They'll hear you coming around the corner."

"Funny funny." And then she sighs. "Will you look after Claren?"

"Holy Name," says Walker.

"Well?"

"Y'all know I always look after the boy."

"Thanks," she says, landing a brusque kiss on Clarence Nathan's forehead.

"Lord," Walker says, as she leaves.

One evening Louisa comes home and wakes Walker, and—with her pupils swimming up near her eyelids—she insists on dancing while the boy is asleep. She puts a finger to her mouth for silence and stands in the center of the room. The seashell necklace lies white against her brown skin. She has wrapped a thin blue scarf around her head. Four other scarves hang from it, down to the small of her back, rippling in with her hair, which is filthy. She spins and whirls and throws out her arms and Walker is temporarily enraptured until—suddenly—she loses control, falls, and, as if in slow motion, one foot goes high in the air, her arms make half windmills, her elbow grazes the floor, and she collapses against the cupboard. Her head slices against a metal handle.

Walker, in his pajamas, struggles up and lifts her from the ground. He leans close and notices a trace of vomit on her breath. He is thankful to see there is no blood, just a scrape on her forehead.

He opens the buttons on the sleeve of her blouse to check her pulse and sees the bracelet of tiny track marks on the inside of her wrist.

"Go back to bed," he tells his grandson, who is awake and standing beside him.

"What's wrong, Mister Walker?"

"Go on now. Your momma's just taken a little turn."

Walker is glad to find the faintest of pulses—like the distant memory of a canoe turning a corner—and he lifts Louisa to a sitting position, gently slapping her face to waken her.

. . .

"The thing about a crane, son, is that when it swallows a fish it takes it down headfirst. Any sort of fish y'all want. The tail never goes down the throat first. If it did, the scales would rip her throat. So she eats it headfirst, and it goes down all nice and smooth. That's a known fact. They just do it by nature. They're no fools. They just do things the way God supposed them to do. I seen that happen."

Balance is the boy's inheritance. While his mother is strung out on a tide of chemicals and his grandfather is strapped to the couch with pain, he likes to go up to the rooftop and look out beyond the architecture of Harlem—past the projects and the red-brick churches and the funeral homes and the intricate plasterwork and the empty lots and the parks—to the sky-scrapers leaping across Manhattan.

Heroin deals take place on the rooftop, wads of money changing fists, but the junkies leave Clarence Nathan alone. When they get high they like to watch him walk the edge of the wall, acrobatically, above a seventy-foot drop to the street below. They urge him to go faster, to run along the thin ledge.

The boy moves like a morphine vision, full of potential. His feet never go astray and he can even do a handstand, a slight quiver to his arms as he looks upside down at the sky.

He never thinks of the danger. His heart is steady anywhere. The blood flows equally to each part of his body.

Once he went to his school gymnasium, climbed the rope from floor to ceiling, and hung upside down—a teacher saw him, dangling in the air with the rope wrapped around his foot, knotted at the ankle. He remained still; his body didn't even sway. The teacher recognized him from other incidents—he'd been cornered at school many times, beaten up by other boys. For a moment he thought Clarence Nathan had strung himself up, but the boy let out a yelp, curled his body, unknotted his foot, slipped down the rope, and dropped to the ground.

Some afternoons his grandfather struggles up the staircase to watch the boy's antics. Walker uses a cane, guiding himself past the reams of graffiti on the walls. His seventy-second year has given him more pain than ever before. A thin gray beard has appeared on his cheeks, his fingers no longer nimble enough to handle a razor. A tobacco pouch is slung around his neck for easy access, tied with a length of cord. It bobs above the silver cross. He labors to open the door at the top of the stairs, eventually just shoves it with his knee, and winces with discomfort.

On the rooftop Walker finds some sunlight and turns his face toward it, sees Clarence Nathan standing on the ledge.

"Mister Walker!" shouts the boy.

Walker glares at the junkies who are slumbering on the other side of the roof, melting cubes in a bucket for shooting ice water into their veins.

He sits on a shabby blue lawn chair covered with the soot of the city. He reaches up to his brow and rubs his temple cool and then nods to the boy. "Go ahead, son."

"Which one'll I do?"

"Any one y'all want."

"Okay!"

"Just be careful."

Walker settles back in the seat. He has seen it often enough that he has learned not to be afraid. The boy waves, rushes to the edge of the roof, and leaps to a nearby rooftop. In the air there is a fusion of ecstasy and danger: one leg straightened way out in front of the other, the rush of wind around him. He lands perfectly, three feet beyond the lip of the next building, looks around, and grins. He leaps back again, sticking to a curious rule he's made for himself, landing on the alternate foot each time. He likes it this way. If he makes a mistake he goes back and forth, back and forth, to ensure balance. The soles of his sneakers are almost worn out. He tells himself that one day he will try it barefoot. Pride thumps in him as Walker gives a slow round of applause, a bit of tobacco spit escaping the old man's mouth and dropping on his shirt. Walker rubs at it, ashamed.

"Good job, son."

"Will I do it again?"

"Sure. Nothing too fancy though, that's all. Go on now."

Walker sits all afternoon, moving the lawn chair according to the swing of the sun, watching the acrobatics.

Even when the boy listens to his grandfather's stories he perches on the ledge, putting his arms around his knees, rocking back and forth above the street.

When the sun goes down, Clarence Nathan hops from the wall and cleans the soot off the back of his grandfather's pants. The soot billows out from the old man's ass, and they laugh as it makes clouds in the air.

The stories continue as they make their way over patches of sticky tar and broken glass and then negotiate the staircase down. There are new faces graffitied on the stairwell wall, Huey Newton and Bobby Seale wearing dashikis, their faces set between two large panthers drawn like petroglyphs. Beside that: PIGS AREN'T KOSHER. Beside that: EAT YOUR DRAFT CARD. Further down, a poster with the face of the late Martin Luther King.

There are two new locks on the apartment door. Inside, dishes are piled high in the sink. The fridge is open, nothing

inside. A half-made wicker chair stands upside down, aban-
doned. Photos are yellowing on the walls. All the frames have
gone missing.

Louisa isn't home. She seldom is these days. Walker sits by his
grandson's bedside. There is a stale smell from the old man,
something like fire smoke, but the boy listens quietly. One of his
favorite stories is about his great-grandfather—Con O'Leary—
who used to hide a bullet in his belly button before he was
blown halfway toward heaven. Some of Eleanor's World War
Two bullets are still kept in the apartment, and the boy likes to
watch his grandfather lift up his shirt and shove one in.

"Do another one."

"I ain't that fat!"

"Go on, try another, Mister Walker."

"Don't push y'alls luck, son."

"Go on. Please."

Walker coughs and brings up a string of black dust from his
lungs, a remnant of the tunnels. He spits into a sheet of newspaper, balls the paper up, and drops it into a wastebasket. The
boy sits up in bed and slaps his grandfather's back to help him
through the coughing. Walker can feel the thumps echo through
him. Recently his body has given way even further, a cough
growing deeper, his limbs tightening, the tobacco spit confound-
ing him, a legacy of dribbled stains on white shirts.

After the fit of coughing, Walker straightens himself up and
reaches for the second bullet. "Abracadabra," he says.

All the taunts scribbled down in a school copybook: halfbreed,
mulatto, Sambo, nigger, honky, snowboy, zebra, cracker, jungle
bunny, coon, Wonderbread, Uncle Tom, Crazy Horse, spade.

. . .

Clarence Nathan takes the subway train—his grandfather has inculcated in him a love of this journey—and he emerges from the station and walks jauntily to the construction sites near Battery Bark. He has been given new sneakers for his sixteenth birthday.

He watches the choreography of commerce toward the sky.

The men who create the giant buildings are only seen as specks moving on naked beams, a series of hardhats going back and forth. They move at the rate of a floor a week. The cranes feed them steel; then the men bolt it together. When the steel is clad, the men climb higher, distancing themselves from the world below. Sometimes Clarence Nathan goes into neighboring skyscrapers, saying he's a delivery boy, then sneaks his way to the top floor for a better view. He has bought a pair of binoculars in the pawnshop. He loves to see the men in motion on crossbeams and columns, climbing without harnesses even. The men move as if on solid ground; their feet never slip; there is no need for them to spread their arms wide for balance. Some even swing through the air on the ends of jib lines. Clarence Nathan falsifies the application forms and says he is eighteen, though it's clear to the foremen that he hasn't even begun shaving.

"Come back when your testicles drop," says one of the ironworkers.

One afternoon two security guards have to drag him from a ladder twenty-three floors up an unfinished skyscraper. They grab at Clarence Nathan's feet and are amazed at the brutal strength in his legs. He shakes free, and they watch him leap the final eight rungs to the steel decking below. He lands with knees bowed, the binoculars swinging at his neck. "You goddamn fool," says one of the guards. He is escorted down to the street and told that if he comes back he'll be arrested. Clarence Nathan nods gravely, leaves the site, and when he is far enough away he punches the air in euphoria. Someday he will climb and they will watch in awe. He will create his own movement in the air.

Clarence Nathan stands on top of a parking meter, balancing, until a cop shoos him away. Further down the street he tries another parking meter on the other foot.

He returns day after day to the skyscraper site, wearing his grandfather's boots and an old flannel shirt. The ironworkers finally allow him to sling chokers on the giant steel beams on the ground as long as he promises not to climb. He attaches the short lengths of cable and watches the beams rise, lifted by the Favco cranes. Weeks later, Walker answers the door to a school official who says he hasn't seen the boy in ages.

Angela stands up quickly when she sees Elijah's silhouette further down the tunnel. She throws the blanket over Treefrog and kisses him on the cheek.

"See you later, Treefy," she says.

"Stay here."

She shakes her head. "Thanks for the picture."

"It ain't a picture."

"Whatever. Hey, man. You got any money?"

"Spare some change and I'll dance at your wedding."

"Very funny."

"No," he says, "no money."

She folds the graph paper carefully and tucks it in her fur

coat, winks at him, and then rubs her tongue along her lips. "I'm thirsty," she says. "Goin' to see the candy man."

"Man," he whispers after her. "Stay here."

He watches her figure move in and out of the light shafts until she has gone, and after a moment he hears shouting from down near Elijah's cubicle—maybe Angela has shown Elijah the map of her face with the disappeared bruise. Treefrog tucks himself further into the tunnel wall, wondering about the ritual of love and fists—how they might square off in front of each other, distant at first, then growing closer, as if in a funnel: Angela and Elijah, slowly spinning downward, the circle between love and fists gradually becoming smaller, until a fist nears love and love nears a fist; spinning ever downward, and then a fist is love and love is a fist, and they are in the mouth of the funnel, both of them, hammering and loving each other to death.

chapter 12

split open with sunlight

*M*oving into the back cave for silence, Treefrog lights a candle. The white wax drips
down to the dirt floor.

He takes his hand-drawn maps from their Ziploc bags—maps
he has made of his nest, his tunnel, of Dancesca, of Lenora—
and spreads them out at his feet. Watching them, he feels them
looking up at him. He folds them all away except for Lenora
and Dancesca, and on a blank sheet of paper he draws a copy of
Dancesca exactly the way he remembers her, constant, unchang-
ing. Her face with all its perfect contours. As if she could suddenly wake and rise from the paper to stand and breathe and
sigh and remember. He touches her neck and then brings his
fingers all the way up to her eyes. With his pencil he draws the
final hollows and then tucks the new map away in the plastic bag.

Treefrog takes another clean sheet and, looking at the old

map of Lenora, he imagines the way his daughter's face might have changed in the four years since he's seen her. He gives her a brand-new landscape, the nose lengthened, the lips just a tiny bit fuller, a little more weight around the cheeks so the contours are pitched higher, a deeper dimple at the chin, eyebrows plucked, a longer ear with the tiniest of lakes on the earlobe, space for an earring. The map takes an hour to draw. When he is finished Treefrog holds the paper up in the air and touches it with his lips and tells her that he is sorry, all the time making absolutely sure that his hands don't stray beneath paper where the rest of her body lies.

Dancesca likes the way Clarence Nathan walks the ledge. She comes up to the rooftop on summer evenings when the sun is sinking through a chemical sky, the smell of hair lotion on her hands, a recent scar on her cheek where a customer cut her after Dancesca nipped her ear—the customer grabbed the scissors and sliced them through the air. The cut was long but shallow. The doctor said it didn't need stitches; he just pinched the cheek together and stapled it with Band-Aids. The cut left a thin creek of pale skin on her face. Dancesca wears a thick swath of makeup on the bumpy ridge.

She sits at the end of the ledge, one foot dangling into nothingness, the other placed on the rooftop.

"Do that little turn," she says, the braids in her hair bobbing.

Clarence Nathan wanders along the ledge, all concentration, his hair curled high and ridiculous. He met her first in her salon in East Harlem. She was slightly chubby, although later she would grow skinny. Brown-eyed. Gorgeous. Skin as black as riverbottom. When she looked at him in the mirror, he darted his eyes away. He felt a flush in his cheeks. When his hair was finished, he left her an enormous tip. There were hoots of derisive laughter on the stoop of his apartment building when he came swinging home, bouncing on the balls of his toes, a comb sticking up from the frizzy outshoot. He met her again two days later in Saint Nicholas Park, and they sat on a bench while she reshaped his hair.

He walks the roof ledge in wide-bottom jeans, so it looks as if his feet aren't even moving, then takes Dancesca's hand and tries to coax her to stand on the ledge. But she can't; she can feel her knees buckling in fear.

"All you have to do," he says, "is forget your body even exists."

"I can't do that."

" 'Course you can. It's all about forgetting where you are. Just pretend you're on the sidewalk."

"You're a looneytune."

"Watch this," he says.

He makes his favorite move—kicking off his shoes and jumping between the buildings. Later, they take a blanket and spread it out on the roof. The pungent odor of tar rises up around them. Sitting at first on opposite ends of the blanket, they make gradual movements until they are so close she can feel his breath on her cheek. He puts a hand on her waist and they lie down together. Opening the buttons on her shirt, he feels the metal wire at the bottom of her bra. He fumbles with both hands at the back clasp, opens it, pulls one strap from her collarbone. She leans back, takes his shoulders in her arms. Lips touching, his fingers tentative, he nudges himself up against her hip. She leans further across and takes the lobe of his ear in her teeth. Earnestly, he slips inside her. When they make love, Clarence Nathan, seventeen years old, feels like he is entering his own history.

In the morning, back alone in the apartment, he is woken by his grandfather.

Walker has prepared a towel and shaving soap and a straight-blade razor on the bathroom counter. Laid them all out neatly in a row, even heated extra water on the stove. Walker's gray beard has grown too long, he says; he hates the way he can grab the ends of his mustache between his teeth. He has begun to find pieces of food dried in there, and he dislikes catching a glance of himself in the mirror.

Clarence Nathan follows his grandfather. Early morning shadows lie on the floor. When the men push open the bathroom door—the lock is broken—Louisa is sitting on the toilet seat, bent over. At first all they notice is a hunched body, but then she raises her head slowly and they see that her skirt is lifted and she is ferreting around her thighs for a new place into which to shove a needle.

"Get out of here!" she shouts.

Walker bangs a half-open fist against the wall. "What the hell y'all think you're doing, woman?"

She looks up and shoves the needle in quickly. Clarence Nathan shivers at the sight of his mother's tired pubic hair peeping out from her white underpants.

"I swear it's my last one, I swear it's the last."

She stands and pulls at the hem of her skirt, rubs a shirt-sleeve over her eyes. She looks straight in the old man's eyes as she passes him.

Walker sighs and bends over the handbasin and washes his hands even though they're already clean. Sitting on a stool in front of the bathroom mirror, he says, over and over again in a mantra, "Lord."

His grandson takes off most of the beard with the scissors first, fingers trembling. Walker can feel the heat of the morning lying down inside his saggy cheeks, then diving further inside him—even his lungs and heart feel as if they are sweating in the disappearing landscape of his body. At the edge of the horizon, he can see a catastrophic gale heading his way: dark winds and a contagion of rain. The forecast speaks to him in his knees and shoulders and elbows. The way of weather. He feels there is not long left. Surrendering will not be difficult. Let it rain, he thinks, as water and lather slip over his cheeks. Let it pour on down. In recent months Walker has given up the trips to the doctor. Pain is his companion. He would be surprised—even lonely—if it left him. It has gathered around him for so many years, donated a necessary order to the hours, to the routine, to the watching of the street. He thinks of Eleanor, the way she once lifted her nightdress by a different bathroom sink.

A small, rude smile appears at the edge of his lips as the beard falls away.

Tiny moments flit back into Walker's mind. He lingers on the rim of these memories. He has begun to say prayers again, long convoluted rhythms, though he's not quite sure if he's talking to himself or not. He recalls the prayer he didn't quite speak in the tunnel, in 1917, that moment of silence before the boys began to throw candles. He can reach out his tongue and almost taste it.

The razor is high around his gray sideburns.

"Say, son."

"Yessir?"

"I heard some rumblings on the roof last night," says Walker. "Sounded like someone jumping around."

Clarence Nathan feels his cheeks flush, but his grandfather laughs long and hard.

"That's a nice girl. Whatshername?"

"Dancesca."

"Yeah, now, she's a catch."

Embarrassed, Clarence Nathan's hands shake and he lets the razor slip and a tiny nick appears near his grandfather's ear. He wipes the remaining soap off the old man's face and dabs at the cut with the towel, watches the cotton soak up the blood.

"Hold on to her," says Walker.

Clarence Nathan tears off a piece of newspaper, licks it, and puts it against the old man's cut, where it dries and stays. The blood darkens the paper.

"Sorry I cut you."

"Can't feel a thing," says Walker. Looking at his reflection in the window, he says, "Nathan Walker, you are still so goddamn handsome!"

Chuckling, he turns to Clarence Nathan.

"Let's you and me go enjoy the day. Just a quick walk."

"Yessir."

"I've got something to tell ya."

"Yessir."

The streets seem split open with sunlight, widened by heat. Walker and his grandson cross the avenues westward and up the hill toward Riverside Drive. Walker feels the silver cross flip at his neck, and the cool side lies against his skin.

As he walks, he looks sideways at Clarence Nathan. The young man wears a dashiki. A red-green-yellow hat perched on his head. Flared green trousers. A harmonica—a present from Walker—dents one pants pocket. Clarence Nathan has gone over the lip into late adolescence: muscles rumbling under the shirt, his Adam's apple big and prominent, a familiar swagger to the shoulders. The boy has been trying to cultivate an Afro, but mostly his hair falls quickly out of it, lying lank and black down to his collarbone.

They sit on a park bench at the rear of Grant's Tomb and look down through the trees along the bluff to the river flowing below. The teenager perches on the high back of the bench. Walker lifts up the flap of his tobacco pouch, puts his nose down close to the bag, drags the scent down, raises his face to the air.

"Feels clean, don't it?"

"Sir?"

"The day, it feels clean."

"Yessir."

"Whatshername again? That girl?"

"Dancesca."

"Hang on to her. Did I tell ya that already?"

"Yessir, you did."

After a long silence, Clarence Nathan says, "They let me go up yesterday to the forty-third floor. With the ironworkers. You can see the rivers for miles: the East, the Hudson. When it's not hazy."

"Y'all making money at this job?"

"Yessir. A little."

"Saving it up?"

"Yeah, yeah, 'course."

"What ya spending the rest on?"

"Bits 'n' pieces."

"That's what I wanted to talk about."

"What?"

"There's two types of freedom, son. The freedom to do what ya want and the freedom to do what ya should." And then Walker says, "Y'all're buying your momma's dope, right?"

"No, sir."

"Don't lie to me, son. Y'all're buying her smack. I know. Ya know how I feel about lying."

"I never bought any drugs, never."

"Then y'all're giving her money."

Clarence Nathan says nothing.

"Don't be giving her any more money."

The teenager lowers his head. "Yessir."

"I mean it. Promise me that."

"Yessir," he says.

"If ya don't stop, there'll be no telling what happens to her. It's the right thing to do."

"I know it is."

"Ya know what she did? She took out all the keys from the piano. I lifted the lid the other day, and they were all gone."

"Sir?"

"I guess she thought they were pure ivory. I guess she thought she could soak 'em. They got ivory tops, but the rest of them is wooden. They ain't worth diddly squat."

Clarence Nathan stares at his fingers.

"Listen up, son," says Walker. He coughs and wipes a dribble of spittle from his chin. "Did I ever tell ya about the first sub-aqua pitch in the history of the world?"

He has heard the story but says, "No, sir, you didn't."

"Y'all promise not to give her any more money?"

"I promise."

"Okay," says Walker, stretching out his hand. "Pretend this is a Bible."

Clarence Nathan lays his palm on his grandfather's hand.

"Now swear on it."

"I swear."

"Swear on your life that y'ain't gonna give her another dime."

"I swear on it."

"Well," says Walker. He coughs again, feels his body snap up in sudden pain, closes his eyes. "It was the first run of the train, and the boys brought down baseballs, see. . . ."

. . .

In the distance Treefrog hears a loud smack of flesh on flesh
and a grunt. The wind blows along the tunnel from the southern
end, slamming into the nooks and crannies, ferreting its way
upward through his nest. Castor sits on his lap, milk frozen to
her whiskers. He breathes on her and wipes off the milk between thumb and forefinger, in case the piece of ice has af-
fected her balance.

Clarence Nathan has often seen his grandfather rifle through
his mother's clothes, taking out small packages and flushing
them down the toilet. Louisa comes home and rummages in the
bowl with a bent coat hanger, finds nothing. She moves through
the apartment, waving the hanger like a weapon. She threatens
to leave, says the heroin comes from a treatment program; she
needs to let it fade gently from her body. There is talk of South
Dakota, a bus journey, a plane trip, but she only portages her
bones between the street and the apartment. Her face is brown
as leather, with an array of wrinkles. The only thing of color
she's seen in years is the rise of red up a plastic tube, a mistake
when she draws the hypodermic needle back too far.

"I need a loan," she says, late one night.

"No more loans, I told you."

"I need it for groceries."

"We got enough groceries."

"Don't you know I have to feed you? You know what it's like
trying to feed a family?"

"You don't even feed yourself. Excepting that other shit."

"Don't say shit." She closes her eyelids. "I need it, Claren.
Please."

"Where you gonna get medicine three in the morning?"

"It's just a loan. Please."

"He'll kill me," he says, nodding at the sleeping form of Walker.

"He doesn't have to know."

She takes his face in her hands and rubs her shaking fingers tenderly along his cheeks.

"No, Momma. I'm sorry."

"It's the last time," she says. "I swear on the Bible."

"Momma, don't do this to me."

"I'll get a job tomorrow."

The whites of her eyes, large and beseeching. A terrible need in the quake of her fingers. She looks at him as if he could crush her, snap her, dissolve her, create her.

"Please," she says, putting her hands close to the whirling blade of an electric fan, no cover on the fan. "I'm begging you. Please."

She pulls her hands back from the fan at the last minute and then she hangs her head, closes her lips, purses her mouth.

"I suppose you'd rather see me on the street."

"Momma."

"My own son. Putting me out on the street."

"I wouldn't do that."

"Then how am I s'posed to get medicine?"

He sighs, hangs his head.

"Did you know that the imprints of bird feet—"

"Momma."

"—are the perfect thing for making peace symbols?"

"You're high, Momma."

"They are, though, they're perfect."

"You're talking crazy shit, Momma."

"You draw a little circle around them. Think about it. I'll

show you. A perfect circle. Like this." She makes a circle with her finger against his rib cage, scrapes three lines like a bird print within the circle, cocks her head sideways, says, "Don't put me out on the streets. Please. I know too much to be on the streets. You know how I feel about losing your father."

Clarence Nathan reaches under the mattress where he keeps his money and palms her a neatly folded twenty-dollar bill. She smiles, shoving the bill into the opening at the breast of her blouse.

"I won't never forget it," she says.

She leaves after kissing him fluently on the forehead. He slams his fist into the palm of his hand.

Clarence Nathan sleeps on the fire escape; he has been told that his father used to do this. He is not bothered by the noise from below: police sirens, record players sounding out through open windows, Jimi Hendrix, James Brown. His body is squeezed up in the small space, his forearms wrapped around his knees. Sometimes the night is punctuated by gunshots. Or the blare of a musical car horn. Or couples shouting as they lean out of windows. A landscape of loving and hating. A palpable viciousness in the air. And yet a tenderness too. Something about this part of the world seems so alive that its own heart could burst from the accumulated grief. As if it all might suddenly stumble under the gravity of living. As if the city itself has given birth to the intricacies of the human heart. Veins and arteries—like his grandfather's tunnels—tumbling with blood. And millions of men and women sloshing that blood along the streets.

Clarence Nathan has often wondered what it might be like to have acute hearing, to listen to that blood slapping against the skinbanks of bodies, that symphony of misery and love.

Down below, he can see his mother passing under the flitting light of street lamps, and she looks so thin, with her arms wrapped around herself, shivering, that her slacking flesh seems to make her retreat into the girl she must once have been.

A few weeks later he is slinging chokers on the beams, on ground level, when word comes that there's a phone call for him near one of the ironworkers' shanties. He walks across the site, tapping out a rhythm against his thigh.

"It's your momma," Walker says. "Come on back."

The door to the apartment opens before he knocks. Clarence Nathan's eyes dart around the room. The gutted piano sits with its lid open. The couch is propped up against the window. A few wicker chairs are forlorn in the middle of the room, their top netting unraveling. Walker rises and grabs his grandson by the lapel and punches him, a slow punch, no power. But the young man falls backward onto the floor.

"Ya didn't keep your promise, son."

Clarence Nathan puts a finger to his mouth.

"Take a seat," Walker says.

"Where's Momma?"

Walker shakes his head.

"Where is she?"

"I knew it was gonna happen," says Walker.

"What?" The young man pulls his knees to his chest and hugs his feet. "Where is she?"

"Get up off the floor."

The young man rises, looks around the room, begins to cry, says, "I gave her all that money."

"It don't matter no more. When it's over, it's over, ya gotta accept that. It's over."

"It's over," says Clarence Nathan, not thinking about the words.

"Come on, give me that hand of yours."

Clarence Nathan stretches out one hand and Walker lays his own shaking hand upon it. "Let's say us a prayer."

After a few minutes' silence, Walker says, "I'm sorry I hit ya, son."

The old man adjusts himself on the couch and takes a little tobacco from the pouch around his neck, stares at it, counts the grains. "Aw, shit," he says eventually. He wipes at his eye, tries to drink from a teacup he knows has been long empty. "I was hoping she'd give it up."

Clarence Nathan looks out the window. "It's my fault. I gave her the money."

"Don't be feeling sorry for yourself, son. She done it to herself. That's the worst thing a man can do. Feel sorry like that."

Walker struggles up, dries his eyes, crosses the room.

"We gotta go down the funeral parlor. Make arrangements to get her back to South Dakota. She needs to be near that lakeside she talked 'bout."

Clarence Nathan closes the buttons on his grandfather's overcoat, helps him wrap a scarf around his neck, bends down to tie the old man's shoes. They triple-lock the door and walk together down the stairs. Clarence Nathan steadies Walker as the old man holds on to the banisters. They emerge into sunlight. Clarence Nathan, still crying, removes his baseball hat and puts it on Walker's head so the brim shades the old man's eyes.

In Saint Nicholas Park on a mucky day, he shows Dancesca the trick of making a symbol from the foot of a bird. "See," he says. "See. Draw a circle here. Just like this."

. . .

Treefrog wakes in the rear cave when a rat scuttles across his ankles. He draws his knees to his chest and whistles for Castor, but she is not around. He wonders if it is night or day, if he has been dead or if he has just been asleep, or if he has been both, and if he may be both forever, dead and sleeping.

He lights another candle and tucks his maps back into their plastic bags. Rocking back and forth in the dark dampness, he waits for the sound of a train to tell him whether it's morning or night. No trains between midnight and seven; after that, the Amtraks come every forty minutes. He singes the bottom of his beard with the lit candle, feels the heat at his chin, and waits almost an hour, curled into himself, his stomach rumbling. Nothing, so it must be night. He drops hot wax on the back of each thumb, where it hardens quickly. Then he presses his fingers into his left side to balance the pain in his liver. He still has some money left from Faraday's funeral and he wonders, perhaps, if he should go and buy gin.

He moves out of the cave into his front room and feels drawn by the tunnel, swings down.

No light whatsoever. The purest and pitchest of black. Treefrog passes by Dean's pile of trash and smells the human filth, steps away so he doesn't get shit on his shoes.

Treefrog knocks against the baby stroller, full now with garbage. He stops and stares into the carriage, reaches out, and rocks it a little from side to side: it was the summer of 1976. Lenora was just born. She was so small. Her hair was fine and thin and dark. Her skin was smooth and mahogany. Clarence Nathan felt like his world had shifted equators, given him meaning, history. He spent hours just holding her. She would lie across his stomach and kick her tiny feet in the blankets.

Dancesca lay with them. There was a new quality given to time—sometimes hours would slip away in simple staring at the child. They felt whole, full, brave, assured. Lenora's helplessness was their depth. They moved together in a trinity, he, Dancesca, Lenora. Every Sunday he paid for a taxicab so that Walker could come and visit. They sat and watched baseball games together. The child slept on a cot close by. It was a time of sweet slowness, even when Lenora fussed and cried. One Sunday, Walker lifted Lenora out of her cot. He kissed the child's forehead. He took her into the bathroom, where he had already filled the sink with warm water. Clarence Nathan watched. The old man was going to baptize the child—a mixture of his own religion and the history of Eleanor's. Just before he lowered the child gently down into the sink, Walker whispered something in her ear. For a moment all was silent, and he dipped the baby in the water. The child cried a little, then stopped. Walker came out from the bathroom with a warm blanket wrapped around her. Later, he said, "I'm gonna bring Lenora for a walk." Dancesca and Clarence Nathan watched from the window as the old man stepped into the street, pushing the baby carriage. By the side of a fire hydrant, Lenora's pacifier dropped out. Walker bent down and, with difficulty, picked it up off the ground. The rubber end was dirty. He looked around for a moment, seemed confused. Then he stuck the pacifier in his own mouth to clean it. He bent over, gently inserting the nipple in the child's mouth, and whispered something into Lenora's ear. From his distance, Clarence Nathan knew exactly what his grandfather was saying to the child.

Treefrog spins away from the baby carriage, moves on, balancing on a rail, left foot right foot left foot right foot. A tremendous urge within him now to speak to someone, anyone, to say anything, to simply let words come from his throat, long and slow and honest. He pauses for a moment by Papa Love's door and then decides against waking the old artist; he wouldn't answer the door anyway.

A mumble sounds from Elijah's cubicle and a small spill of light comes from under the door. Elijah must have reconnected the juice. Treefrog puts his ear to the cubicle and hears Angela crying. There is a sharp thud. The sound strikes Treefrog low in the stomach and rests there, gnawing at him. He takes the spud wrench out from his pocket. His throat is dry, his feet unsteady. He wants to open the door and burst in, but he holds himself back, paralyzed by inaction. The thumping and crying continue, and he hears Angela saying, in long high pathetic gulps, "Why you hurt the ones ya love, why you hurt the ones ya love?"

Treefrog remains at the door and knocks the spud wrench rhythmically into each palm. Then he hears Elijah move.

Slithering away from the cubicle, Treefrog stands beneath the grate at the opposite side of the tunnel. He waits for Elijah to emerge, but nothing happens. And he hears the thuds again, the whimper, the intake of Angela's breath. Treefrog lets himself slide down along the wall until he is sitting on the tunnel gravel. Slowly, he removes his gloves and takes out his penknife. He presses the blade down against the palm of his hand. All this nothingness, he thinks. This cowardice. This solitary life as an ear—listening, always listening, only listening.

With the knife, he makes a nick in his right palm, then his left, is amazed to flick his lighter and see two thin streams of blood running parallel down his raised wrists. He shoves his overcoat sleeves high on his arms, and a small globule of red collects in the crook of each elbow.

Under the grate, looking upward, watching the irrelevant stars, Treefrog knows that the light hitting his eyes left years ago; there is nothing up there but the movement of the past, things long imploded and forever gone: it was years later, a Friday, and he finished his shift at the skyscraper, descended in the elevator, showered and tucked his hair into a short ponytail, and they were waiting outside in a brand-new rental car, a Ford. Walker had insisted on an American-made car. Dancesca got in the backseat with five-year-old Lenora. Clarence Nathan drove. It took them four days to reach South Dakota. Clarence Nathan had sent on hundreds of dollars for a gravestone, a twenty-dollar bill each week, but there was nothing in the graveyard except a plain wooden cross marked TURIVER. Louisa's family had moved. Weeds were in bloom in the old shack where she had once lived. They went down to the lakeside together, all four of them. The lake was immense, the only movement that of a speedboat out in the middle of the water. They had brought food for a picnic, and they sat in silence over soggy cucumber sandwiches. The boat threw waves and a skier tumbled. For the first time all day they laughed, watching the skier vaulting through the air. Walker's body was just about crippled with rheumatism by then, but he took young Lenora down by the lakeside and stretched one arm out and bent a knee and toed his foot out in the air and every movement was imitated by the child, and there wasn't a stir in the sky or mud prints in the ground. They stayed like that, dancing. Clarence Nathan touched his wife's arm, the South Dakota sun pouring down generously around them.

Treefrog hears a sudden startling thud and he opens his eyes, gets to his feet, feels for the spud wrench. The top hinge of the cubicle door cracks and the wood splinters.

Electric light slips out from the smashed door.

He wonders for a moment where exactly he is—in a tunnel or a car or by a lake—and then Angela stumbles from the cubicle, pushing at the broken door, her body heaving, her breath rapid.

Elijah follows her.

"No!" she shouts.

The bare lamp in the cubicle swings.

Elijah punches the back of her head and she stumbles again, turns, spins in the light, falls.

Angela crawls to her feet, blood from her mouth and blood from her eye and blood down her cheek. Even in the patch of pendular light, Treefrog can see that her body is a sad broken mess. She limps in the gravel near the edge of the tracks, her fur coat half on, her handbag swinging in the air to keep Elijah at bay. "No!" And then Treefrog comes out from the far darkness with the spud wrench tight in his fist.

Elijah—standing back from the range of Angela's handbag— looks across the tracks, takes down the hood of his sweatshirt, says, "Look who's here." He beckons Treefrog with a curled finger. "Come on, man, come on, motherfucker."

Angela whimpers by the tracks, the bag clutched to her chest. Treefrog is aware of every step he takes, as if he is floating through the dark.

The cubicle door swings back and forth and light leaks into the tunnel, licking into the dark corners, touching Treefrog's body, sliding off once more, until the door stops swinging and he stands in a definite circle of light.

No need for balance, the pump of certainty through him. He moves across the tracks and stops.

Elijah grins.

Treefrog grins back.

Elijah puts one foot out in front of the other, holds his fists up.

Treefrog steps closer.

Elijah makes a quick spin.

Treefrog steps back from the arc of Elijah's kick, moves forward, ducks beneath the second kick.

Elijah's leg slices above him as if in slow motion.

Treefrog's body seems set on springs, and he rises from his crouch and the spud wrench swings upward and—with perfect accuracy—catches Elijah in the crotch. Elijah falls back against the cubicle, holding his balls. He cries out in agony and takes four huge gulps of breath.

Putting one hand on the ground, Elijah slowly uncoils, reaching for a knife in his back pocket.

Treefrog steps closer.

Elijah's eyes grow wide. He prods the knife out, jabs with it.

Treefrog keeps coming.

The whites of Elijah's eyes look huge.

The knife slices the air.

Treefrog steps aside.

Elijah's body follows the curve of the knife.

Stepping into the created space, Treefrog grins. The swing of the spud wrench into Elijah's elbow is swift and graceful, and the crack of bone echoes the splinter of the door, and the knife clatters to the ground.

When the spud wrench swings a second time, it catches Elijah on the shoulder and he lets out an animal howl, his face creased in terror. He totters, puts one hand to his elbow, the other to his testicles, and then the spud wrench swings again.

This time it catches Elijah's knee, and in one smooth movement Treefrog kicks the knife away.

As Elijah falls, Treefrog plants his boot firmly into Elijah's teeth and a monumental joy whips through him as Elijah's head slams back against the broken door. Treefrog's boot connects with Elijah's crotch and the man accordions in massive pain and emits a groan that Treefrog thinks might reverberate off the walls and last forever in the tunnel.

He picks Elijah's knife up, tucks it in his pocket, leans down, and calmly says, "Good morning, asshole."

Elijah spits up some blood and turns his face away, coughing and moaning. Angela, watching from the tracks, pulls her hand from her ruined mouth and cheers. All the time, it feels to Treefrog that this is the first thing he has ever done in his life.

chapter 13

where the steel hits the sky

*H*e slings her handbag up into the nest and climbs to the first catwalk easily. Removing his gloves for a better grip, he leans down to grab her by the wrist.

She places her leg against the column, but the soles of her high heels are slippery and he must use all the strength of his forearms to haul her up. Her face is already bloated and bruised; there is blood from her mouth where a tooth has cracked; her eye is lacerated and bleeding. With one leg against the concrete column, she sobs. "Treefy." Her arms flail and she breathes nervously. "I can't do it. I can't do it, Treefy."

She seems to want to fall—it is only a few feet to the tunnel floor—but she stretches and catches hold of the crossbeam and his arms curl under her armpits. He leans dangerously over the beam and drags her up through the darkness until she is lying on the lowest beam, whimpering. He remembers lifting his daughter off the swing, and his stomach feels huge and hollow.

"Bring your legs across," he says.

"Why don't you—"

"Rest easy, Angela."

"—have a goddamn ladder?"

He steps across her in one smooth movement and takes her hand in his. "I wanna get down," she says.

"Stand up," says Treefrog. "I got you, you won't fall, I promise; you gotta trust me."

"I don't trust nobody."

"Just try."

"Nobody, I said."

She remains with one leg on either side of the icy beam and her hands clasped at its edge. Her body begins quivering, so he leans down and puts his arms around her to warm her. He looks down at her high heels and says, "Wait a minute."

And he is gone, twelve steps across, up to the next beam, into his nest and down again, holding some sneakers and three pair of socks. Treefrog hunkers down, removing Angela's shoes.

"Here," he says.

He flings her high heels all the way across the tracks toward the mural, and they land and roll in the patch of snow beneath the grill. "Stay still," he says, and he pulls two sets of socks over her feet. He ties the sneakers—they are still way too big—and then tells her, "Now."

Shoving the third set of socks into his pocket, he steps over her crouched form, stands behind her, lifts her up, and holds her waist.

"Treefy!"

"I got you."

"It's icy."

This he recalls as he walks behind her: he arrives after dawn, a man in motion toward the sky. He climbs the steps from the subway station, walks down a street cantankerous with car horns. He is pinned in by businessmen and women on the way to Wall Street, but soon he joins other men, construction workers, who look as if they might have stepped out of advertisments for very strong cigarettes. Their eyes are bleary from nights of love and drink and television and cocaine. The back pockets of their jeans have taken on the logic of what they carry—the imprint of a pack of cigarettes, a small circle where tobacco tins jut, the bump of a plastic baggie of cocaine, the mark of a wallet. In the wallets they carry photos of their mothers and their wives and their girlfriends and their daughters and sometimes even their fathers and their sons. If they get hurt, it will be close to those they care about; it's better to die close to family than to commerce. Still, death is seldom mentioned—even at funerals they say nothing about the way the dead man fell forty feet, or how the elevator shaft collapsed, or the attempted suicide that was caught by the net, or the single bolt that fell from up high and created a corridor of blood in a bricklayer's head. Instead, they talk of women and girls and waitresses and the gentle curve of buttocks and flamboyant asses and the appearance of summer nipples and the way a shoulder is bared to sunlight.

They curse loudly as they move through the streets. They never give way. The businessmen seem small and useless and feminine around them.

Sometimes one of the workers puts a finger on one nostril and blows a stream of snot to the ground, and a businessman is disgusted and curls his upper lip, but the workers move on, indifferent, through the morning rush hour.

Clarence Nathan's new tan construction boots have already been worn so much that rings of hair have been rubbed away where the leather uppers touch his legs. A talisman of sorts. A charm. His blue T-shirt clings tight to his torso. In the wallet in his back pocket he carries his grandfather, his dead mother, his wife, and his three-year-old daughter. His hair has fallen out of the Afro that Dancesca gave him, become long and straight once more. Up above, if he raises his head, a skeleton of his own creation rises toward a cloudless Manhattan sky. Some of his fellow workers will remain at the foot of the building, slinging chokers; others will hang clips to ropes and lean out dangerously over the middle section of steel; others will reside all day in its corridors, fixing elevator shafts, twisting electric wires, grouting, hammering, painting, sheet-rocking. But Clarence Nathan will go higher than any other walking man in Manhattan.

After coffee in the shanty, he joins the ironworkers at the elevator and they rise, aristocratic, in the air. Fourteen men, two teams of seven. The cage rocks in the wind. There are no glass panes, just bars across their knees, hips, chests. Beneath him, Manhattan becomes a blur of moving yellow taxis and dark silhouettes. There is something in this rising akin to desire, the gentle rock from side to side, the cooling breeze, the knowledge that he is the one who will pierce the virginity of space where the steel hits the sky.

All Clarence Nathan's colleagues are sinewy. A couple of them are Mohawks, their blood distributed in such a way that it is balanced in all parts of their bodies: it comes from their history, it is a gift, they have pure equilibrium, the idea of falling is anathema to them. Others are from the West Indies and

Grenada, and there is one Englishman, Cricket, who serves his vowels as if holding them out on a set of tongs. He is thin and blond and pockmarked and wears a lightning-bolt earring. Cricket was given his nickname for trying to teach the other workers his native game while standing at the top of a crossbeam. After shining an imaginary ball at his crotch, he put his head down, ran along the narrow beam to display the technique of bowling, making his arm spin in a giant circle. His watchers sat and stared as Cricket almost fell—there was thirty feet of space beneath him to metal decking—but he caught himself by the strength of his arms, dangled, grinned, pulled himself up, and said, "Leg before wicket, gentlemen!"

The elevator clangs and stops. Clarence Nathan finishes his coffee, tosses the paper cup, and walks across the metal decking toward two ladders that jut up in the air. For a joke the men call this area the POST, the Place of Shriveled Testicles. No ordinary man will go further.

The nimblest—Clarence Nathan and Cricket—take the ladder two rungs at a time. Their leather belts are filled with tools, and their long spud wrenches knock against their thighs. They climb three ladders to the very top of the building, where columns of steel reach up into the air. The foreman, Lafayette, in thick-rimmed spectacles, pokes his head up from the top of the ladder and says, "Another day, another dollar."

Careful with how he steps, Lafayette walks across the loose decking. Cricket goes with him, saying, "Another day, another dolor."

Clarence Nathan remembers his mental maps of yesterday: where certain pieces of equipment were left, where the holes in the decking might be, where on the roof he might accidentally kick over a bucket of bolts, where a can of beer might have been discarded at the end of the last shift. Radios crackle and voices babble over the airwaves. The men watch the huge yellow Favco cranes swing into action, bringing up beams and columns of steel. The metal is inched through the air. When the steel is laid on the decking, Lafayette decides in what order the men will build. The ironworkers wait and chat.

The quietest among them is Clarence Nathan. He says hardly a word, but sometimes, when the foreman is not around, he and Cricket challenge each other to walk blind across the beams. They move as if on solid ground. If they fall they will not go far, but thirty feet are as deadly as one hundred. Eyes closed, they never miss a beat.

On the decking, Clarence Nathan turns his hardhat backward, tucks his hair underneath. The signalman speaks in a language of coded radio signals to the engineer in the crane. A huge steel column is hoisted; the men jostle the column into position, and then it gets bolted in at the bottom. The column jags up against the sky. The crane swings a jib line with a spherical ball on the end of it—the men call it the headache ball. Lafayette whistles for a man, and Clarence Nathan gives him a thumbs-up. The line comes toward him.

He reaches out to grab the cable, steadies it, and, with superb insouciance, steps onto the small steel ball.

Suddenly the jib line moves and he is swinging in the air, in nothingness. He adores this feeling: alone, on steel, above the city, his colleagues below him, nothing on his mind but this swing through the air. He holds on with just one hand. The engineer in the crane is careful and brings him slowly up toward the top of the column. The headache ball swings slightly, then stops. Clarence Nathan shifts his weight and moves lightly out onto the thick steel flanges of the column—for one single second he is absolutely free of everything; it is the purest moment, just him and the air. He wraps his legs around the column. On the opposite column, Cricket is waiting. Then the Favco swings a giant steel beam toward them and it inches through the sky, carefully, methodically, and both men reach out and grab it and bring it toward them. "All right?" shouts Cricket. "Okay!" They wrestle the beam into position with brute strength, sometimes using large rubber hammers or their spud wrenches to knock it into place. The sweat rolls quickly down their torsos. They insert bolts and turn them loosely; the bolter-uppers will crimp them tight later on. And then the men unhook the chokers—the beam now sits between the two columns, and the skeleton of the building is growing. Clarence Nathan and Cricket walk along the beam and meet each other in the center. They step off into space and onto the headache ball, arms around each other, and descend to the decking, where the others wait. Sometimes, for a joke, Clarence Nathan takes out his harmonica at the top of the column and blows into it, using just one hand. The wind carries most of the tune away, but occasionally the notes filter down to the ironworkers below. The notes sound billowy and strained, and for this the men sometimes call him Treefrog, a name he doesn't much care for.

"All right!" Treefrog says, when he and Angela reach the end of the first beam.

Angela is breathing hard. Even in her fur coat he can see her chest rising and falling. "No way in hell you gonna get me up there!"

"It's simple."

"Get me down. You just wanna knock. You just like all the rest. I don't feel good, Treefy. Oh. Treefy."

"It just looks higher than it is, that's all."

"I want my shoes."

"Just imagine you're on the ground."

"Well, I ain't."

"If you think you're on the ground it's easy-peasy."

"I ain't a child," she says, as she wipes a stream of blood onto her fur coat.

"I never said you were."

"I'm staying here. Get me my shoes."

"They're down there, goddammit."

"I ain't leaving till I get my shoes."

"All right, then, stay here."

"Don't leave me, Treefy. Please."

"Just watch me."

He places his hand in the hold that he has chipped from the column and, within seconds, he is up on the second catwalk. Five feet below him, Angela still has her arms around the concrete column as if she's bandaged there. Treefrog wraps one leg around the beam and leans down and takes her hand and— close to violence—he swings Angela through the air and grabs her at the waist and tugs her up. He expected her to shout and scream and kick, but all she says is, "Thanks, Treefy."

Angela sits shivering on the beam. She has stopped crying and she blinks her good eye several times, wipes more blood from the other.

"I don't feel good."

"All you gotta do is walk across here. Relax. See? Up there. Don't look down. Don't look down, I said!"

"He hurt me."

"I know."

"Did you kill him?"

"No."

"I want you to kill him," says Angela. "Kill the asshole. Stuff his throat with a blue washcloth."

"Okay."

"Don't kill him, Treefy."

"All right already. Whatever."

"You're gonna let me fall."

"Trust me. I worked on the 'scrapers once," he says.

She stares at him. "I'm scared."

"It's okay. I promise nothing will happen to you."

"You're weird."

"You ain't exactly normal yourself."

"I'm normal! Don't call me disnormal."

"All right all right all right. You're the normalest woman I ever saw. Come on."

"You're cute, Treefy."

He stands behind her and guides her across the narrow beam. Her steps are slow and precise, and he keeps his arms wrapped around her: only weather stops him—the steel becomes slippy with fog and ice and rain, and lightning is the most dangerous of all. The men have a makeshift rod at the top of the building, but at the first sign of heavy storms they are given the day off. When weather is good, they go at the rate of a floor a week. The sun bounces off the metal, but at least there is a wind to cool the ironworkers down. Although it's against the rules, Clarence Nathan often works without a shirt. He has a body still free of stab wounds and scars. The foreman, Lafayette, talks of frozen waterfalls in Canada, of climbing on thick ice with special shoes and ropes and carabiners and ice picks, of staying in sweat lodges and incanting chants to the sky. Clarence Nathan likes the thought of it—suspending himself on a river— and he imagines himself halfway up the face of a fall, water trickling behind the ice.

On Fridays, at the end of the shift, the men drink beer together on the top beams, sit in a row, let their legs dangle over, and drop the beer cans into the nets way beneath. They like to achieve this appearance of nonchalance; nonchalance is their greatest gift. They will not be seen without it. Even if they become aware of moist cloud settling around them, they will stay and sit and talk. Beer cans pop. Hardhats are clipped onto carabiners at their waists. Many of the hats have stickers: Harley Davidson insignias, badges from the New York Mets, an emblem from Yellowstone National Park, a circular sticker from the Hard Rock Cafe, and, quite often, Canadian flags with marijuana leaves in the center. The men chat about their upcoming weekend—who they will see, how much they will spend, how many times they will get laid. Their guffaws get carried off by the wind. Only the faintest of sounds rise up from the city; an odd siren, a truck horn. They wait until Lafayette is gone and then take out bags of coke and thin red straws and sometimes a little dope. Matches flare the end of joints. Razors chop through large white grains. One man cups his arms around a fat line of coke so none of it blows away.

High on marijuana—he doesn't snort coke—Clarence Nathan talks to the helicopters that come across from the East and Hudson rivers.

After work, he takes the train to 96th Street and walks the rest of the way home with the sun arcing downward in the west. His spud wrench hangs from his construction belt and taps in rhythm against his thigh. He still feels as if he's up on the beams, floating, and he makes absolutely sure his feet don't touch the cracks in the pavement. It's a short walk home to where he lives with his family in a small apartment on West End Avenue and 101st, but he goes down to Riverside Park first, smoking as he walks. Sometimes—before he reaches the park—he stops at a parking meter and works on his old trick, balancing on top of the meter on only one foot.

He keeps his head down and counts his steps as he goes. A curious thing, he likes to land on an even number, although it's not absolutely necessary. It is just a game of his. In the park, he often gets bothered by male hookers offering him a blow job. The park is one of their favorite haunts. "Not today," he says, and sometimes he is whistled at; they like it when he wears sleeveless T-shirts, his arms are fretted with muscle. At the door of his apartment there is the traditional joke—"Honey, I'm home!"—and Dancesca appears as if she's just climbed out of the television set, makeup precise, hair in beads, dark skin, white teeth, their young daughter holding on to her leg. In the hallway, Clarence Nathan takes off his shirt and Dancesca rubs her fingers over his chest and pinches him playfully. Lenora stands outside the shower room as he cleans off the day's work. When he emerges, he lifts her and spins her in the air above his head until she says, "Daddy, I'm dizzy." After dinner, he puts the child to bed. On her bedroom wall Lenora has tacked up a huge sheet of see-through blue plastic, which she calls her aquarium. Beneath the plastic there are cut-out photos of fish, shells, plants, people. A Polaroid of her parents, at their wedding, is positioned near the top of the aquarium where her favorite people go. Photographed outside a registry office in 1976, Clarence Nathan wears a wide brown tie and flared trousers. His hair is short. Dancesca is already in a maternity smock. They look embarrassed, bewildered. She folds her hands over the stomach bulge. He has his fingers knotted together nervously. Their shoulders barely touch. But vaguely triumphant in the background is Walker, who, without a hat, is pointing comically at his own bald crown.

There is also a black-and-white of Walker posing with other sandhogs in the mouth of a tunnel. All the other men seem stern under their large mustaches, but Walker, covered in muck, looks happy. A shovel leans against his hip, his hands are folded beneath his arms, and his muscles bulge.

Before she goes to sleep, Lenora shifts the photos around in the aquarium. Clarence Nathan sits by her bedside. When she finally nods off, he blows her a kiss from the doorway. Sometimes, for fun, he closes his eyes and walks blind through the rooms. The apartment is small and old, yet clean, with a stereo, a flowered couch, an old-fashioned television set, a kitchen full of red and white machinery. The bathtub had once been situated in the living room, but it is discarded now, filled with junk now and covered with a tarp. Along the walls there are framed sketches of New York storefronts, presents from Walker.

Popping open a beer, Clarence Nathan sits on the couch beside Dancesca and they watch television. In the late evening they make love, and Dancesca moves under him like a river. Afterward they settle into television shows once more and he likes this dullness, this rhythm. He wants his grandfather to come live with them, but Walker says he will die in Harlem; he will die in the room where he spends his days chatting with the only ghosts in the world worth their salt; he will die with a whisper for each of them: Sean Power, Rhubarb Vannucci, Con O'Leary, Maura, Clarence, Louisa Turiver, and, most of all, Eleanor, who gives him a rude and lovely smile as she adjusts her hair and shunts herself up onto the bathroom sink.

Treefrog's foot moves forward to steady Angela as he guides her on the beam.

"Just a couple more steps," he says to her. "A couple more and you're there."

Her arms flail wide, and he pins them to her body. He wraps his own arms around her and feels the warmth of her fur coat. Her feet inch along the beam, and just before they reach the low wall of his elevated nest she lunges forward and grabs it with both hands.

"I made it," says Angela, as she climbs across the low wall and smiles. "That's easy."

He swings in front of her, takes two steps, lights a candle on the bedside table.

"Wow," she says.

"It used to be a storage room. They kept their tunnel stuff up here. I think there musta been a ladder or a stairs up to it one time, but there ain't anymore. Hardly anybody ever been up here."

"What the hubcaps for?"

"Plates."

"Man," she says. "A traffic light!"

"Faraday found that."

"You got the electric?"

"I told you, no."

"Wow. How big is this place?"

"Goes all the way back to a cave there at the back."

"Treefrog the Caveman."

"Gonna draw a petroglyph."

"What's that?"

"Nothing. Listen, we gotta fix those cuts, Angela. Your eye's bleeding."

"It don't hurt me none," she says, touching her eye.

"It's just 'cause you got your adrenaline going," he says. "We should fix it before it begins to hurt."

She picks her handbag off the floor. "Do I look okay, Treefy?"

"Yeah."

"You're lying."

She rummages in her handbag and then she begins sobbing. "Elijah's gonna kill us."

"We'll hide in the back," he says, and he grabs a candle and they duck into the rear cave. He puts the candle on the makeshift shelf, and the light makes strange flickers against the blasted-out rock. She puts her hand to her nose.

"Man, you shit in this place," she says.

"No, I don't."

"Smells like shit. I don't like it here. I want my shoes. I want my mirror."

"See, all my maps," he says, pointing to a row of Ziploc bags.

"I don't care about maps. Elijah's gonna kill us."

She moves out from the cave into his front room once more. There is still a tiny bit of light from the grills across the tunnel. "I ain't staying here, no way. He'll kill us."

"Sit on the bed," he says.

"No way, Treefy."

"I won't touch you."

She fingers her loose front tooth. "He'll definitely kill us."

"You should see a doctor."

She thumbs the tooth back and forth in her gums and whimpers, "No."

"Why not?"

"I don't like doctors. Excepting Doctor Treefrog."

He smiles and motions to the yellow canister at the foot of the bed. "I'll boil some water, and then I'll clean your face."

"I'm thirsty."

"I don't have any drugs."

She moves tentatively across the dirt floor to the carpet, and then she sits on the bed. Treefrog lights the remnants of the firewood and newspapers. Angela warms her hands over the fire and then fidgets with an empty cassette box that she finds on the ground. She uses the edge of the inlay card to clean the gaps in her lower teeth. She picks the plaque from the card with her fingers and flicks it away into the fire.

He moves backward, not wanting to frighten her, and sits on the floor at the foot of the bed while the water boils.

"It hurts now," says Angela, and she climbs into his sleeping bag.

"Gonna fix you up when the water boils."

"It really really hurts."

"I know." Then, after a long silence he says, "Wonder where Castor is? I haven't seen her for a few hours."

"How she get up here?" Angela asks.

"I have to lift her."

She tucks herself further into the sleeping bag. "You gonna look after me, Treefy?"

And he remembers how, when Lenora was five, she got a high fever and he stayed home from the skyscrapers for a week while Dancesca worked. He bought groceries at the local supermarket. He heated cans of chicken soup on the stove. Lenora lay in the bed next to the blue plastic sheet. Father and daughter, they went through every photo in the house. She picked out the ones she liked. He got extra copies made, so Lenora could arrange them in the aquarium. When her fever climbed higher, he smoothed a damp cloth across Lenora's brow and spooned the soup delicately, blowing on it first to make sure it wouldn't burn her tongue.

"Treefy."

"Huh?"

"You listening to me?"

"Huh? Yeah."

"You gonna protect me?"

He dabs his bandanna into the boiling water, turns, and says, "Of course I'll protect you, Angela."

On Sundays, Walker takes a gypsy cab down from 131st Street and gets the driver to blow the horn beneath Clarence Nathan's apartment. It's a five-floor walk-up, no elevator, and Walker's legs and heart rebel against the idea of climbing. Clarence Nathan and Dancesca come down the stairs with their daughter, and Clarence Nathan leans in the taxi window and pays the driver, tips him well.

He helps Walker out of the taxi and has to hold Lenora back from bowling the old man over. Walker has fashioned himself a wooden walking stick, and he leans against it. His remaining hair is herringbone-colored, and wrinkles have etched into other wrinkles.

"How's my lil' pumpkin?" asks Walker, bending down.

"Hi, Paw-Paw."

Walker stretches up. "Hey there, beautiful."

"Hey, Nathan," says Dancesca.

"My-oh-my," he says to her. "You're getting finer lookin' every day."

The four of them descend the hill to the park with infinite slowness. Walker wears a new hat, a Hansen, with a tiny feather sticking out from the band above the brim. Lenora skips ahead of the three adults as they go over the mundanities of the previous week—baseball scores, basketball matches, the vagaries of the weather. The chat is light-humored and sometimes even turns to Walker's ghosts. Dancesca is fond of the stories he tells about Eleanor. Clarence Nathan, who has heard the stories many times, often walks on ahead with his little girl.

They are splendid days, the finest of days.

Even if it's raining they go down to the park and huddle beneath umbrellas. Clarence Nathan uses the flap end of a shirt to wipe the seat of the swings and occasionally Dancesca will bring a towel for her husband to slide down the chute and dry it for Lenora. Everything about the Sunday visits revolves around Lenora. The adults take turns pushing her on the swing. They gather at the end of the slide to welcome her. They lift her onto the fiberglass dinosaurs. Walker gauges her height by how she measures up against his walking stick. Sometimes he removes a bullet from his belly button, but the young girl doesn't like the trick too much; it frightens her.

In springtime all four of them spread a blanket on the ground, sit under the cherry-blossom trees, and eat cucumber sandwiches, Walker's favorite. When the evening sun goes down across the Hudson, they trudge to the edge of the park and Clarence Nathan hails a cab and slips his grandfather twenty dollars, and then the old man is gone.

One Sunday afternoon, when Dancesca and Lenora are visiting elsewhere, Walker takes Clarence Nathan down to the edge of a railway tunnel underneath Riverside Park. There is a gate at the tunnel entrance, but the lock is broken. The two men open the gate, slide inside, and stand on the metal staircase. Walker kicks away a bloodied hypodermic needle, and it drops to the tunnel floor. "Damn things," he says. It is dark at first, but their eyes adjust and they see the grills in the ceiling and the murals painted below. Petals of cherry blossom fall steadily through grills. They see a figure emerging from the shadows, a man with several cans of spray paint. Grandfather

and grandson look at each other, then leave the tunnel, Clarence
Nathan wrapping his arm around Walker's shoulder and help-
ing him up the steep embankment.

"I dug there once," says Walker, pointing back at the tunnel.
"I dug and grouted in that place."

He cleans the cut at the side of her eye meticulously, dabbing
the bandanna in the boiling water, twirling the cloth's edge,
rinsing it out in the pan until, even in the half-light, he can see
that the water has turned red. What was she like as a child when
the water was iron-colored and warm? Did her father take her
down to the swings to play? Did she sit in the backseat of the
car with her arms folded in her lap? Did she ever think there
was somewhere darker than even an Iowa cornfield at night?
And what sort of map could he make of her flesh if he used the
tiniest of little scales and became a cartographer of the corpus-
cles there in the little rim of violence at her eye?

He can feel Angela's breath at his neck as he touches the
wound. Across the tunnel the morning rays shine through—light
enough now for Elijah to come calling. He should have buried
the spud wrench down Elijah's throat; he should have hit him
harder, like his own father did, his unknown father who buried
that cop and that car mechanic. For a moment a vision flits
across Treefrog's mind and he sees a shovel handle get buried
deep into a white man's head. His father winks at him and says,
It's all right, son, I hit a homer.

Treefrog wets the clean end of the bandanna with his tongue.
If he had some gin he could sterilize the cut, but no matter,
it will heal soon. He folds the bandanna into a square and
gently presses the cloth against the side of her cheek. Leaning

across, he kisses the top of her forehead. She says to him, "You stink, man."

"Go to sleep," he says.

Treefrog pulls the zip of the sleeping bag, grabs a couple of blankets, and moves back to his chair. He removes the pot of bloodwater from the fire pit. As the flames jump, he warms his hands, thinks about the harmonica, but Angela's eyes are fluttering and soon she will be off to sleep.

Tightening the blankets around himself, he lets the fire die down and listens in the silence for Castor. Angela turns a little in the sleeping bag, her lips touching against the pillow. He smiles and echoes her: "You stink, man." Sometimes, when he lay in bed next to Dancesca, she would smell the sweat from the construction site even after he showered. She would toss away from him and say, "Traffic violation!" "Huh?" he'd ask. "Parking ticket!" "Huh?" "You smell, Clar." "Oh." And he would rise to bathe again, shave himself close, splash cologne around his cheeks, get back in bed, and snuggle close to her. She had grown thinner since they married. He missed the bigness, the ample bosom, but he didn't mention it to her; he sometimes even carried the idea with pride—while other men's wives fleshed out and away, she came in toward him.

She went with him once to Houston where he was working on a skyscraper with his crew. Lenora was left with Dancesca's family. It was Dancesca's first time on a plane; she loved the thin red straws in the drinks. She collected seven of them—one for each of Lenora's years. The Texas heat was oppressive even in winter, and it weighed down on them. After a day's work they mostly stayed in the hotel room—the good times, the best of times. The air conditioner hummed. Dancesca was fascinated by the tiny bottles of shampoo in the bathroom. The plastic glasses were sealed in Saran wrap on the bedside table and they stayed unopened. Dancesca and Clarence Nathan poured gin straight into each other's mouths. She loved to let ice cubes melt on her belly. They wanted to send a telegram to Walker but could think of nothing to say except, "We're in the Lone Star State."

In a suburban bar one night, he, Dancesca, and Cricket sat drinking cocktails. The music was loud. Alcohol thumped in them. There were some oil riggers sitting at a nearby table. Cricket challenged them to walk the roof of the bar—it was, Cricket said, a question of balance. The bet was for one hundred dollars. Everyone stepped out into the night. The building was a two-story affair with a roof shaped a sharp inverted V. He and Cricket walked with their eyes closed. The nervous oil riggers stumbled behind, amazed. Back inside, he and Cricket collected their winnings, drank shots together, slapped each other's backs. Suddenly a pool cue smashed down on the back of Clarence Nathan's head. He fell to the floor, tried to get up, slipped in his own blood. Dancesca screamed. Cricket was set upon by a group of four. A knife slashed hotly across Clarence Nathan's chest. He was taken to the hospital. His first scar. Dancesca stayed at his bedside and for months afterward— when they got home to New York—she attended to him with a special poultice smeared lovingly across his chest. She would rub the yellow paste over his chest, and then her fingers would meander lower to where they would pause in their ecstasy.

He opens his eyes and looks at Angela as she sleeps.

Tenderly, Treefrog touches the side of her eye where blood still oozes from the cut. He cleans it once more and then retreats back into his own pungent darkness. He blows on the fire to rekindle it. Only a small amount of rice and some cat food in the Gulag. He takes out the rice, apportions it in a cup, washes out the saucepan, and wipes it with the flap of his second shirt, the cleanest one. He stirs the rice with his finger, waits for it to cook, and then wakes Angela with a kiss to her cheek. She eats hungrily and, when finished, says, "What're we gonna do, Treefy?"

Treefrog looks at her and shrugs.

She reaches down into her coat pocket and unfolds the piece of graph paper he has drawn of her face, and she looks at it, touches her cheek, and says, "I bet them mountains is even bigger now."

"I could make a map of you without any bruises," he says.

"Why d'ya make maps, man?" she asks.

"I make maps of everywhere. I even make maps of my nest."

"Why?"

"In case God comes calling."

"What?"

"So He can follow the contours all the way back here."

"You a Jesus jumper or something?"

"No. It's just so He can find me."

She turns in the sleeping bag and sighs. "You're weird." Touching her loose tooth, she bites the top of a long thumbnail off with the other front tooth. She uses the slice of nail to pick out the remaining plaque in her lower teeth. "I used to have the nicest teeth," she says. "Everyone said I had the nicest teeth."

"You still got nice teeth."

"Don't lie."

"I ain't lying."

He watches her through the candlelight as she spits the slice of thumbnail away. "Treefy?" she says. "I'm thirsty. I wanna get some candy."

And all at once Treefrog knows that this will not last, that soon she will be gone, that she will not remain in his nest, that there is nothing he can do about it; she will leave as quickly as she came. Knees to his chest, he pulls the blankets tight, feels the dull thump of his heart along his kneecap. His liver gives out gentle jabs of pain. He asks her for a cigarette and she rumbles in her handbag, comes up empty-handed.

"Shit," she says. "I'm gonna go see Elijah."

"You can't."

"Why not?"

"Blue washcloth," he says.

They remain in silence for almost an hour, and he wonders if perhaps they will remain like this forever. Maybe someone will come down and find their bones, bleached high in his nest. If he had a clock he could put a value on all this silence. One cent for every twenty minutes. Three cents an hour. Seventy-two cents for a day. He could be a millionaire by the end of his life. He rocks the chair from side to side and flicks a long hair out of his eyes.

But suddenly he sits up and claps his hands together, reaches down into his pocket, and takes out his Swiss Army knife.

"Watch this," he says to her.

Treefrog touches his beard, runs his fingers along it. He slips open the scissors, sits on the edge of the bed, and begins. He is surprised at the way the cold chews at his chin when he takes off the first chunk of beard.

Angela says, "Man, you look younger."

He smiles and from the middle of his chin he works his way up to the left sideburn, continues on the opposite side. The hair falls down into his lap, and he looks down at the strands and says, "I remember you." The scissors are dull; he can feel his cheeks tearing and stretching. Even so, he continues to cut the beard tight to his skin. If he had a razor he could shave even closer, get down to the very element of himself, maybe even cut all the way to the bone. As he works, he tells Angela that he sometimes carves his real name in the snow, topside, so he doesn't forget: Clarence Nathan Walker.

His thumb and forefinger work the tiny scissors, and he doesn't even have to switch the red-cased knife from hand to hand. When his beard is gone, he removes his wool hat and touches his hair.

"Aw, man, not your hair, I like your hair."

"Just a minute."

To save the blade he hacks with a different knife, a sharp kitchen knife, and throws the long tangles of hair into the fire, smells it burning. He goes at it again with the scissors, until the top of his scalp feels tight and shorn.

"Come here," says Angela.

"Meet me," he replies.

He goes across to the bed and nestles in beside Angela, pulls the blankets over them both. He keeps his clothes and overcoat on. She flips around to face him and her hair touches his head and he reaches his tongue out and he can taste it, all the subterranean filth, but he doesn't mind, just keeps his tongue at her hair, and she smiles and touches the stubble on his face.

"You're cute, Treefy, you're really cute."

She puts her arms around him, and he nudges up against the closed sleeping bag. Treefrog breathes in deep and makes an X of his arms across his chest and pushes his body in further. She rolls in the sleeping bag and moans. He leans down to untwist the bottom of the bag where her feet have tangled and—when her breathing eases—he moves so that the whole length of his body is against her. The tunnel is lit with the headlights of a train and his nest is flooded with the blaze of oncoming lights and he moves in cadence with the *clack clack clack* of carriages against the rail.

The light from the passing carriages splays out moving shadows, a webbed pulse against the wall of his nest. He coughs quietly as he hauls the scent of her down. Lifting up the flap ends of the blankets, he removes his gloves and holds the zip of the sleeping bag. She turns a little, and a dryness settles in his throat as he inches the zip down, tooth by tooth.

Opening the bag down to the high part of her stomach, he reaches, feels the warmth of Angela's fur coat.

"Treefy," she says.

The coat is cheap; he knows from the imitation plastic around the buttons where his hands roam. With the top three buttons open, he fingers the fourth, and then he relaxes. He opens her three blouses, spreads them out. His hand touches the thermal shirt and he is aware of the soft, beautiful round-ness of her flesh underneath. He hears Angela's hand rising—it swishes against the sleeping bag—and her hand is clasped against his and she guides his hand in under the thermal shirt and there is the shock of his hand on skin and she says, "Your hand's cold, man." He pulls away, warms his hand by rubbing it on his own skin, and works his way under the thermal once more. The fabric of the shirt is tight, not much room to maneuver. Angela guides his hand, and the thermal shirt rides way up her belly. She drags the shirt up over her breasts. His fingers hover close to her nipples and his hand moves as if to cup her, but he keeps it hovering above her breast, then lets it retreat to touch her belly button, and he can hear the slightest wheezing into the dirty pillow as he caresses her.

"Treefy," she whispers again.

"Clarence Nathan," he says.

And then she says, "Ouch" when his hands touch her ribs.

Angela keeps her hand pasted over his, high on her stomach, fingers meandering, and he can feel the pounding of her heart—she is the first woman he has touched like this in years—the zip of adrenaline through him, the lightness of thought, the levity of blood, the lavish erection. His hand makes circles to the side of her breast but he doesn't touch it—he can't touch it—and he leaves his hand to hover above the bumped landscape of her nipple. "Hold on, Treefy," she whispers. She fumbles as she removes her sweatpants and underwear and lies back in the sleeping bag. Her head touches the pillow and she smiles up at him and he moves his body slightly—take it easy, don't crash—and she clasps his hand against her breast, and for a moment Treefrog feels no need even for balance, and she doesn't say a word, not a single word, nothing, she just takes hold of his shoulders and pulls him closer and he squeezes her breast—he has forgotten all—and then he is closer and she has unzipped him and she is warm and he moves within her and she moans in all the vast agonies of a woman on the border of both boredom and some ferocious human passion.

In the evening, Elijah shouts from beneath the catwalk and then slings a bloody plastic bag up into the nest, where it lands with a thump.

Before they leave the nest he chooses a section of floor that he hasn't done in a long time. His hands trembling, he takes a new sheet of paper and draws a horizontal graph on one side and a long straight line below it, using the edge of a cigarette box to guide the pencil.

He walks through the nest, feeling the landscape with his boots. He shows Angela how to mark it. As he walks he calls out to her and she makes dots with the pencil where the floor of his nest rises, each half inch an increment on the graph, and she flicks the lighter and marks the paper carefully. He shuffles backward, knowing exactly what his heels will touch. He has to stoop low to step out of the cave. His feet touch against his collection of hubcaps, and Angela's pencil traces the rim of a half circle. Toward the front of his nest, he steps on the mattress. It seems like a huge drop from the bed down to the floor once more. He feels his way with his hands over the bedside table, touches the length of a Sabbath candle, zooms down again, just misses bumping against the smashed traffic light, and comes to the end of the nest and the dropoff to the tunnel below. He returns along the same journey, making sure it is all correct, lingering over the mattress with his eyes closed.

The candle leaks down to its very last, white wax seeping into the dirt.

He finishes the graph—the cave, the bed, the Sabbath candle, the little hump of dirt where, in his grief, he just buried Castor—and, when he is done, the geography is one of massive valleys and cliffs and mountains and canyons, a difficult journey, he knows, even for God.

He winds some duct tape on his boots where a flap has come loose, swings his way onto the catwalk, and then helps Angela down to the tunnel floor. She comes tentatively, slowly. He carries blankets. "Where we going?" Angela asks. "Somewhere I been thinking about," he replies. "I'm thirsty," she says. And he whispers to her that they're going to a place where she can find the candy man. She asks if he has enough money and he nods, yes. She skips across the tunnel and collects her high heels and shakes the snow out of them, and then she comes back and leans up on the tips of her toes and kisses him and says, "Come on. I hope you ain't lyin'."

He wipes his eyes dry. And then he says that if he sees Elijah he will kill him this time without a doubt, he will crush his skull, he will strangle him, he will mash him into the ground beside Castor's body. But as they move along the tunnel through all the dimensions of darkness they don't hear a soul, and when they reach topside it is cold and clear without any snow. They walk through the park and up the street and, out-side an all-night store where he buys cigarettes, Angela pulls up her collar and touches the bruises on her face and then she stops for a moment, smiles—"Candy," she says—and overdoses her mouth with lipstick in anticipation.

chapter 14

now that we're happy

*H*e was living up there on 131st Street. He'd got himself mostly silence for a life now. But you see I loved him more than anything else in the world, so we'd all visit much as we could. Like I told you, he'd been making furniture. But for some reason he took to deciding, right at the very end of his life, that he'd make a fiddle. And he got some wood and he carved it out and it was shaped like a fiddle—like this, ya know? Some people call it a violin. He had garnet paper, and he wrapped it around a cork and he sat out there all day, varnishing and carving and sanding. Then he got some horsehair, shit knows where, and strung himself a bow. He said that music'd been some sort of gift in his life, there'd been this important piano and all. My grandmother even played a piano down the tunnels, but that's something else altogether. Wrap yourself in that blanket there, sister. Anyways, yeah. So he'd be there making tea in his apartment and waiting to go down to the stoop to work on his fiddle and he had this thing, this tea cosy, to keep the pot warm. It belonged to my grandmother's mother, Maura O'Leary. And one day when he's making tea he just leaves it on his head! It was something his kids did to him once. Even did it for me when I was a kid. Just cause he liked it, it was funny to him. And maybe he liked it there, on his own head, like it was keeping his memories warm or something.

And he'd go on down and sit there on 131st with his half-made fiddle and this goddamn tea cosy on his head. He got laughed at, but he didn't care; he was dying, he allowed hisself some of that there eccentricity, ya know? I bought him a Walkman once—I had money back then—but he didn't take no truck in those sort of things. Damn, he even got a small cosy for my Lenora, but she didn't like to wear it, can't rightly blame her. We was visiting lots and sitting out there with him on the stoop and those were the good days, the best of days. And we was all there—Lenora too—when he played that fiddle for the first time. Man, he played so bad, it sounded terrible, man; it was awful, right? But it was beautiful too. And he sang this song which is a blues song which don't go with no fiddle, and it goes, *Lord, I'm so lowdown I think I'm looking up at down.* We was so happy sitting there on the stoop that we went changed the words, and we were singing, *Lord, I'm so high up I believe I'm looking down at up.* Cars going by. We even heard some gunshots far on down the street, but we didn't pay no mind.

Which is one of the things I always do find myself thinking about. Looking up at down and looking down at up. I never heard nicer than that, no matter which way you believe it.

I know you're cold, sister, but I'm cold too. And, man, it was

the coldest day when I went to his apartment. Dancesca and
Lenora, they're making visits to her family; we all of us got two
families no matter which way we think on it. Like ol' Faraday.
I went on up the stairs and I was smoking then—no, no—
cigarettes; cigarettes, sister—and so I always made sure that I
stubbed it out in the flowerpot just one floor down from his
apartment, 'cause I told him I'd given up the smoking.

I told you. Later.

Anyways. Listen up.

Just me on my own, knocking on the door. Normally he'd be
curled up on the couch or something, in some amount of pain,
but this time he just opened the door for me—it was 1986 and
he was eighty-nine and he was shoving close to timber. But this
time he opened up the door and said, I saw you coming down
the street, son. He was all done up in his overcoat and scarf and
that damn stupid tea cosy. I went on in and took off my coat and
sat myself down and turned on the TV and this baseball game
came on, see, the Yankees and the Red Sox. He asked me who's
winning? And I told him the Yankees just scored, even though
they hadn't. He had this old friend who liked the Dodgers and
the Yankees. So it made my grandaddy happy if the Yankees
won. Yankees just hit a homer, I said. And then he just came on
over to the couch and said, Let's you and me take a walk. I says
to him, It's cold out, but he says, I'm feeling good today, I could
walk a million miles. Let's watch the game, I said, but then he
just reached out and dragged me up from the seat—he had
some power still—and we put on our overcoats and went outside. Here's this old man with a tea cosy on his head and outside
it's colder'n fuck and the only ones about are a couple of guys
selling smack and sprung.

We went on down the deli and bought ourselves a copy of

the *Daily News,* and I never seen him with so much energy. I heard sometimes if you know you're gonna die then you get energy.

Y'ain't gonna die, Angela, come on.

And then, see, he shoved some tobacco in his mouth but I didn't say nothing even though I wanted a cigarette. He always said he was old enough to be allowed a vice, said the one thing an old man regrets in his life is that he behaved hisself so well. So, anyways, we went on to the subway and changed a couple of times and went all the way down to that tunnel that he dug way way back. We went out and we was standing by the East River near a pile of rubbish by the old Customs House, when he says to me, he says, There's a gold ring under that there river. Your own great-grandmomma's, he says, and I says I know, 'cause he told me a million times. And then he says to me—you know what he says?—he says, I'd like to walk through that there tunnel and say hello to my old friend Con, he says, that's what I'd like to do.

And I says, Huh?

I'd like to walk under that there river, he says.

And, course, I says, You're crazy. And he just sighs and says, Come on, we'll go down and just ride that train.

We can't walk the tunnel, I says.

I said ride the train, he says. Ride, son.

So we went on down the steps—I won't never forget it—we put in the tokens, and I helped him on down the steps. He still had his walking stick. At the edge of the platform we waited for the M train—it's the M train, isn't it? Yeah. And when it arrived, brakes squealing, he held me back by the elbow and stared at me in the eyes like this and said, he says, How about it? And I said, You wanna walk under the river? It's Sunday, he said, let's wait for the next one and see how long it takes 'tween trains. Might be much as half an hour. On Sundays they don't run so good. I don't know how long it took, but it was damn near thirty-five minutes and—I swear to whoever be up there, I swear—we looked at each other and laughed, my grandaddy and me. Then the door of that train closed and the platform was left empty save us. And we went nodded at each other. Right, he says, just a few short yards, that's all. And we slapped hands. I was quick then—quicker'n now—and I vaulted on down onto the tracks and reached up to take ahold of him, help him down. We don't have to do it, I says, and he says, I'd like to. It's what I want to do. Just a couple of yards.

Watch out for the third rail, I says. And he's all happy, saying, I know what the third rail is, son.

And then he asks me, Y'all got a lighter? And I asks why. And he says in case the train comes early, we can flick it so's the driver sees us.

I gave him the lighter and asked him how long it'd take us to walk, and he says fifteen minutes give or take. And I says, We best hurry.

We moved on down a few feet beyond the platform and made our way into the dark. Darker'n any tunnel. I ain't ashamed to say we went hand in hand.

Gimme your hand there.

I know you're cold. Here, take my gloves.

Along the middle of the track, down the slope of the tunnel, he let go of my hand and held on to my shoulder, walked behind a pace. It was like we was blindfolded. I don't know why we didn't stop, but we kept on going. And all the time I'm thinking, We shoulda brought a flashlight with us. And then he's pointing out all sorts of things in the tunnel: the strip of red and white

metal on the wall, the curves, some place where a welder went
on fire.

That tunnel—nobody living there, of course. Nobody could
live there. Too narrow. But there'd been people through there,
graffiti artists; there was that guy, COST REVS 2000, and all sorts
of other graffiti, except nobody like Papa Love; ain't nobody in
the world can draw like Papa Love. We stayed close together.
And I'm thinking, Up there, there's boats on the water, and
Brooklyn and Manhattan, and we're walking under the river.
We were shaking with the cold and damp. I was looking back
scared over my shoulder. I was all right then. I mean, I wasn't
fucked up. I wasn't fucked up in the head.

I know I ain't, Angela.

Yeah, you're cute too.

Sunshine and cigarettes.

But listen.

Just listen.

We shoulda gone back, but we didn't. The tunnel was all
curvy and quiet, and he takes the lighter and flicks it close to
the ground a few times. Roundabout here, he says, is the wedding band. All I see is nothing but a pile of gravel and a few
pebbles, but he looks up to the roof, the ceiling, whatever, and I
asked him if he found the ring and he says, Just a minute. The
top of the lighter was burning his thumb. Come on! I says. Just
a minute, he says, I'm having a look here. Come on come on
come on! He went closed the hood on the lighter, looks up, and
says to the ceiling, Yankees are one up as we speak! I was getting scared then, and I was feeling bad, 'cause the Yankees
hadn't hit a homer at all, but I didn't say nothing. I'm scared.
So I grab the Zippo and take ahold of his overcoat and drag
him along the flat part of the tunnel. No rats, no Skagerak, no

Barents, nothing—just our breath—and he says, I remember, and I says, Remember what? and he says, I disremember.

And I says, Come on.

Holy Name, he says, which is what he said sometimes.

Move it! I says. So I reach backward and drag him by the sleeve. I'm trying to keep the Zippo lit, but it keeps flaring out on me. Keeping well away from the third rail and all. Down the center of the tracks. Faster and faster, me tugging at the overcoat. He can hardly move, and, me, I'm wondering if I might have to carry him.

I'm all right, leave me alone, Angie. I'm all right.

Angie. Angela. Whatever.

Just listen.

Maybe he felt some youngness going on through him, some shit like that, eighty-nine years old but suddenly nineteen; he mighta been following himself into his past—one, two, three, strike, return—and he mighta been rising once more—through the tunnel and the river and all—but he's not. I'm just dragging him along, and in the distance we see the lights from the subway station—they're still a ways away—and I'm screaming now, screaming, Come on! Come on! He stops for a moment and puts his hands on his knees and bends over and says, I haven't felt this good in years.

And then he was just standing, staring. Maybe he recognized the corner. Maybe he was remembering things. But he weren't moving. So I tugged him harder and harder. His feet going thump-thump on the ground and I see the platform and I'm thinking, Man, we're home free, we are home free. We get there, right? We've walked under the river. All the way, one side to the other. He puts his walking stick up, and then I hear the rumble and a big blast of horn explodes from a train and two headlights flare far away, and me—I'm quick—me, I'm up on the platform and reaching down to grab him, under the armpits, pull him up—lights of the train coming—and one hand slips and he grabs again and the hat falls—that's what's horrible, you know, it's the tea cosy; it's the stupidest thing in the world—and he reaches to get it, and I try to grab him, and him, he looks at me, and I swear to whatever be up there—I swear, I swear it, I loved him, I loved him, I loved him, Angie—he was looking up at me, and his face was wanting to be saying, it was like it was saying, What do we do now, son, now that we're happy?

There is this dream: Clarence Nathan is chopping his hands off and sucking out the marrow in his bones until there is a hollow corridor along which he walks, as high with despair as Manhattan.

Dancesca looked after me. She was sad as hell too. And Lenora, there was no end of crying. She even put his walking stick in her aquarium, but it kept falling out. I mean, nobody been missed more in the world more'n that old man been missed. I keep seeing it in my head—the train dragging him along and along. And me there on the platform screaming. And the train wheels screeching. And then all of a sudden the biggest silence you ever did hear. I couldn't do nothing after that. I was paralyzed. Nothing there in my hands. I loved him more'n any man can love a man.

No, I ain't sad.

I ain't crying.

I said I ain't.

And see here, see this—see—this is when I first done this. See, I'm thinking about murdering my hands and everything I touch—shit—I touch everything twice like this. Or this. Still do it sometimes, but not that much. Just habit now. But—back then—if I can't touch it twice I go crazy, like someone's gone hollowed out half my body. I went back to the 'scrapers but I weren't doing much good, took me a long time to climb, my head's going thump thump and I know they're thinking about firing me. So, one night, I stayed up there on the top of the 'scraper—we were up to forty-seven floors then—with this friend of mine, Cricket. He gave the guards a few bucks so they'd leave us alone. It was cold, the stars were out. I was feeling terrible; my head was going thump thump thump thump. The steel was treacherous 'cause it had rained earlier and froze a little. The city was all lit up, like it is sometimes.

You see, to me it was like one of those photos where all the lights are blurry 'cause the shutter's left on, know what I'm saying?

We went up the ladder, we was buzzing a little, we drank a couple of beers. Cricket kept saying, You must be out of your mind. But I was thinking about my grandfather and nothing was gonna stop me. We got to the decking and I went up one of the beams that goes like an X. No problem, but Cricket he's a bit jittery on account of being a little buzzing. Eventually he came on up too, I never seen him climb so slow. I took the cigarettes outa my pocket.

Anyways, I lit one of them and tossed it in the air to the other end of the beam where Cricket was, but he kept missing them mostly. I didn't have any candles, but you shoulda seen those little red ends going through the air. Once or twice Cricket caught one and he'd cup his hands around it, but most of them cigarettes fell right over the side of the building, caught by the nets down below, I suppose. But you shoulda seen those little red ends. Like this. I musta lit two packs. Flinging them through the air. And I sat on that beam all night long, and I ain't ashamed to tell you that I cried like a baby. I just sat there and kept trying to throw those cigarettes all night long, 'cause it was the only thing I could think of.

And that was when I stamped a cigarette down. That was the first time, I s'pose.

Shit, yeah, it hurt but I didn't feel it.

Burnt a little hole on the back of this hand, like a crater. Then this hand, before Cricket could stop me. He took ahold of me and he said, I'm sorry, man. Put his arms around me and said, It's gonna be all right. Before morning we went home and Dancesca, she's all frantic, she's going crazy, sits me down, she's all loving me and all, she put some of her poultice on my hand. She had this family poultice recipe.

Yeah, it's like yellow healing stuff.

Oh, she got brown eyes and beautiful, looks a lot like you.

Nice teeth, yeah.

I told you we'll get the candy.

Three in the morning maybe.

But Angie. Angela.

You shoulda seen those little red ends going through the air.

He watches the patterns the paper clips make. He straightens the bends fully out, holds the elongated metal over the flame from the gas stove.

The metal heats and reddens and he uses tiny pliers to bend the metal around. It curves very slightly, and he blows on it to let it cool and harden. Clarence Nathan swipes a hair back from his eyes. He must be careful; it is easy to break the paper clip. He uses the pliers to hold the clip over the gas flame, makes patient curves in the metal. When he is finished the clip looks like the body of a slinking snake. There are other patterns too: the shape of a boat, a tiny eye, a pyramid, a shovel.

Clarence Nathan moves away from the stove to the kitchen table—bare feet feeling the cold nailheads in the wooden floor—where he sits and smokes, watching the spirals of blue air above him. In the corner, a television sizzles with gray snow. All else is fabulously quiet. He lays the paper clips on the kitchen counter to cool, and when they are ready he heats them individually until they are red hot and glowing. He puts the clips to his arms and presses down on them with his fist until the pain shoots itself through him.

Closing his eyes, he clenches his teeth and the tendons in his neck pop and a massive roar comes from his throat. Dancesca has heard it often enough that she doesn't even stir from the bedroom anymore.

His heart doesn't feel in any way involved, only his body. The sensation of it. The deliciousness. He welcomes it, greets it: the body as his form, the pain as its content. His skin looks like a desert scape of these imprinted patterns, equally scorched on both sides of his body, burnt on with the curiosity of an onlooker.

He has even melted them into his feet, so that, at night, when he walks barefoot along the floor it looks as if these patterns are moving all over him. He tries to remember how many months it has been since Walker's death—and if it is three, he decides that it's four; and if it is five, he decides that it's six; and if it is September, an odd month, he decides that it has become October.

Outside, when he walks on sidewalks, he always makes sure

that his feet don't touch the cracks. He counts as he walks; his footsteps end on even numbers. Occasionally he even retraces his steps just to get the number correct. Then he must go back and forth to make sure there is even pressure on his left and right foot. At the entrance to a grocery store, he steps up and steps down. The clerks watch him closely. After buying cigarettes, he says to them, "Thank you thank you." He returns home to his paper clips. Continues to scrimshaw his torso.

Dancesca creates big dinners to punctuate the evening hush. He sits at the table and taps his forks against empty plates. Lenora asks him why he eats with two forks. He tells her that it's a special game and she too begins it, until her mother whispers in her ear.

Later his daughter says, "Daddy, are you crazy?"

"Go to the bedroom, girl, right now," says Dancesca.

She looks at Clarence Nathan and says, "She just gets these notions."

At work the foremen have noticed something curious: he must touch everything with both hands. On his thirty-first birthday, in 1986, he insists that he is thirty. They have heard about the cigarettes. It has become a ritual now. They fire him and, in the unemployment office, he fills out the forms twice.

At home, he turns off the television set. He needs to turn the knob with his left hand for balance. But the knob won't turn any more, so he switches the set on. Then turns it off again. Realizes that his right hand has been neglected. He reaches out for the knob once more. The screen flares to life.

On off on off on off.

On.

Off.

Until he can't remember which was first. Was it on? Was it off? He grabs at his hair. He lies on the floor, puts on his boots, laces them equally tight, and then smashes the television with both feet. The glass splays. He reaches inside the set and is delighted to count an even number of shattered pieces. Taping them back together, he smashes his feet through the glass once more.

Clarence Nathan sits on the floor, rocking back and forth, his head in his hands.

In the morning he must prepare two cups of coffee. Drink them alternately. Paste butter on four slices of bread. Make sure the strawberry jam has an even number of seeds.

There is a gentle throbbing in his brain if he doesn't portion himself out equally. Return and collection, return and collection.

In the room, there is something about the couch that makes him uncomfortable. He sees a ghost there and he avoids it.

"Now swear on it," he says aloud to nobody.

"I swear."

"Swear on your life that you ain't gonna give her another dime."

"I swear on it."

All repeated twice.

Once he dials Information and gets a number for a Nathan Walker in Manhattan; he hears a voice answer and he replaces the receiver without saying a word. Then he picks up the receiver with his left hand, dials, lays the phone down a second time. For a moment suicide scratches the side of his brain. He lets it rest there and gouge a ditch into his thoughts.

We had a nice apartment, see. On West End Avenue. Up on the fifth floor, except we didn't have a view or anything, but it was nice. I'd been making money on the 'scrapers. Back then an ironworker could make fifty grand a year. We had money in the bank. We were doing okay, even though the money's going down some. The union had good insurance.

Thirty-two or so.

Now? Thirty-six, I think. How old're you?

Take it easy, don't crash.

Anyways, I was staying in Lenora's room. It's with this yellow wallpaper and the aquarium and all, and she's getting older; she's got movie stars in there now, boys from school, singers too—Stevie Wonder, Kool & the Gang. She don't like being away from the aquarium, but the room is for me to get my head together; that's why I'm staying there. So she's sleeping with Dancesca. But Lenora, she comes in and visits all the time. I rig a blue light there above the aquarium and it goes shining down into the plastic, and she likes that. It was bright at the top and darker at the bottom, just like a real aquarium. Even ol' Faraday woulda liked that. Once we went together down to Penn Station, me and Lenora, and we got ourselves one of those photos in the photo booth with the swivel seat, four pictures of her and me, and they went on top of the aquarium. See, I still got one, see?

Yeah.

And, see, every day she brings in plates of food to me. Sandwiches and coffee and all. Milk in a nice little jug. Even the crusts cut off the sandwiches. And she's there, looking at me and asking me, Daddy, why can't you have any knives with your food? Daddy, how come Mommy says you can't have shoelaces?

Sometimes Dancesca comes in too, and she sits on the end of the bed and she cuts my hair and says to me, she says, It could happen to anybody. It weren't your fault. And she'd bring Lenora in to kiss me good night and all. She's the best child. I mean, she got that aquarium on her wall, right? And there's Walker, at the very top. I found the negative in the kitchen cupboard, went to the photo shop, made another copy, then another and another, until he was swimming all around me. I made I don't know how many copies. I suppose I shoulda gone to the nut-house but I paid a couple of visits, outpatient. And they was telling me that I was fine, that I was just inventing this all for myself. They had all these speech people and psychologists and all saying how I'm very interesting, 'cause there's no chemical imbalance, when they give me drugs it just gets worse, so they don't give me drugs anymore, and Dancesca, she tells them she'll look after me. And she does. She looks after me real good. She makes sure I'm okay. And dinnertime, she lays out the table real nice with a cloth and she doesn't say a word even though I'm doing that switch with the fork still. And we're talking small talk and happy enough, I'm getting my head together. But I'm drinking some, getting the money from Dancesca's purse. Going up to the liquor store where they got it cheap. Sometimes a bottle a day.

Uh-huh.

She's cutting hair to make money, and Lenora's at school, and I'm home most of the time and we even bought a new TV after I smashed the first one.

I don't know, Angie. Maybe I was.

Shit, everyone's a bit crazy, ain't they?

What?

No.

Don't leave.

Stay here. The sun'll come up. Here, look, I got three pairs of socks. Put 'em on. Put 'em on your hands, I don't care. I don't care about nothing anymore. I never told nobody this story. Here. Put them on.

Why don't you want the blue ones?

Oh. Yeah. No problem. I forgot.

But they ain't washcloths.

Whatever.

Don't get frostbit.

Look, look how it is. Ain't it nice? Don't leave, Angie. Just sit here till the sun comes up, then we see it real nice.

Uh-huh.

Tide's out.

Yeah yeah yeah, cold sand, ain't that something?

Don't leave, Angie.

Elijah?

Elijah's got nothing but a fucked-up shoulder. He'll kill you anyway. You saw what he did to Castor. Just pull the goddamn blanket up and listen.

Angela. Listen. You gotta tell me something.

You gotta tell me that y'ain't gonna hate me.

Just tell me.

'Cause I don't want you to hate me.

Just tell me that, 'cause Dancesca she hates me, Lenora too. They went off, and I never even seen them since. So you just gotta tell me that you ain't gonna hate me.

At the Port Authority bus station he meets Dancesca and Lenora. They have spent two weeks in Chicago with relatives. The three of them take a taxi home together. He asks the driver to stop near a parking meter and he does his trick, but Dancesca doesn't watch; she keeps her head down as he moves from one parking meter to the other. He stretches his arms out, imploring her to watch, until Lenora rolls the window down and says, "Mommy wants you to get back in the car."

It's been bad, see. I been going a little crazy. Lenora, she's been asking questions, like, Why you don't have a job anymore? And, Why does Mommy say you're sick? And, Why does Mommy want to go see her cousins in Chicago all the time? Little things like this. She's about nine or ten and she's looking up at me and asking me these questions. Sometimes, when I go to the bathroom or I'm watching TV or something, she'd go switching my photo around in her aquarium, so sometimes I'd be at the bottom where all the plankton was. That's making me feel bad, but I don't say anything, not a word. She's got these small eyes for a little girl, most kids got big eyes, but hers are small. And a scar on her ear where she fell off a tricycle. She's looking up at me. I know it sounds stupid, but it's the little things break your heart.

Yeah, I remember the story. You were in the backseat.

Now you see it, Angie. Well, almost. When the sun is up fully.

Yeah. I remember that too. Your old man.

That Cindy girl sure can dance.

But listen. I have to tell you this.

Listen.

See, a lot of the time we go down the park and it's all three of us, and if it's wet I slide down twice with the towel underneath my ass and if it's dry she climbs on up, but she's getting a little old for the slide, she don't like it too much, but she likes the swings, maybe they remind her of when times were all right with us, before I was so fucked up in the head. Maybe she's remembering that. Sometimes Dancesca and me sit on the benches and she says to me, You gotta pull yourself together.

And I know that. I mean, it's not me that's doing this to me. It's just my head. It's just, you know, the playground—

The one on 97th there.

Yeah.

All right, already. Just take it easy, okay?

Put your head on my shoulder. There you go. That's nice. Don't that feel good?

I ain't whispering.

I ain't crying.

Angie.

I'm in the room, ya know? I been in the room a few days. Just laying there. Alone. And then I hear all these kids coming in and I say to myself, What the hell's that? I came outa the room and all these kids are there with nice clothes on and all. Lenora's friends. It got all silent when I came out. And there's this big cake on the table. Lenora, she comes up to me and says, It's my birthday, Daddy. And then I get that hollowness in my stomach like I told you about, and I says, Happy birthday, happy birthday. And I see this huge cake on the table. So I go into the kitchen and get some money out of Dancesca's purse, the last five dollars. We don't have a lot of money, even our savings gone down. I weren't working on the 'scrapers no more. Hid that money in my pocket. Went on outside and went to the supermarket where they got a cake shop. But when I came back it wasn't as big as the first cake. So I go to the kitchen drawer, and Dancesca she grabs me by the wrist and says, Put that knife back. I'm only gonna cut the cake, I says. And she says, It's Lenora's birthday, let Lenora cut the cake. And I says, Please, I just wanna arrange the pieces.

I don't know why. But Dancesca she gives me this smile like she understands and she kisses me on the cheek.

So I cut the cake and arrange all the pieces on two plates so that they're equal size. Put 'em on large white plates.

'Cause I like things equal.

Yeah.

And I think that mighta been one of the times I felt the very best, just sitting there in that room watching the kids eat that birthday cake, even though Lenora didn't have a chance to cut it and there was just one piece with all the birthday candles on it. And I was happy. Just sitting there, being a father. And after all them kids left, Dancesca she was cleaning up and she says to Lenora, Why don't you go down the park with your daddy?

Now, she's getting older, Lenora, but for some reason she still likes them swings. Getting taller and filling out and puberty coming along and all, but she loves them. She could go on them swings all day long. So we went down. It was summer. Garbage in the playground. Cherry blossoms out along the walkways topside. We're at the swing together. Her hair is done in braids. She swings happily and calls for a push. All I wants to do is give her a greater lift. I stand behind her. She just about fits on the small wooden swing, and her feet make these curves in the air. At first I'm just pushing the metal chains forward. She's laughing. It's not on purpose.

I swear it.

It's just that my hand—this hand—comes around the chain. I only brush her on the very edge, just a light finger touch, and she doesn't even notice and she's calling again for more height— she's wearing her birthday dress—and, shit, I don't mean to, I'm just pushing her, hands at her armpits, and Dancesca is coming along the pathway, carrying three cans of Coca-Cola, but I see her and my hands rest against the metal chains once more. But you see, I did it again.

And then I did it again. At the swings.

And then I did it one night in the bedroom and she was wearing a little nightdress and I says to Lenora, It's our little game, but it's just around her armpits, that's all it is, it's just that I'm stroking around her armpits.

No.

No fucking way.

No.

I ain't gonna tell you again.

It's not that.

I ain't crying.

It's just that I'm cold, that's all. Cold making my nose runny.

Listen up. Please.

This woman, see, she had made an appointment 'cause she said something was happening at school with Lenora. And I remember 'cause when she came in she looked at my hands and they was all scarred up and all. With cigarette burns and them paper clips. I went tucked my hands in under my ass and I was just sitting there waiting. I'm sitting at the table with Dancesca. The social worker, she came in and she seemed nice to Dancesca, but she wouldn't say nothing to me; she just said, If you'd give us a moment, please, Mister Walker.

It's the first time in years anyone called me that: Mister Walker. But, see, that name makes me feel like I got nothing in my body, like I been carved out, so I just leave the room. I was drinking pretty heavy then. I had this gin in the room. I'm just climbing into the bottle. Not even listening at the door or nothing. Then the door closes and I hear Dancesca in the kitchen. She's rumbling in the cupboards. I'm looking at the aquarium. She has a knife when she comes into my room but she doesn't use the knife, it's just in case. She stands in front of me with the knife. And then she just slaps me and leaves my face in my shoulder, and then she moves away and the sting of her hand is in my face and I'm thinking, Slap me on the other side, slap me on the other side, but she's gone. She's in the other bedroom. Slap me on the other side, slap me on the other side. I went and stood in the doorway. I'm watching her. She reaches for the suitcases. She loads her clothes without folding them, stuffs two of the suitcases tight. She clamps down the locks. Then she moves past me as if I'm nothing but air. Lenora's not around, she's still at school. Dancesca, she opens Lenora's cupboard and holds up a training bra. You recognize this? she says to me, and then she buries her head once more and goes to filling the suitcase. She loads all of Lenora's clothes and then rips the sheet of blue plastic off the wall, gathers the photos from the ground, and throws the one of me at me. And she says to me, Pervert. You're nothing but a pervert.

And I can't say nothing.

I'm paralyzed, like I told you.

She ain't a bitch.

She ain't a bitch no way.

No, I didn't touch her there.

No!

Yeah, just the armpits. Not anywhere else.

I never touched that. Not the nipple.

Just around there.

I didn't—

She was just a child.

Just a child, Angie. Just a child.

I didn't mean nothing by it.

I never even saw her once after that. Dancesca, she took her from school and went to her folks and she won't listen to anything I got to say when I try to phone her and then she disappears altogether; they say she's not around, both of them gone, they say she's in New York, doesn't want to talk to me, but I know where she is, I know she's in Chicago.

I been thinking about goin' up there, yeah. Sometime.

Angie.

Angie!

No. No way. I never touched her there, I swear, I never did, I swear on it, and that's the truth, never there.

It wasn't that, it wasn't a hard-on, it was nothing like that.

I wasn't touching her like you think.

No.

Listen!

I mean, it's what I been trying to say. I'd be there in her room and I'd be touching her shoulders and my head'd be spinning and I'd be out of control and thinking something else. I mean, it wasn't a hard-on, you don't have to believe me if you don't want to, it was something else, but Dancesca wouldn't listen and nobody would listen; I guess I didn't listen myself, I was pretty fucked up in the head it was going thump thump thump thump like I told you.

I been thinking on it more and more. I ain't never told anybody this before. I mean, we all got a history in us, yeah? A man is what he loves and that's the reason he loves it.

That ain't shit.

No.

Ah, Angie, no.

No, Angie.

Don't do that.

I mean, look.

Out there.

Can't you see? See, I told you the sun'd come up. See. Now you can see it. It's gray and all, but ain't it nice? Hey. Angie.

Shit, I mean that's what I meant. You said you hadn't seen it before, Angie.

Angie.

You said you wanted to see the sea.

Fuck candy.

Yeah, that's my goddamn candy. I ain't got any goddamn candy. And I ain't gonna get any either. Fuck candy.

Fuck candy!

Angie.

Hey, Angie. You can't go there.

He'll kill you. Angela!

You dropped my goddamn sock.

Angie.

Angela.

It wasn't like you think.

Damn, Angie. Angela. An-ge-la!

I was lifting him out of her.

For weeks after Dancesca leaves, Clarence Nathan sleeps out in other parts of the city. His hair is short, and he can feel the cold bite at his ears. In Riverside Park he stuffs a red-haired man with his Swiss Army knife. He has seen the man before; he is homeless too. Clarence Nathan is sitting on the park bench by the Hudson, and Redhair taps him on the shoulder—"Spare a cigarette, bud?"—and Clarence Nathan asks him to tap him on the other shoulder for balance. Redhair laughs and reaches forward and steals the lit cigarette from his mouth. The blade is small and pathetic, but it slides in and slides out and Redhair stands there as a small patch of blood spreads on the stomach of his T-shirt. Clarence Nathan runs off and later stabs himself while on a bus. He sees Redhair a few weeks later and Redhair says he is going to kill him, but Clarence Nathan tosses him two packs of cigarettes and that is it; he never sees Redhair again. He wanders around the city in an ache. The sole of his construction boots undoes itself and he sticks it with glue that he steals from a drugstore. One afternoon he sees Cricket in the distance, walking through the park, and he hides in weeds down near the embankment. Junkies and male hookers are in abundance in the park, but they don't ask him if he wants a blow job anymore; he is broken down and head-hung and dirty and covers his muscled torso with long shirts so he doesn't have to stare at his scars.

Sometimes there is a mother and child in the park. He moves up quickly behind them and then covers his face and passes them, waits by a lamppost or a park bench, turns around, and sees that it isn't them.

On an afternoon of torpor he sees a pigeon wing its way through the park; it swoops down toward the bottom of the hill and flies through the ironwork gate, and he wonders if the pigeon lives in the tunnel. He descends the embankment that leads to the gate. Some flowers are in bloom by the crab-apple trees. His feet slide in the muck. The gate is locked. Clarence Nathan gazes at the ironwork and at a bar that is bent backward. He waits a long time for his heart to quiet itself; then he bends his body and nudges his way through the gap. He stands for a long time on the metal platform, like he and his grandfather had once done. All is quiet. The tunnel is high and wide and gracious. Goose bumps on his skin when he descends the steps. He moves into the shadowy depths, across a heap of garbage. He opens a bottle and sips from it and looks up at the ceiling. He gazes along the tunnel and then he feels it: it rises right through him; it is primitive and necessary; and he knows now that he belongs here, that this is his place.

Shuffling along, he sees a dead tree planted in a mound of dirt and he sees murals lit from above. Further up the tunnel, he wonders about the world that is walking above him, all those solitary souls with their banalities and their own peculiar forms of shame. Dancesca is up there. And Lenora. Somewhere, he doesn't know where. He has tried calling Chicago, but the phone gets slammed down. He has even thought of buying a bus ticket, but the ache is too tremendous within him; he can go nowhere except here; he likes it here, this darkness. He steps on a rail and can feel a slight rumble in his foot, and a few seconds later there is a train with its horn blasting and he steps aside to watch it pass and all the commuters are at their windows unaware and then the train is gone and all that is left is the imprint of its red lights on his eyes and he goes over to the wall and he lies beneath a mural of Salvador Dali's Melting Clock and he has no idea what time it is.

He looks up through the ceiling grill, watching as the light leaves the sky. He runs his hands over his body and then punches a fist into the tunnel wall and does it again, and each time he can feel a crack in his hands. He keeps on thumping until there is blood on both fists and then he mixes the blood together and keeps on thumping until he is exhausted—he even slaps at it with his elbows—and then he stumbles into the blackest blackness and there is not a sound in the tunnel.

Clarence Nathan can feel the pain in his hands but he doesn't care; he wishes he could murder them, annihilate them, suicide them; they form no meaningful connection to his wrists—more than anything he wants to get rid of his hands.

Returning to where he saw the pigeon flying, the cantankerous dark all around him, he bumps into a pillar. With all his remembered gymnastics, he climbs the pillar and finds himself on a narrow catwalk and walks along it, welcoming the pain in his hands—he doesn't even feel it anymore, it is part of him, organic—and he is high up in the tunnel, all spectacular balance still in him; there is no sign of anything or anyone, it is cold and quiet and otherworldly, and he is amazed to find that the walkway leads to an elevated room, and he opens his hands to the dark room and falls there and curls up into himself and he doesn't sleep.

The thing about it is, Angie, a man needs time to bury his hands. You listening? I could go bury my hand right here if I wanted to. Just watch me. See how it disappears. Right down here in the sand. Both of them. Angie. Angela. Where the goddamn hell you gone, anyway? Angie? See how they disappear.

chapter 15

our resurrections aren't what they used to be

*H*e wakes alone on the Coney Island sand, high tide just five feet from him, pieces of plastic and filthy foam carried on the waves, all unaccustomed water noise around him, an anemic wolfhound sniffing at his feet. The dog runs off when he stirs. His toes are freezing in his boots, and he remembers giving Angela his socks. Moving to rub the sand from his hair, he is shocked at its shortness. He stands and shakes the sand from his clothes and the blankets, reaches in his pocket for his sunglasses, but they have been smashed, cracked into two pieces. He tries to balance the glasses on his ears but they fall off and he leaves them in the sand and looks out to sea, sensing a shift in the weather, morning redness far out on the horizon. It is strange to him how quickly the sun rises, the one abrupt moment before it moves into lethargy, its arc of slowness, its daily grind.

He turns his back and walks from the beach.

Up on the boardwalk there are some early joggers. A few straggling lovers hung over from nightclubs. A Russian Jew with a black hat and long beard and ringlets. A man with a silver cart is selling coffee and doughnuts.

Reaching inside his overcoat pocket, he still has, from Faraday's funeral, a five-dollar bill with pins through it. He buys coffee and a bagel, walks a short way along the boardwalk, coughs and spits. More blood in his phlegm than ever before. He feels the heat of the coffee sear through him, and his stomach has shrunken so much he can eat only half the bagel. He tosses the rest to the wolfhound, which is still down below on the sand. The wolfhound sniffs at the half bagel and then turns and lopes away. In the distance, he hears the rumble of trains on the elevated track. He counts out a dollar twenty-five cents and makes his way toward the station. Slush at the edge of the sidewalk. The palms of his hands are scabbed over now from where he cut them.

He tips the rim of his wool hat and allows two old ladies to go past him.

"Good morning, ladies," he says, and they ignore him, scuttle on.

He vaults the turnstile and nobody stops him. In the train he sits in the second carriage from the front, in the middle of the row of seats, away from the subway map. The train is full of well-dressed suits and skirts, one woman powdering her face. He notices that all the seats are taken except those around him, and he knows how badly he must smell, and for a moment he thinks about standing up and giving his seat to a woman—any woman—and then going to stand between the two carriages to let the wind drive the scent of him away. But instead he stretches out on the seat, curls his body, puts his hands in under his head, and rocks with the rhythm of the D-train. He has emptied himself of history, and everything Clarence Nathan Walker has ever known in his life stands between here and a tunnel.

"And ol' Sean Power, Lord save his soul, ol' Power said to me once that God just went ahead and let one go, God went ahead and farted. But I don't like to think on it that way, son, even though it's funny and it makes me laugh. Me, I think on it as something else altogether. And sometimes at night, see, I can still feel my whole self rising up through that river."

He waits at the gate, in the sharp silence of a last snowfall, picks up a clump of snow and scrubs his face, feels refreshed, vital, alert. He has spent the morning at the bus station—fifteen dollars one way, they told him. In his pocket he has twenty dollars. Bottles and cans. Redemption money.

There is a single set of footprints in the snow, and he knows they belong to Angela. He places his boots in the prints and lengthens them.

Removing both his overcoats, Clarence Nathan squeezes his way through the gate, stands on the metal platform, and catches his breath as he puts the coats back on. Along the tunnel the brilliant blue light shafts slip in and out of the darkness. The flakes of snow make their long familiar journeys through the light—their spin, their fall, their gathering. He moves down the steps and walks quickly from light shaft to light shaft, enjoying the brief rage of brightness.

A shorn man wrapped in the darkest of coats, the inside lining flapping down beyond his thighs, he looks thin and sculpted by some terrible human degradation, his construction boots wrapped in tape, his purple hat tight down over his ears, motes of dust in the light shaft crashing off him at all angles as if the light itself mightn't even want him. Yet he moves with a strange fluidity, a sureness, balancing on the edge of a rail as he goes. Clarence Nathan has revisited himself, arrived full circle, each shadow of himself leading to the next, which is just another shadow in the fun-house darkness. He shivers when he sees a small rat moving at the side of the tracks as if it might accompany him the rest of his life. Picking up a handful of pebbles, he flings them at the rat and walks on.

Thirty-nine days of snow and ice and ferocious cold. His feet so numb there is hardly any pain. Already the stubble beginning to darken his cheeks. But he moves quickly, with intent, solitary and sure.

At Elijah's place he stops and puts his ear to the door and is not surprised by the sound of radio music drifting underneath the giggles of Angela. With his eyes closed, he can imagine Elijah and the thump of love moving through his body, even the smashed shoulder and the shattered kneecap, and the tender way Elijah might be preparing to strike her pure and hard in the low part of her stomach. Clarence Nathan notices that the door has been fixed and that Elijah has appropriated Faraday's toilet seat. For a moment a smile flickers across his lips, until he thinks of Castor and the smile is gone, and he wants to burst in upon them, but he doesn't and he knows he won't; he never will. He will leave them to their own brutalities and all the winters yet to come.

"Angela," he whispers. "Angie."

He throws a shadow punch and moves on, past the pile of cans and the shopping cart and the baby carriage and the dead tree and the scent of shit and piss and every other ounce of imaginable worldly filth. He touches his fingers against the dead tree, wondering if it could someday bloom. He chuckles at the absurdity, fabulous petals erupting like the sound of some distant piano played years ago underneath the earth. There was a tree once in Harlem, the Tree of Hope—his grandfather told him—and it was chopped down when Seventh Avenue was widened. A slice of it still remains in an uptown theater.

A memory whips through Clarence Nathan as he moves through the tunnel. All that ancestry of song. *Lord, I ain't seen a sunset since I come on down.*

He sticks a hand in his pocket, finds a pink handball in the depths. As he rolls the handball around in his palm he spies a movement in the shadows, and his eyes are so well trained now that he sees it is a man, long-haired, bearded, filthy, and he realizes that he is looking at Treefrog. "Heyyo," he says, and the figure nods back and smiles. Clarence Nathan turns his back and slams the ball against the wall. The slaps on either side of his body begin to heat him and he feels the figure still staring. Clarence Nathan keeps the ball in the air, back and forth over the dead tree, and, as he plays, all inheritance moves through him: Walker in Georgia staring at a snakeskin hung on a wall, Walker putting his face to a pillow that moves in his dreams, Walker by the East River with men in their hats, Walker in joy painting halfness on pigeons, Walker with his fingers over a rib-boned piano, Walker pounding his fists into an automobile, Walker by a lakeside with a tiny girl, Walker with garnet paper wrapped around a cork, Walker looking up at him from a subway track, Walker in a red hat, Walker on a massive torrent of water, what do we do now, son, now that we're happy?

The rubbery thump against the wall is the only sound in the tunnel as Clarence Nathan keeps the ball aloft.

Catching the ball in his right hand, he bites the inside of his cheeks. He looks over his shoulder and down the length of the tunnel with all the light shafts spilling through. Still in the shadows stands Treefrog, watching him. Theirs is a silent communication, a nod to each other, an understanding. Clarence Nathan flings the ball against the wall and allows himself a laugh as he catches it. He places the ball in the crook of one of the branches of the tree and walks away, toward the nest.

The stalactite has begun to drip. He stretches out a hand, just one hand, and holds the drops in his palm, scrubs his face, and his eyes shine with alacrity: Walker pressing his thumb down on the skipping needle of a phonograph, Walker driving his shovel into the brown bank, the swish of paddle as Walker sits knee-bent in a low boat of moss, Walker reading a newspaper to a tunnel ceiling, the spoke song of Walker on a bicycle with cages balanced delicately on the handlebars, Walker carving initials on a shovel.

Clarence Nathan crosses the tracks and comes to the column, grabs the handhold, and drags himself up. His body is assured, each move comes around to the same move, he could walk these columns and beams endlessly. Ten feet in the air, he knows that—even if he wanted to fall—there would be a difficulty in it, his arms would fight against memory and the limbs would catch and hold and he would be dead but his body might still be alive. The beam is still cold to the touch. Maybe his skin will stick to the beam and leave the imprint of his hand forever. He walks across the beam, not counting the steps, up along the second column, and across the final catwalk. He shunts himself fluently over the low wall, near the traffic light, and looks down at the shadow of Treefrog, alone now in the tunnel. Clarence Nathan sits for a moment with his eyes closed and then feels about on the floor for a candle, finds only one stub, which he lights. A small ring of light around him: Walker with a billy club leaving a scar on his forehead, Lenora tumbling from a tricycle, Walker in a shop full of tuxedos, Lenora coming home swinging a schoolbag, Walker with the heel of his palm smashing into the teeth of a welder, Lenora pulling her bedsheets around herself, Walker dressing himself in front of a mirror, Lenora shifting the old man's photo on a wall, Walker winded under the awning of a cigar shop, Lenora staring at pieces of a birthday cake, Walker dipping down to catch a hat, the straps of a girlhood nightdress falling, Walker guiding a canoe down the tunnel, return and collection, return and collection, Walker swiping parts of Lenora from the trees, Walker on a geyser of water, rising, rising, rising.

Leaning over the side of his nest, Clarence Nathan looks down into the shadows, and with half a grin he says to the darkness, "Our resurrections aren't what they used to be."

It doesn't come to him like a burning bush or a pillar of light, but he grins and then he touches the end of the bedside table with his foot.

The candle wax lies in a hardened puddle on the table. He nudges the table again and watches the white lake move with the sway. Then he hits the table harder with his foot and it feels good to him, it feels right; he hits it harder so that it topples for a second and then rights itself. A morning train rushes through the tunnel, but he ignores it, steps back. He swings with just one foot and the bedside table crashes against the wall and the white lake is upside down now, and—with tremendous energy—he lifts the bedside table and smashes it against the wall, hears the crack and splinter. Reaching down for the pieces, he breaks them into different bits. He throws the pieces down from his nest to where they land in the tunnel, away from the tracks.

Clarence Nathan swings his boot at the traffic light. It vibrates against the barbed wire and hook that holds it in the wall. He takes off both his overcoats and throws them on his bed and begins wrenching at the light. The light trembles minutely, dust leaks out from the hook hole, and he keeps pulling until it frees itself. He falls backward with the light in his hands and chuckles. Lifting the traffic light—take it easy, don't crash—he puts a fist hole in each piece of glass, green first, then yellow, then red. He grins as he hefts the traffic light and throws it over the catwalk. The light spins through the air and goes down and smashes, and the colored glass shatters further and splays in the tunnel gravel.

He reaches for the line of ties strung to the ceiling, tugs it down, thinks briefly about putting one across his forehead, but there is not time to undo the knots, and he just balls the line up and flings it and watches it spin and unravel out, all its colors, until it hits the ground and bunches up. He takes his harmonica and it too is gone, sailing along, maybe some whistle of wind within the reeds before it smashes to the tunnel floor. Over the side of his nest he dumps the contents of the piss bottles in a long yellow arc. The empty bottles follow the stream. He lifts his mattress and tilts it in the air and flicks his lighter and sees the wiggle of maggots in the damp side of the bedding, but he continues searching underneath for change and tobacco, finds a few half-smoked butts and a small bottle of unopened gin. He grins and pours the gin out on the floor. Then he lashes out at the sleeping ghosts of himself and Angela, overturns the mattress once more, and drops it down from his nest.

It lands with a sad thud.

One sweep of his hand into the Gulag to make sure there is nothing left. Then the hubcaps spin away from his fingers and glide across the tunnel and make a strange high sound when they hit the wall. He kicks a rock into the fire pit and he feels alive and powerful and a million movements are within him and he steps with calculation through the nest, getting rid of every-thing, even some of his hair and beard that lies on the floor. When he throws it down, it makes great feathery motions on the air.

Clarence Nathan moves into the rear cave, careful not to dis-turb the mound where Castor lies. He moves to the shelf and pulls it down in one smooth motion.

The books are first to go; he shuffles in and out of the rear cave and throws them down from the front of his nest, most of them landing spine open on the tracks. Dean will probably come and collect them. He stares down at his maps among the frozen mud. Dozens of them. He is well aware of how they will burn and what that will mean. A dozen Ziploc bags flutter to the ground, and he is out by the fire pit and seaching for his Zippo. He crumples the maps together and—by the light of God's journey and the faces of his own—he looks around at the nest and chuckles and there is no grief in it, the maps coming down to ash, the contours consumed. The smoke drifts across the tunnel and away to the topside world: four years of maps in a single burning. He goes over to his pile of clothes and stuffs a plastic bag with the only things he might need—nothing except a couple of shirts and some pants and one pair of sneakers— and the plastic bag goes tumbling and lands near the tracks and he will pick it up later and the bag will be heavy enough to just throw away.

To desire is to not have, he thinks, remembering Lenora and

the way he touched her, but there is not this hollowness any-more; he has stayed alive for the calm of this moment.

He should remain awhile and savor the empty nest, but he doesn't. He is out on the catwalk, and a small tremble runs through his calves. His elbows are held in at his sides. The twenty-foot drop beneath him is a vast chasm of blackness. The catwalk is still a little icy. A burning half cigarette is perched in the side of his mouth. He closes his eyes, smiles, and manages to turn himself a half circle on the catwalk, moving in tiny, gradual increments, clicking his tongue as he goes. The ciga-rette bobs up and down in his lips. His boots crunch the ice. He knows that to be blind means that everything is abrupt, that nothing announces its approach except memory. All true light recedes with the memory of light.

Halfway there, his face set in a peculiar grin, up on one leg, one arm out, then the other out, switching legs, tucking his head down to his shoulder, crane-dancing in the country below.

He sways a little, hops, and turns around, his arms out wide for balance. The idea of himself without his hair and beard is fantastic to him now, and he tells himself that if he had a mirror, which he doesn't, it is the one time he might dare to look at his shut eyes. He chuckles at the absurdity, turns on the catwalk, completes the full circle. He knows now that he will try to go see her, that he probably never will, but—when he does—he will ask for nothing but will tell her he hadn't meant what he did, he had been searching for ancestry, the gift of blood, and he will tell her that, when she was younger, he had been lifting his grandfather up, he had been lifting the shoulders of Nathan Walker up from her body.

I was lifting the shoulders of Nathan Walker out from you.

But for now he stretches both arms wide and he puts one leg

out in front of him and he tucks his head into his armpit and lifts it again and, changing the structure of his body, Clarence Nathan smiles at his own ridiculousness—one, two, three, strike, return—and he says once again as he stretches his arms wide, he says, "Our resurrections aren't what they used to be."

But he turns and he hops and he knows it might be untrue, and, landing on the ground, in the tunnel, amid the detritus of his life, knees bowed, heart thumping, he lets a word rest upon his tongue, just once, it rests there, a thing of imbalance. He moves on out through the light shafts and into the darkness, into the light shafts again, along past the cubicles, stopping for a moment to listen to the sound of Angela's breathing. He blows her a kiss and goes on, past the dead tree, beyond the murals, a great lightness to his body, not a single shadow cast in the tunnel. And at the gate he smiles, hefting the weight of the word upon his tongue, all its possibility, all its beauty, all its hope, a single word: resurrection.

Acknowledgments

Some of the incidents in this book are based on historical events—in particular the river blowout—but they have been adapted to suit the purposes of fiction.

I would like to thank sincerely the New York Transit Museum in Brooklyn, for allowing me access to their archives; the Schomburg Library in Harlem; the New York Public Library; and the American-Irish Historical Society. I would like to thank the many sandhogs who gave me access to their hearts and memories. Thanks to the men and women of Harlem who gave me their time and remembered with such honesty. A very special thanks to Sean and Sally McCann, Roger and RoseMarie Hawke, Captain Bryan Henry, Barbara Warner, Ledig House, Terry Williams, Jean Stein, Christy Cahill, Darrin Lunde, Rick Ehrstin, David Bowman, Billy "The Mule" Adare, Shaun Holyfield, Shana Compton, Leslie Potter, and Ronan McCann, many of whom read the manuscript in its early stages and provided invaluable advice. Also to Arthur French, who graciously helped me with many sections of dialogue. My sincere gratitude to all and sundry at Metropolitan Books and Henry Holt and at Phoenix House. I'm blessed with two very fine editors, Riva Hocherman and Maggie McKernan.

Of course, this book would never have been written without the love, advice, and support of my wife, Allison. To her, all thanks. And for Isabella too.

Finally, my thanks to the men and women of the tunnels of New York who allowed me into their lives and their homes, most especially Bernard and Marco. Neither of them are in this book, but it would have been impossible to write without them.